LEWIS SINCLAIR ~~AND THE~~ GENTLEMEN COWBOYS

LEWIS SINCLAIR AND THE GENTLEMEN COWBOYS

D. M. S. FICK

CamCat
Books

CamCat Publishing, LLC
Fort Collins, Colorado 80524
camcatpublishing.com

Hardcover ISBN 9780744308815
Paperback ISBN 9780744308822
Large-Print Paperback ISBN 9780744308839
eBook ISBN 9780744308877
Audiobook ISBN 9780744308891

Library of Congress Control Number: 2022947378

Book and cover design by Maryann Appel

5   3   1   2   4

To Frankie and Lawrence Fick.

Good citizens, witty company, generous parents.

The best of the best.

—«⸨•⸩»— —«⸨•⸩»— —«⸨•⸩»—

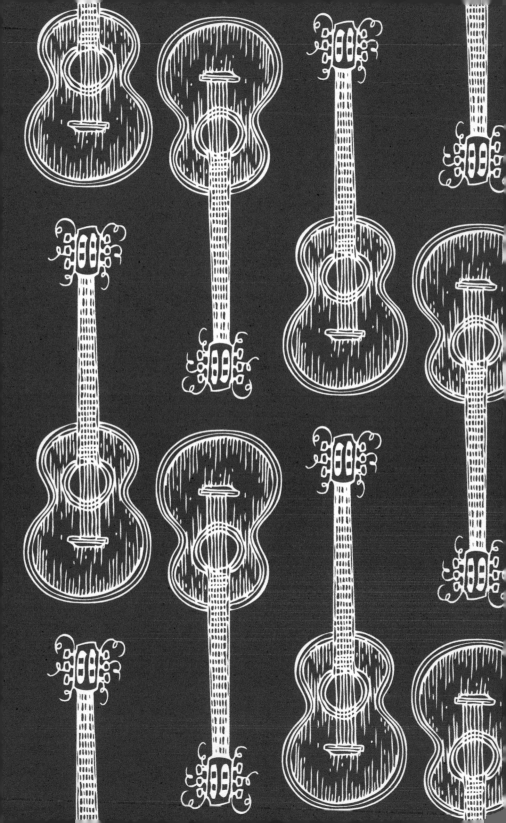

PROLOGUE

The treasure hunter hunched over the desk rifling through the leases and rent receipts piled higgledy-piggledy across it. He looked over and under the paper, scattering army souvenirs, watches, and jewelry as he searched. He was so intent on his quest that he didn't see the observer lurking behind the office door. Neither did he notice that the baseball bat—usually standing sentry on the wall behind the desk—was absent from its post.

In time, the offending clutter was parted and the treasure revealed. The man transformed from stooped desperado to exalted king. He raised the azure velvet box to the bare light bulb hanging just above the desk. He held it with tenderness and even a little reverence. If he'd been a man who could cry, he would have. He opened the tiny treasure chest. Its contents sparkled under the humble light bulb. The treasure hunter's eyes sparkled too. So pleased was he with the glittering, glowing contents and the joy it would bring that he was oblivious to the lethal blow of the traitorous bat as it descended.

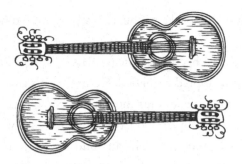

CHAPTER ONE

He should have seen it coming, but she was just so darn pretty. Love can make you blind like that.

Ann-Dee met up with Lew Sinclair in New Orleans a little over a year ago. Lew's keyboard player had a side gig over at Tipitina's. Lew and the rest of the band, the Gentlemen Cowboys, were in the audience having a few beers and enjoying the music. Ann-Dee, well, she asked Lew to slow dance. By the end of the night her demo was in Lew's shirt pocket. He should have known right there what the story was, but it was already too late. He was that much in love.

And now she'd dumped him. Five minutes ago, to be exact. The day before the last stop of the tour. This was an important show for Lew too. It was at FallsFest, one of the biggest country-music festivals in the world. With a third national tour under their belts and a new album, Lew and the Cowboys were poised on the precipice of stardom. This FallsFest appearance, in front of forty thousand of the world's most enthusiastic country fans, could be the one to break them. Now Ann-Dee broke his heart instead, just a day before their big chance.

Lew stared into his open suitcase. His white Stetson rested beside it on the unrumpled hotel bed. He shifted his gaze to the uneaten room service on the desk just beyond it. Two cups of coffee—one with Ann-Dee's rose lipstick on the rim—just a few sips emptier than when they were poured. The air conditioner rattled on with the rusty metallic rasp of a trash can with a bad cold. Its uncoordinated rattle insulted Lew's ear and sense of rhythm. Its cold blasts of air gave him shivers. He rubbed his hands to warm them, then tossed his lucky socks into a suitcase. They landed with an inconsequential thud.

Yeah, he should have known better. He'd kicked around the music business for two decades honing both his Hank Williams covers and his Jimi Hendrix virtuosity in small venues and even smaller recording studios. By now his music was as natural as a cold beer on a sunny afternoon with a dog snoozing at your feet. He should have seen Ann-Dee coming.

He caught his reflection in the hotel mirror. You might call what he saw a hangdog face: turtledove eyes that had seen enough misery to belong to a cynic but enough love to nourish a romantic. Now, courtesy of Ann-Dee, they'd seen a little more of both.

Yes, he'd been foolish to think a woman as young and bewitching as Ann-Dee could really fall for a guy like him. Then again, he was not an unattractive man. And both of his grandfathers had been twenty-odd years older than their wives, so the age difference wasn't an entirely taboo concept to him. Of course, that was another time, and those men had lived in small Texas towns where the dating pool was limited. If you fussed over a little thing like age, you might never get married at all.

So, Lew hadn't thought twice about Ann-Dee's affection. Of course she loved him. She said so. And of course he passed her demo on to people he trusted who could do her some good. And now, of course, she didn't need him anymore, so she'd called it quits. He should have seen it coming.

⋘•⋙ ⋘•⋙ ⋘•⋙

Lew tipped his Stetson to the driver as he climbed into the Gentlemen Cowboys van. Gary Schroeder, the ever-punctual bass player, was taking the first shift at the wheel on the considerable drive to the festival. Gary was a Germanic straight razor of a man, just as thin and not a rounded line on him. Lew sometimes startled when Gary reached overhead or bent low to handle luggage or a monitor. Despite the fact that the sensible Gary always lifted with his legs, Lew feared the youth would snap in two from the burden. It was an illusion. Gary was actually quite sturdy. It was just his stature that made him seem slight, his head perched far up in the atmosphere like an eagle in its aerie or a fasting mountaintop saint. Lew chose the seat right behind Gary because the analytical thirty-three-year-old was clever at crossword puzzles. Lew removed his Stetson and placed it on the seat next to him. He opened his attaché case, removed a puzzle book, and settled back, hoping the crossword would distract him from his woes.

His concentration on forty-two down (his age and mood) was disrupted by the gleeful shouts of the band's Irish drummer, Finbar Mitchell, as he bounded toward the van. "Mitch," as most people called him, wore a cheesehead, a large foam hat resembling a wedge of orange cheese popular with cartoon mice and Green Bay Packer fans. Flips and spikes of wavy hair stuck out from under the cheesehead. His chin sported a perpetual three-day growth of beard. He had that musician's poetic scruffiness that many women find irresistible.

"Gary!" Mitch called to the bass player. "Look at my hat! A fan gave it to me last night after the show. Wisconsin is brilliant!" Mitch pulled a stick of string cheese from a pocket and began peeling strips from it and casting them at Gary and Lew through their open windows. "And they've got confetti made out of cheese!"

"Mitch," said Lew, "if I find string cheese in my collar when I get out of this van, I'm getting another drummer."

"Aw Lew, you'll never find another drummer like me."

"That may be a good thing."

"Naw," said Mitch. He rounded over to the passenger side of the van and threw himself into the seat next to Gary. "You'll not find another drummer who can play the pipes the way I do. You'd never fall asleep on tour without me."

It's been said that the uilleann pipes will make the most gawd-awful sound known to man if played without skill, and that the banshee herself would have no need of wailing if she took up the instrument. Mitch, however, had the gift to conjure from the pipes ancient songs of longing and truth—songs so beautiful they caused Lew to weep, then fall back in his van seat, his hotel bed, his bar chair, and relax as he never could without those blasted pipes—or Mitch playing them. And Lew enjoyed the drummer's antics. Within Mitch roiled the energy and joy of youth amplified by a true musician's spirit and a vigorous imagination. Lew would certainly miss all those positive ions bouncing around their music and on the road. String cheese or no, Mitch had job security. A little chastisement from Lew was part of the game for both of them. It gave Mitch a challenge, and, mercy, who knows what would happen if there were no restrictions on his activity.

Boarding next was Slim Pontchartrain, the most gentlemanly of the Gentlemen Cowboys. He touched the brim of his straw boater to Lew and took the seat behind the Stetson. Slim removed the jacket of his oyster linen suit—it went so well with his sage silk tie—and gently put it to bed on the seat to his left, next to the baseball bat the band kept on the van for security. He kept his hat on. Slim rarely removed it in public. For all Lew knew, Slim slept in the stylish top-per. Lew suspected it was due to Slim's bald pate. He didn't consid-er Slim vain at all, for, being the most gentlemanly of the Cowboys, Slim always removed the boater in the presence of women. Perhaps he was just an extreme fan of Maurice Chevalier. (Lew had heard him sing in French on occasion.)

Slim sat back and opened up a food-and-entertainment guide to the Twin Cities. St. Paul was an hour or two away from FallsFest. Slim had already mentioned to Lew that he might stop at that de-lightful Thai restaurant by the Fitzgerald Theater—oh, and that su-perlative jazz club just two blocks south.

He thumbed through the guide.

Lew returned to forty-two down. Three letters. That should be easy. "To tease with a comb," read Lew. He concentrated his thoughts.

"Lew! I've got some news for you!" Archie Grant, the band's man-ager, threw open a door and heaved himself into the seat next to Lew. Gary slid Archie some sinister side-eye.

"Want any coffee, Lew?" asked Gary. "I'm heading to the front desk." Lew shook his head and Gary picked up a travel mug from the center console and departed for the hotel.

Archie shifted about. He zipped and unzipped his kelly-green track suit. He drummed his fingers on his thigh. He tapped his foot on the floor. Lew felt a bubble of indigestion.

"So I booked Ann-Dee into FallsFest."

"Aw Archie, I wish you hadn't done that. What day is she on?"

"Friday. The slot before you and the Cowboys."

"Archie . . . Ann-Dee and I broke up."

"Yeah, I know. Couldn't be helped. The booking, I mean. I made it before you two were splitsville." Lew often enjoyed the music of Archie's East Coast accent. Sometimes he was so used to it he didn't even hear it. But right now, it didn't do Archie any favors. "And I can't cancel it now. You don't jerk those FallsFest people around, you know what I'm saying? That owner, Morgan? He's a tough nut, let me tell you. But if you show up and do a good show they'll keep you in mind for other years. Book you kind of regular, so to speak. FallsFest is a very good audience for you, y'know? This could be the concert that pushes you right to the top of the old heap. So I don't want to tick anybody off, see, especially not Gordon Morgan. Ann-Dee's just gonna have to stay on the roster and that's all there is to it. You understand."

"You know we broke up?"

"Yeah. Ann-Dee told me. Sorry, buddy. But like I said, I can't change the booking."

"Ann-Dee told you ..." Lew's heart sank further than he thought it could sink. He realized he was possibly the second man to find out he'd been dumped. Slim reached a large dose of antacid tablets in between the seat backs into Lew's receptive hand.

"You're taking it too hard, Lew," said Archie. "Forget about her. You'd be trading her in for a new model pretty soon anyway."

"What?" asked Lew. "Archie, you know that's not my style."

"It's every man's style, Lew. You're gettin' to be that age. Midlife crisis, y'know? You can bet *I* know. I swear I got hot flashes."

"Men don't get hot flashes."

"I'm telling you, I got an eye for the ladies five times what I used to. It's the middle age. I think I'm losing my looks too. Old Archie's gotta move in on the ladies while he still has a hairline. I got Botox last week. Can you tell?" Archie shoved his round face closer to Lew's.

Lew looked out the window and wondered why he'd ever chosen such a manager.

"What I'm saying is, it's a great time for you and Ann-Dee to break up," continued Archie.

Lew whipped his head around to glare at Archie, nearly bumping foreheads with him. Archie pulled his pumpkin cranium back.

"Don't worry about it. There's gonna be babes aplenty at this FallsFest, Lew, and you are now free as a bird to enjoy them as you please."

The heat in Lew's glare did not reduce in temperature.

"Hey, don't look at me like I said the Pope's made of cheese," said Archie. "FallsFest is where Gary met Nancy, ain't it? And she's a babe and a half, I tell you what. Hell, I'd look at her twice if she walked down the street, know what I'm saying?"

"Don't let Gary hear you say that," whispered Lew as if Gary could hear all the way from the hotel. "He'd knock you sideways back to Memphis. Anyhow, Gary first met Nancy at college in Boston. They bumped into each other at FallsFest the next summer."

"Well he didn't bump into her in church, did he? He bumped into her at FallsFest, 'cause that's where the babes are—hundreds of 'em. Doesn't matter if you meet 'em at FallsFest or Timbuktu. All I'm saying is you oughtta take a look around. I know I would. Right now, I got the music business thing going for me, but someday, might be pretty soon, when the Botox wears off and the hairline leaves town, even that won't turn a young filly's head. I gotta make hay while the sun shines, maybe clinch the deal with some young thing before I'm totally bald. You're lucky. You got hair. You got time."

"If you don't mind, Archie, I'd like to be alone right now. Breaking up with Ann-Dee and all."

"Sure, Lew. Just don't forget old Archie's pearls of wisdom. There'll be a quiz later. Oh, and I'm not riding with the band today. Gotta drive Ann-Dee. I figured you wouldn't want her in the Cowboy-mobile, am I right?"

Archie slithered out of the van and strutted over to a scarlet Mustang convertible with its top down. He waved at Gary, who'd just emerged from the hotel with a now steaming travel mug. Archie waggled a thumb toward the Mustang. Gary tilted his head. Even from this distance Lew could see Gary's jaw muscles tense up.

Gary looked at the van, at Lew. He gestured with the mug toward the van, then toward Archie. Coffee sloshed out of the mug. Archie skipped backward, saving all but his shoes from the scalding joe. Gary lunged at him, shoving the mug into Archie's chest and knocking him backward into the front seat of the convertible. Ann-Dee strolled out of the lobby. She looked at the Mustang, at the puddle of coffee. She glanced up at the van. She scowled in Archie's direction, turned around, and strode back into the hotel.

Lew watched after Ann-Dee. He looked down at his flattened Stetson in the seat beside him vacated by Archie. It took a very insensitive man, he thought, not to notice he was sitting on another man's hat.

Later, during the drive to Big Pearly Falls, Lew and Slim were the only two awake. Gary and Mitch, like infants, tended to fall asleep in the van when not driving, even on a bright day such as this one. Lew envied them. Slim had taken over the wheel, much to Lew's relief. In between Gary and Slim had been Mitch, who made one too many jokes about not knowing which side of the road he was supposed to drive on. In addition to that, his pressure on the gas varied depending on the beat of whatever song was on the radio. They nearly rear-ended a Volkswagen during Queen's "We Will Rock You" as Mitch treated the accelerator like the pedal of a bass drum. But now that his good old, steady friend Slim was at the helm, Lew could relax, gaze out the window, and contemplate their set list for tomorrow's performance.

His thoughts were rudely and consistently interrupted, however, by a jumble of melancholy memories featuring Ann-Dee, and irksome remembrances of Archie's tone-deaf handling of Ann-Dee's booking and the breakup.

Lew thought of sunny picnics with Ann-Dee, cozy weekend mornings with robust coffee, cinnamon-rich rolls, and the Sunday paper; helping each other write songs; tracing her dainty fingers over a tablecloth while candlelight limned wisps of her golden hair. He would miss watching her perform. He was so proud of her natural talent and how she practiced her craft. She could be a faerie singing enchanted songs when she was on stage. He saw how she could charm an audience.

But now, for Lew, she'd been a siren luring him to the brutal rocks of heartache. How could Archie be so callous to have missed how smitten Lew was with her? Well, Archie was a pretty callous fellow—that or he was just plain dense.

Lew wouldn't put it past his manager to have nudged the breakup along. He'd seen him eyeball her, not caring who was in the room. Archie was never one to suspect his behavior was being observed or considered. Probably more than pleased to be her manager now. Well, Ann-Dee was a smart cookie. She might not want old Archie for a manager, let alone a paramour. Lew had a good mind to discuss sacking Archie with the other Cowboys. He was pretty sure Gary would be on board with that. And Archie had sat on Lew's hat!

At that moment Lew noticed in the van's side mirror a semi barreling up to pass. It was a deep purple with flames painted on its hood and exhaust pipes growing out of the cab like metallic bull's horns. It drew up next to the van and the noise it made caused the windows to tremble. Lew searched the cab but couldn't see the driver. Sweat gathered on his brow. The semi edged past the van, leaving a miasma of diesel in its wake. Without thinking, Lew began chewing at a bit of his right thumbnail.

"You all right, Lew?" Slim met Lew's gaze in the rearview mirror. "I don't mean to nag, but if that's a hangnail you're nibbling at, you could end up with a sore thumb tomorrow. Not the best condition for a guitar player."

"Don't know what I was thinking," said Lew. "I haven't bit my nails since high school. Broke that habit when I took up the banjo. Thanks."

"Not at all."

Lew wiped his brow. He leaned back in his seat and wished Mitch was awake and playing his pipes. He stared out the window at the rows of soybeans. The visual effect caused by the van rushing by them turned them into a continuous pair of running legs. Eerie. Lew thought about the driverless semi. He made a mental note to add "Ghost Riders in the Sky" to their FallsFest set.

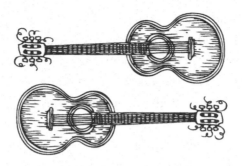

CHAPTER TWO

C huck Nelson studied the road ahead. He glanced now and then out the passenger window. Corn and soybeans and corn and soybeans and more corn and soybeans. Chuck and his traveling companion hadn't spoken much since they'd left the Cities. Chuck had been occupied with his phone, and the driver—Chuck's one-time mentor, John Turnbell—didn't seem to mind. He looked glum now though. Maybe John was tired of driving, and they still had an hour to go before they got to FallsFest.

"John, old boy, how about some tunes? Let's hear this sound system you've told me so much about."

John looked at Chuck. His face brightened. He turned on the stereo. It began playing "Tangled Up in Blue."

"This is from a USB drive. You can set it to play by album, artist . . . right now it's in alphabetical order." He smiled and shook his head. "Man, I bought this album when I was in high school," said John.

"Classic," said Chuck.

"Cl—" John did a double take at Chuck. "Yeah. Classic." His shoulders slumped. "At the time, I just thought I should own a Dylan record. Little did I know how important this one would be, or that at least half of it was made right in the Twin Cities."

Chuck studied John. Dress shirt. Chinos. Trimmed beard. Jaw-length hair with a side part. Same cut he'd worn since Chuck first met him three years ago. It was a good look for a music journalist in the seventies. Chuck himself looked like an old-school beatnik. He wore a striped stretched-out T-shirt from Ragstock, shorts, and Vans low-top sneakers. He needed a shave and sported a soul patch that he rubbed sometimes for luck but mostly out of habit. He caught himself doing so now. His hair was short and tousled. He cut it himself. He wondered if John ever cut his own hair.

The Dylan song ended and the Eagles' "Tequila Sunrise" began playing. John actually blushed. He pressed a button on the steering wheel and the stereo skipped to the next song. "Thank God I'm a Country Boy" chirped away. John pressed the "skip" button again.

"Dude," said Chuck. "This is fine, but you got any more of that Dylan? I'm blogging about *Blood on the Tracks* next week. Love to get that playing in my subconscious over the weekend."

"Sure," said John. He muted the audio via the steering wheel. His index finger hovered over the menu screen.

"I usually just play the USB straight through," said John. "It's been a while since I . . ."

The stench of a feedlot entered the car. John pressed buttons on the dash until the air vents closed. He returned his finger to the audio screen and scrolled and pressed and scrolled. Thankfully, *Blood on the Tracks* eventually returned to the screen and their ears.

"Dude, do you have heated seats?"

"Sorry," said John. "Must have pressed the wrong button when I was trying to close the vents." He turned the heat off.

"Yeah. I didn't remember drinking barium this morning." He laughed.

John sunk into the driver's seat. Chuck followed suit. The leather was soft, much cushier than the Green Line seats of Chuck's usual commute.

A piercing chime jolted both John and Chuck a centimeter out of their comfy leather seats.

"Sorry," said John. "Lane departure warning. It's a safety feature. My wife and I wanted the safest car we could find once our son started driving. This model has superb airbags." John stared straight ahead, not talking, just driving for a solid minute. He sighed. "I don't know if you've heard, but there've been rumblings at the paper about downsizing. New owner and all that. Doesn't look like any department's safe. I'm not gonna lie, I'm a little worried. You get to be my age these days, you've got a target on your back. I need the health insurance, and there's no way we can afford college for Toby if I get laid off." He checked the rearview mirror. "So I'm going to have to be a little more on my toes at FallsFest this year, find something readers will interact with. I need comments. I'm gonna keep an eye on the lesser-known acts this year. Maybe I can help break one or two. That'd look good."

Chuck rubbed his soul patch. John lifted a finger to the space below his lip.

Chuck remembered being in high school and looking forward every week to John's columns. He'd lived vicariously through the reviews, imagining all the venues and concerts he himself didn't have access to.

John was the reason Chuck sought an internship at the *TC Record* in the first place.

He remembered waiting in the *Record* lobby for his interview. John's books on The Replacements and the Minneapolis Scene were displayed in a case alongside the paper's Pulitzers.

A tinkling flourish of bells drew Chuck's attention back to his phone. He muted it and opened a text from his roommate—the common-law kind—Moira. The text read:

Look Toots! We made it into Scene Monthly again. 3 pix in the Party Poop!

A link took Chuck to the magazine's photos. He scrolled through the schmooze-fest. The last photo featured Chuck and Moira yakking and laughing with the owner of the *Record*. Wasn't John at that party? Chuck swore he was. He swiped through all of the photos again. Yes, there he was, blurry, and far in the background—behind Chuck. Chuck remembered his conversation with the owner that night. He'd hinted that John's job might be opening up in the near future and suggested Chuck would be a good fit.

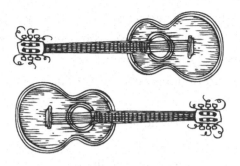

CHAPTER THREE

The van with Lew and the Cowboys reached the outskirts of Big Pearly Falls, the town outside of which FallsFest was being held. Lew looked out the window at the rolling hillside of people, campers, and tents. They passed six campgrounds (originally five pastures), three information checkpoints with off-duty police officers, and the amphitheater itself. He was impressed by the scale of the festival. Lew cast an eye over the rippling flag of humanity that covered the valley in T-shirts, bandanas, and jeans. The brilliant sun heightened every red, white, and blue (and even a smattering of yellow and purple) set against an emerald field. A thrill shot through his spine.

A grand hollow surrounded the amphitheater. Here's where the audience stood, sat on folding chairs, ambled, or danced. In three days' time the grass would be matted and dull, but today it stood perky and green. A short skirt of food stands, clothing tents, and various other vendors wrapped around the hollow, anchored by two grand turrets. The first turret was the saloon, a former machine shed that now provided drinks for those who needed either darkness or protection from the sun. The second was the StarWalk, the jewel in the festival's crown. It boasted the handprints and signatures of many country legends (and a few bonus features in the case of some rascally participants). Beyond all this was a swath of pasture wide enough to drive RVs through on their way to the campgrounds.

The van continued a few more miles into Big Pearly Falls proper, a resort town that had grown up around farmers, families, and fishermen. Its outskirts held plenty of chain restaurants and box stores for those leery of the unexpected. Just beyond that ring of franchise, however, lived homegrown cafes, corner bars, and bait shops. Big Pearly Falls worked for just about anybody who ventured into it.

The Cowboys arrived at their motor lodge. Archie had managed to arrive before them. (The Mustang might have had something to do with it.) He greeted them and dealt out the room key cards, then left to take care of other "business." The band congregated in Lew's room. He watched the different personalities on display. Mitch flowed through the room like water, checking amenities and flicking light switches. Every inch of him was ruffled and animated. Slim looked over the gift baskets on the writing desk. Serene. An aura of calm reached out seven feet from him on all sides. Gary, by the window, stood with a soldier's posture in his tailored clothes, not a scrap of extra material, not a hint of lint or dirt.

Gary extracted his phone from an inside jacket pocket and called Nancy. He was staying at the motel with the rest of the band instead of at his family's nearby resort because he liked to keep his band hat on when they were performing. Family can get under your skin—no matter how loving—and he wanted to take the stage at FallsFest as a Gentleman Cowboy, not the Schroeders' son.

Gary often played the lionhearted knight to his fair maiden Nancy, protecting her often from the unwanted notions of lesser men.

Not that she needed any help. She was genial, but Lew sensed a will of steel beneath her polite exterior. Still, despite their fierce and stoic natures, they were capable of billing and cooing after a prolonged time apart. Lew listened with a wistful ear.

"Lew!" said Gary, putting his phone back in his jacket. "Nancy says Ann-Dee's playing the set right before us tomorrow. Did you know about that?" Lew threw his flattened Stetson onto the bed. Slim walked over to Lew and put a hand on his shoulder.

"Yeah," said Lew. "Archie told me in the van. There's something I ought to tell you boys—Ann-Dee and I broke up."

"Sorry, Lew," said Gary.

"She's a mad fool, and that's a fact. You're well rid of her," said Mitch. Lew winced. It was obvious Ann-Dee broke up with him and not the other way around.

"Come with me to Mom and Dad's for supper, Lew," offered Gary. "Mom's cooking will do you a world of good."

"You know he's right," said Slim. "Mother Schroeder's cooking has magical powers."

"That's high praise from you, Slim. I believe I'll take you up on that offer, Gary. A night of hearth and home might be just what I need."

"Since your life is already in turmoil," ventured Slim, "perhaps I could raise another vexatious matter." Gary and Mitch began to fidget. "Our tour ends after FallsFest. Maybe this would be an opportune time to investigate new management."

"You mean get rid of Archie?" Lew's stomach cramped. His thumb twitched.

"It's my opinion," said Slim, "that our bookings are based far more on good word of mouth and our own contacts than on Archie's hustle."

"And he does no promotion," said Gary. "We have no digital presence at all. He's letting us down."

"He's a bastard!" said Mitch.

Lew looked to Slim, to Mitch, then to Gary. Gary looked away.

"Archie is not only lazy," said Slim, "he's trouble. Neither quality is a positive managerial attribute."

"Gary's mam could line up better gigs," said Mitch. Lew looked at Gary.

"Well," said Gary, "I'm sure Nancy could do better."

"The fact is," said Slim, "Archie's been coasting on the talent of his client and giving nothing in return. A composer, a singer, a musician such as yourself, with a band as solid as the Gentlemen Cowboys, should have hit big by now."

"Archie's holding us all back by not doing his part," said Gary.

"And he's just not a pleasant person," said Slim. "He sat on your hat, Lew."

"He's a bastard," repeated Mitch.

"Really Mitchell," said Lew, "once was enough."

"And where is he now?" asked Slim. "Why isn't he here with us?"

"Well . . ." said Lew, "he said he had business."

"Probably making sure his new client got to her motel room okay," said Gary. Lew glanced at him. Was Lew the last person to know everything? What else didn't he know?

A loud knock shook the door.

"Is my boy Gary in there?"

Mitch sprang to the door and flung it open.

"Mother Schroeder!" he cried. Mitch pulled Gary's mother, Beatrice, into the room and twirled her about like a carnival swing. He was surprisingly strong for such a wiry fellow. Drumming will do that.

Gary swept his father in with a sound embrace. Mrs. Schroeder disentangled herself from the enthusiastic Mitch and looked her son up and down with motherly pride and a hint of worry.

"You need a good meal, Gary. Let's get you out of this hotel room and sitting down at the kitchen table."

"Um, Mrs. Schroeder . . ." Slim sidled up to Gary, his straw boater in his hand. "Might there be room at your table for one or two more?"

"You know I cook for twenty, Slim. And there's always a plate set for you. Why I'd be insulted if you didn't join us. That means you and you too," she said to the remaining Cowboys. Lew nodded. Mitch cheered.

The phone on the nightstand rang.

"Yes," said Lew into the receiver. The room watched him. He nodded a few times, said "I see. Well, tomorrow I expect will be too busy, maybe tonight sometime?" Lew looked to Mrs. Schroeder. "Bea, the folks at FallsFest want me to put my hands in cement, what they call their 'StarWalk.' Suppose we have time for that before supper?"

"Supper's always at six in the Schroeder house. I think that gives you plenty of time to cement your place in country-western history. But I'll only allow it if we get to come along and bear witness."

"Yahoo!" cried Mitch. "You've made it, Lew! Only stars get their hands in cement at FallsFest!" He bounded over to Lew and nearly knocked him over with his hug. Gary rushed over and slapped Lew on the back. Slim grinned ear to ear. Lew returned to the caller as best he could.

"I guess any time in between now and five thirty would work for us, Ms. Flynn." He listened. "Well then, we'd better clean up a bit. It's been a long ride. Thank you. See you then." He hung up and looked at his boys. "They like to take photographs at this thing: put them on their website, send them out to TV stations and newspapers and the like. We oughtta spruce up a bit, don't you think?" Cheers burst forth from all around, excepting the quiet Mr. Schroeder, who merely nodded with a minute smile. "They want us to do some radio IDs too, maybe some other things."

"This is it, Lew," said Gary. "This is how it's done."

A white shuttle bus with black-tinted windows arrived to take the Gentlemen Cowboys to FallsFest. They invited Mr. and Mrs. Schroeder to ride with them. Archie sauntered out of the motel lobby doors just as Gary stepped onto the vehicle's lowest step. Gary's cold stare stopped Archie in his tracks. Archie spun around and skittered back into the lobby.

The shuttle's first stop was the FallsFest onsite office, a double-wide trailer sitting twenty feet behind the main stage. An auburn-haired dynamo burst out of the right-hand door. Her gaze darted to each and every Cowboy. If she'd had a tail it would've been an impressive but concise plume that twitched in symmetry with her eyes, warning all lesser forest creatures to keep watch over their acorns and secrets.

"Mr. Sinclair." She greeted Lew. "Welcome to FallsFest. I'm Ruby Flynn, second-in-command at FallsFest. We spoke on the phone." Lew, the Cowboys, and the Schroeders shook her hand. "Come inside. We can do the ID records here. I'd also like you to look over the media requests and see what works for you."

They followed Ruby into the trailer. Gary's girlfriend, Nancy, sat behind the first of two desks. She stood as they entered the office. She was surrounded by stacks of papers, in- and outboxes, staplers, and tape dispensers. Every kind of office supply formed a skyline at the apron of her desk.

Behind the desk hung a baseball bat. Lew wondered if it was for security like the one the Cowboys kept on hand or if she was just a fan of the sport.

"I believe you know Nancy," said Ruby with a wink, nodding to the smashing towhead. Mrs. Schroeder beamed at her potential daughter-in-law. Ruby gestured them past the empty second desk to the next room, where a makeshift recording booth had been set up. "This is Gordy's office, but he's rarely here, so we put up some acoustic panels and use it for records." She pulled four stools, each with a headset and wireless lavalier microphone setup on top, to the desk. She walked over to a mini fridge in the corner and unplugged it, then locked the nearby door to the outside. "Don't want anyone walking in during the record," she said. "Remind Nancy to unlock it when you're done." She picked up a remote from the top of the fridge and muted a sizeable TV. "Have a seat. I'll let the audio guy know you're here. There's some scripts on the desk or you can wing it if you want to. I'll be right back."

They looked over the scripts, every once in a while looking up and taking in the décor of the office. Foam baffling was mounted on the walls so as to make the sound of the room less "bright." Taped to one of the mics was a note saying, "PLUG FRIDGE BACK IN AFTER RECORDING." Next to the mini fridge, the TV showed roadies setting up audio equipment on an outdoor stage. The picture changed to a jumbotron screen featuring the roadies at work. Then it changed to an audience of empty folding chairs. The TV appeared to be a monitor of the stage area of the festival.

A tall, muscular man sporting a thick mane of hair, sunglasses, and Doc Martens entered the room, followed by Nancy.

"Hi, I'm Gordon Morgan," he said holding his hand out to shake. Mitch sprang to his feet.

"You're the king of FallsFest!" he said as he bowed. The others merely stood and shook his hand in turn.

"Majority shareholder," replied Gordon. "We're more of an autonomous collective than a kingdom." He towered over everyone. Despite his giant biceps, his handshake was gentle and brief. No sense spraining a musician's main source of income—especially before Gordon's own festival—with some pseudo-alpha male grip. "I've been following your work. Good stuff. I'm glad we could book you."

"Why, thank you," said Lew.

"Listen, I've gotta leave right now, but I'll catch you at the Star-Walk. We should talk. I have some ideas you might want to listen to. I understand you'll be in Big Pearly for more than a few days?" He glanced at Nancy, who stood taller and smiled. "Feel free to enjoy the festival and let one of us know if you need anything or want to check out any of the other acts. Just call or stop into the trailer. We're all connected with walkie-talkies. Eventually, the right person will get back to you."

He smiled, then ducked out of the office.

"A powerful man, I believe," said Mrs. Schroeder.

"You definitely want him on your side," said Nancy.

"And when did you move up to the main office, young lady?" asked Lew. Nancy blushed. "And you, Gary, you couldn't tell me?" Gary blushed.

"I guess I forgot," said Gary. "But I'm proud of you, honey," he said to Nancy. "I didn't forget because it was insignificant. I mean it is. Significant."

"Well, I think I can see how we made it to the StarWalk," said Lew.

"Oh, I don't know about that," said Nancy.

"Take the credit if it's due, girl," said proud Mrs. Schroeder.

"I mean, Gordon thinks a lot of you, Lew," said Nancy, "and the Cowboys too. I just . . ." A phone rang in the next room. Nancy left to answer it.

Ruby returned to Gordon's office.

"Bobby's ready with the record. The mics are on. Put on the headphones and you can talk back and forth. Anytime you're ready."

"Ruby," Nancy poked her head in through the door. "Archie Grant"—she nodded to Lew and the Cowboys—"their manager, is on hold. He wants to set up some media for them."

"Tell him I'll call him back."

"Any time in particular?"

"No. Let him stew. Thanks." Nancy looked around the room and returned to her desk. Ruby cast a gimlet eye at each of the Cowboys. "Pretty bold talking about your manager like that in front you, huh?" She looked right at Lew. "I tried to set things up for you through that guy weeks ago. You might want to look for new management. That Grant's more red light than green."

Slim and Lew exchanged glances.

"You're lucky you have Nancy on your team," continued Ruby. "She's been talking you up to Gordy nonstop. Gave him a thumb drive with your songs on it. I swear he plays it every time he's in the office or his car."

"See what the right word here and there can do for us?" said Gary. "We need someone with hustle."

"Hustle for us and not his dance card," said Slim.

"No sense airing dirty laundry in front of the lady," said Lew. "Thank you, Ms. Flynn. Your advice is well taken."

"Well, I've got some more advice for you. Show up and shine for every kind of media we line up for you. This is the time people will pay the most attention to it." She checked her clipboard. "I see here that Nancy has tentatively booked you local radio, a music columnist from the *Twin Cities Record*—oh, that's John Turnbell. He's a great guy, you'll like him . . . and let's see, some blogger wants to do an interview."

The band—except for Gary—stood stunned. They'd never had such publicity.

"We'll be there," said Lew when he regained his power of speech. "Just tell us where and when."

"Good. That's what I like to hear."

"Don't forget the StarWalk!" said Mitch.

"Oh, we won't forget that. I'm glad you spruced up. You'll look good in the photographs. Although I don't know why you"—she looked at Lew—"aren't wearing a hat. You're at FallsFest, for crying out loud. Where's your cowboy hat?"

"There was a mishap," said Lew.

"It's Archie's fault," said Slim. "He sat on it. It was a beautiful hat."

Ruby walked over to a file cabinet, withdrew a white Stetson from the top drawer, and placed it on Lew's head. "This is Gordy's. He never wears it, but he's particular about his toys, so don't let your manager near it." She adjusted the hat's tilt, nodded her approval. "It's a fit. Now take it off. Bring it with you to the StarWalk. In the meantime, I'll confirm this other media while you do the record. Any times I should stay away from?"

Lew removed the hat and placed it on the desk. "Frankly, I haven't thought about our schedule," said Lew.

"Your manager should have worked with you on this."

"Whatever's physically possible, I guess."

"I'll figure it out. You'll be surprised what can happen when people who know what they're doing start doing things. Tell Bobby to buzz my radio when you're done here." She marched out of the room. Lew traced the brim of the Stetson with his thumb. Mr. and Mrs. Schroeder kept quiet despite clearly being thrilled to witness all this backstage music business. Mitch tried on the Stetson. It perched atop the swells of his hair like a nesting bird. Lew gingerly removed it and placed it out of reach. Slim couldn't stop chuckling. The result was a most jocular series of IDs.

The shuttle bus delivered the Cowboys, Schroeders, and Ruby to the opposite end of FallsFest from the offices. Here was the world renowned FallsFest StarWalk. Much to Lew's surprise, the Walk looked like a small post-apocalyptic cathedral. The handprints weren't visible from the bus, only the plastic-tarp-encased scaffolding surrounding the concrete walk. Lew caught a glimpse of Gordon Morgan mixing the cement through the scaffolding doorway.

"Gordy feels very strongly about mixing the cement himself," said Ruby, seated next to Lew. "He sees it as a metaphor for how he built this festival." Lew raised his eyebrows. "He told me that directly. He's a great one for metaphors. He told me that too."

Nancy ran up to Gordon and showed him something on her phone.

"That Nancy's a pistol," said Ruby. "She looks mild mannered, but boy oh boy, let me tell you, she's a pistol. The way she's been talking you up to the *TC Record* columnist, he thinks he's about to see the reincarnation of either Jimi Hendrix or Hank Williams—with Bob Wills thrown in there to boot! You must be talented, Lew, if you can get people this interested despite your lousy manager."

"Well . . ." said Lew.

"On top of it all, you should know"—Ruby's eyes narrowed—"that Archibald Grant called Gordy at the eleventh hour and strong-armed him into taking that floozy girlfriend of his as your warm-up act."

"Girlfriend of *his?*" asked Lew. Mercy, even FallsFest staff knew more about Lew's breakup than he did. And Archie had used Lew to promote Ann-Dee. Were they really a pair now? That's low—lower even than Lew's heart sank.

"You're lucky Gordy likes you. If he didn't, you wouldn't be playing tomorrow. In fact, you probably wouldn't be playing anywhere for a long time to come. I can't believe he put that blonde joke on before you."

Blonde joke? Floozy? Lew had never thought of Ann-Dee as anything other than an exalted angel. Even when she dumped him, he assumed it was his fault, at least at first.

"Yep," said Ruby. "Get rid of Grant. But before you do, tell Gordy you're going to do it. And apologize for that boob's behavior. Tell him now while the cement's still fresh. He's always in a good mood when the cement's fresh. Now put on the hat." She zipped out of the shuttle.

Numb, Lew stumbled after her. Gordon emerged from the tarp-encased scaffolding. Lew shook Gordon's hand again for no good reason.

"Mr. Morgan," said Lew, "I understand my manager spoke with you in a disrespectful manner earlier. I want you to know that he did so without the knowledge or consent of myself or any of the band. Lewis Sinclair and the Gentlemen Cowboys have the utmost admiration for what you and FallsFest have done for country music," said Lew. "We could not be happier to play here."

Slim, Gary, and Mitch disembarked from the van. A golf cart drove up the hill.

"Great," said Gordon. He paused a moment and studied the Stetson on Lew's head. "Well, Bobby's here to take the photos, and he's brought someone I'd like you to meet." He waved to a man climbing out of the golf cart. "John, this is Lewis Sinclair. I told you about him yesterday."

John Turnbell walked up the hill to Gordon and Lew. They all took turns shaking hands.

Bea Schroeder trotted up to the three men.

"Gentlemen, I've prepared a feast for the Cowboys' arrival back at the resort. I'd be thrilled if you both would consider joining us."

"Let's get Lew's hands in cement first," said Gordon. "It sets pretty quickly. C'mon Lew."

The trio passed through the scaffolding to the section of fresh cement where Bobby was at the ready with his camera. Laughs, flash, immortality. John Turnbell took a few snaps of his own. Smiles all around as Lew shook some of the excess concrete from his hands. A speeding golf cart drew their attention outside to the view down the hill.

Archie Grant tore up to the StarWalk in a golf cart with the now infamous Ann-Dee beside him.

She clutched her pink shantung straw hat close to her floozy flaxen locks.

"Careful, Archie!" crabbed Ann-Dee. "If you screw up my hair, you're dead meat." The cart lurched to a stop. Archie helped Ann-Dee to the ground. Lew took the scene in. His fingers began to tremble. His palms grew hot.

"Mr. Morgan," said Lew, "I want you to know that I had nothing to do with Archie Grant's request that Ann-Dee join the FallsFest bill. The Cowboys and I are in fact terminating our management relationship with Mr. Grant because of this behavior."

"Brilliant!" said Mitch.

"I hope you accept my apology," said Lew.

In a rare display of emotion to someone other than his parents or Nancy, Gary shed his Teutonic frown and embraced his fellow Cowboys about the shoulders, smiling ear to ear.

"Glad to hear it," said Gordon.

Archie strode toward the trio with Ann-Dee on his arm.

"Listen, Gordy, you have enough cement there for Ann-Dee to put her hands in? I mean, as long as we're here and the cement's still wet . . ."

Lew leaned back and threw a solid punch that packed all the pain he'd been containing straight into Archie Grant's abdomen, knocking him to the ground and causing him to roll down the hill.

"Archie, Lewis Sinclair and the Gentlemen Cowboys no longer require your services. Your management position with us is terminated."

"Aw Lew," gasped Archie. He staggered to his feet. "Clear your head, man. Think this out a minute." Lew started to lunge toward Archie, but Gordon Morgan caught him and held him firm. Gordon nodded to Ruby, who immediately activated her walkie-talkie.

"Security. Flynn here. Send Brad to the StarWalk, please. Not an emergency, but don't dawdle."

The Cowboys gathered around their leader. Lew shifted his gaze from Archie to Ruby, who had cleared her throat ever so softly. Their eyes met. She nodded toward John Turnbell. Ann-Dee was sidling up to him. She placed a note in his hand.

Brad from Security drove up to Ruby.

"Brad," said Ruby, "get the blonde and that gasping blowhard down the hill out of here."

John Turnbell was not so bold as to take any more photos, but he did reach for the shirt pocket where a small notepad peeked out.

"Well now," said Mrs. Schroeder, "who's hungry?"

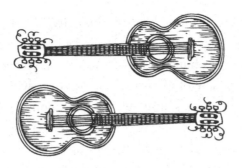

CHAPTER FOUR

E veryone, including Ruby, Gordon, Nancy, and John Turnbell,
drove to the Schroeder homestead for supper. The Schroeders owned and ran a resort close by the FallsFest grounds on
the shore of Big Pearly Lake. (Big Pearly Lake being the walleye-rich
pool that the actual Big Pearly Falls empties into from the Big Pearly
River.)

The Schroeders lived in a humble wood-frame house, built from
a kit by a long-ago Schroeder family, walking distance up a hill from
the beach. It was merely handy in the days before indoor running
water was installed, but now made the present-day occupants the
proud owners of the best-situated and most picturesque resort in
the area. It was wildly popular with fishing guests and, for four days
every year, the prime hostelry for country-western music fans who
were reluctant to pitch a tent or drive an RV.

The resort's knotty pine office/store/soda fountain connected to
the Schroeder family kitchen. Once you walked through the common

door you entered a world of cozy domesticity. Bea Schroeder was a lover of the homely arts. Dish towels hand embroidered with peaches and strawberries hung by the sink. Colorful crocheted potholders adorned the side of the oven. The off-white-with-a-hint-of-saffron walls made a fine showcase for a collection of African violets and Thanksgiving cacti on the counter. The sizeable kitchen table was sheathed in a lemon-hued oilcloth upon which nested a bluebird-decorated teapot and an apple and pear set of salt and pepper shakers.

Next to an avocado-tinted refrigerator (decorated with a celebration of family photos held in place by a medley of ceramic fruit magnets) was a second door to the kitchen that led outdoors. It was a roomy kitchen, despite all the decoration and plants. The result wasn't claustrophobic; rather, one felt nurtured by its abundance.

Warming on the stove was a blue speckleware pot of coffee. How the Schroeders drank coffee morning, noon, and night and still fell asleep at a decent hour (according to Gary) was a mystery to Lew. No serenade from Mitch's pipes could lull Lew to slumber if he'd had so much as a sip of the strong post-lunchtime brew that the Schroeders drank by the mugful. The aroma of coffee wove itself through the smell of baked bread and the cooking supper.

Bea Schroeder's roast beast with onions, potatoes, garlic, and basil had been cooking low and slow in the oven for hours. The moment the group entered the house they were intoxicated by the aroma. This certainly was what they'd been living their whole lives for. Mitch swooned and melted into one of the kitchen chairs.

"Oh Mother Schroeder, I'm that sure I'll die if you don't give me a plate of supper right this instant."

"Such a good boy, Finbar." Mrs. Schroeder patted Mitch on the shoulder and pulled a tray of dinner rolls from a warming drawer in the oven. "Put some butter on that." She emptied the rolls into a basket and placed it on the table. "It'll tide you over till the roast's carved." The men fell helplessly on the freshly made baked goods, juggling the piping-hot rolls with their fingertips until cool enough to hold.

"So, John," said Ruby, "where's this blogger guy you told me about? He hasn't picked up his credentials yet."

"War Zone," mumbled John Turnbell as best he could with a mouth full of warm buttery dough.

"Oh, please no!" said Ruby. She buried her face in her hands. "I hate that place. I'd close it down if I didn't think it'd just pop back up somewhere else."

"What's this War Zone?" asked Mitch.

"It's the campground where all the party animals go," replied Ruby. "Nudity, mass quantities of alcohol. It's a real Sodom and Gomorrah."

"*Where* is this War Zone?" asked Mitch.

"No War Zone for you," said Lew. "Not until after our set. Even then."

"I won't let my daughter come within fifty yards of the place when she's here," said Ruby.

"How old is Lana now?" asked John Turnbell.

"Seventeen," replied Ruby. "She's looking into colleges. Don't get me started. I don't know how we're going to pay for it. Tuition is completely out of hand."

"Tell me about it," said John. "My boy's looking at Boston College."

There was a knock on the door. The knocker didn't wait for an invitation. Archie blew into the kitchen.

"Lew, we have to talk . . ." Archie was distracted by Nancy, who, startled by his entrance, stood quickly and gasped. "Nancy . . ." Archie changed direction and strode toward her.

Gary stepped forward and stopped him with a firm hand on his shoulder.

"It's business," said Archie. He tried to wrench himself out of Gary's Vulcan grip.

"You don't have any business with us," said Gary.

"No, I do," sputtered Archie. "Not the Cowboys. FallsFest stuff. I really need to talk to her. I swear." Archie shook his shoulder free. He stepped toward Nancy.

Gary leaned back like an ace closer and sunk a line drive pitch into Archie's strike zone, sending him staggering backward and onto the floor.

Mrs. Schroeder stooped down to him.

"Mr. Grant, it might be better for your health if you take your supper at the motel tonight." She slipped a warm roll into his hand, helped him up, and guided him outside. She returned to the kitchen brushing her hands together as if removing unwanted flour. "You boys watch your hands now. You can't play music with swollen fingers. Remember, never aim for the hard parts, and use your right hand."

"I could have handled him, Gary," said Nancy.

"There are times," said Gary, "when a man has to show another man where he stands. Archie should have known that already."

"I expect he does now," said Slim.

Lew sent a brisk nod Gary's way.

John Turnbell reached for the notebook in his breast pocket. Gordon shook his head. John's arm fell back to his side.

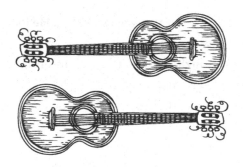

CHAPTER FIVE

----◦◦◦◦----◦◦◦◦----◦◦◦◦----

Chuck Nelson and John Turnbell walked toward the FallsFest trailer.

"Dude, you seriously have to check out that War Zone campground. It is the wildest place I've ever experienced—and I've been to Burning Man—twice!"

"It's more about the music, Chuck," said John.

"Oh, I know," said Chuck, "but, dude, seriously, the War Zone."

"Anyway, remember, FallsFest is very generous to the media. Not bribes, just in letting us hang around the whole festival. The music, the fans, backstage. Just don't be aggressive with the artists. They're very protective of the artists."

"That's cool," said Chuck. "I like these people already. Where's this Ruby? I want to meet her."

They ascended the trailer steps and opened the door. Gary Schroeder sat on the edge of Nancy's desk. A shaft of light limned his angular cheekbones and jaw. Chuck was struck by the tension in

Gary's face, which, even at rest, was imposing. He looked still, like a man who knew how to wait.

"I just think it might be wise to check in on him, see how he's reacting," whispered Nancy. "Maybe not you . . ."

"You're not going anywhere near that monster," said Gary. They noticed John and Chuck.

Silence all around.

"Um," said John, "this is Chuck, you know, the blogger. He's here for his press credentials."

"Ruby has them," said Nancy. "She's in Gordon's office. Let me see if she's available." Nancy pressed a button on her walkie-talkie. "Ruby? This is Nancy. John Turnbell and Chuck Nelson are here to see you. Chuck's getting credentials." She released the button.

"Good deal," said Ruby. "Send them through."

Nancy nodded toward the door. John and Chuck walked into the next office.

"Welcome to FallsFest." Ruby extended her hand. Chuck shook it. "Stay away from the War Zone."

"Too late," said Chuck.

"Well, if you're there again, and you see any naked people, call 911, okay? We want to keep FallsFest family-friendly."

"Right-o," said Chuck. "Consider me your devoted hall monitor." He bowed.

Chuck noticed a guitar lying on the desk—a Martin acoustic with mother-of-pearl inlay. Just like Elvis used to play! Several prominent country-western signatures adorned its body. He reached out to trace his fingers across the names.

"Don't touch that," said Ruby. "It's a prize. The ink's not dry on the insurance policy yet."

Chuck pulled his hand back.

Ruby opened a desk drawer and took out a lanyard. "Here. Wear this. You can go anywhere except the tour buses, even Artist

Hospitality. But if you bug any of them, if I sense one iota of tension from talent, you're out of here and you're never coming back. Falls-Fest rules. But we're glad to have you here. Have a good time."

Chuck received the lanyard. After a few moments, he closed his mouth and took in a breath.

"I'm pretty direct," said Ruby. She laughed. "You'll always know where you stand with me. If I'm smiling, I'm happy. If I'm frowning, I'm mad. There's no second-guessing with me. I don't have time for it. You'll appreciate that someday. Now really, have a good time. You seem sweet. I want you to have fun."

"Yes, ma'am," said Chuck. He started to salute, but caught himself. "Thanks."

"And watch out with that hat cam. John told me all about it. Don't record any of the acts. I mean it. No phone video either. We'll throw you right out."

"Oh, I rarely use my phone camera anymore. People act way more normal when they don't see the camera." He tapped his hat.

Ruby's eyes served him a hard warning. Chuck removed his hat.

"No recording the acts. I won't."

Ruby nodded. "Now, John . . ." She turned her attention to Mr. Turnbell. "Has your son taken his SATs yet?"

"Funny you should mention that," said John.

"I'll just pop out now, then, if you don't mind," said Chuck. "Check out the StarWalk."

"Be careful," said Ruby. "We're redecorating it. Whole new design. Concrete's the same of course. That part's set in stone. Ha!"

"Is that what all the scaffolding's for?" asked John. "I was surprised about that. If you're not familiar with the Walk, you might not know what it is. Is it open to the public this year?"

"Kind of, yes. Kind of, no," said Ruby. "We wanted it to be open for the festival, but we ran out of paint. I had it mixed specially to match the FallsFest logo. I took them a PMS chip. We call it FallsFest blue. They dropped a couple new cans off this morning. I'm debating whether to finish painting today or not. I'd just hate it if some fan leaned into the fresh paint. I'll let Gordy decide."

"I'll just look around," said Chuck. "I won't touch anything."

"You're a good kid. Have fun." Chuck left Ruby and John to discuss their children's post-secondary future.

⸲⸲⸲ ⸲⸲⸲ ⸲⸲⸲

The StarWalk perched at the crest of a rolling pasture. Chuck ascended to it and stood outside the scaffolding and its flapping plastic. The wind breathed through various tears and whistled around the framework of pipes.

He enjoyed the vast scene assembling below. Fans exited various campgrounds and parking lots, forming a human chain to the concert area.

Some hearty settlers had already homesteaded their claims with lawn chairs. Hats and bandanas dotted the pasture like confetti. Festival stage managers and roadies checked gear on the distant stage. A stray laugh arose now and then above the wind. *Not a bad vantage point to contemplate humanity from,* thought Chuck. He crawled to a sheltered spot in the scaffolding safe from the wind. He looked out down the hill and adjusted his hat so the camera could take in the entire scene.

"All I'm saying, Gordy, is that you could do worse than book Ann-Dee for next year."

Chuck realized that in his new location, he could make out voices inside the scaffolding. He scrunched in closer to the plastic.

"You don't call me 'Gordy.' You call me 'Mr. Morgan.' Preferably you don't talk to me at all—ever."

"Hey, I'll call you Mr. Tibbs if you like. What's the big deal?"

"You don't lean on me. Nobody leans on me. Got that?"

Hmm, thought Chuck. *This Mr. Morgan sounds tough—tall too. Is it possible to sound tall?* Chuck found a small rip in the plastic and peeked through it.

"No leaning. Got it. No problem. Not my style anyway."

"I know it's your style, Grant. It's been your style all your life. It sure as hell was in Memphis! Now get off FallsFest property."

Memphis? wondered Chuck. *Where Elvis lives?*

"What?" said the smaller man—Grant. "You got the wrong guy."

"I'm done talking to you. Go."

"Hey. Did we meet once? In Memphis? I'm not good with re-membering names and stuff. I did a lot of stuff in Memphis. Help me out."

"How many people have to take a swing at you before you get the hint? Your act can play tomorrow, but *you* are gone—now!"

"I don't know what you're talking about. Did you live in that apartment building? Over on Van Heusen Street? Yellow brick, fan-cy curlicues on the windows? I worked for a guy owned that place. Oh . . . did you work in a club? There was this one with an Irish name. I collected rents over in that area."

"Rents," scoffed Gordon.

"Oh, wait. Were you that skinny kid? At Kennedy's? Listen, that was a long time ago. All that could have been avoided if the old guy who owned the joint had just made his payments."

Gordon raised his walkie-talkie to his mouth. Pressed a button. "This is Gordon. Brad, you there? Over."

Chuck withdrew from the tarp. He scrunched down. *Whoa. This Grant guy is a punk!*

"*This is Brad. Over.*"

"Brad, I need you to come up to the StarWalk. Archie Grant's here and I need him removed from the grounds."

"*Again?*"

"ASAP. Over."

"*I'll be right there.*"

"No need," said Archie. "No need." Archie raised his palms like a prisoner and edged his way to the entrance. "I don't want any trouble. But if you don't mind, I really would like to stay and see Ann-Dee perform. If I keep a real low profile, like, it should be okay. Yeah? I won't go near the trailers or the talent or . . ." Archie scrunched his shoulders and backed toward Chuck's hiding place.

I'm outta here, thought Chuck. He jumped away from the scaffolding and ran down the hill toward a more genial part of the festival.

⋘⋙ ⋘⋙ ⋘⋙

Ruby stood stalwart at her post by her desk. She would not be cowed by this man—although her forehead would be in far less danger from the onslaught of his saliva if she'd just agree to his demands. He towered a good head over Ruby, yet still the spittle threatened. How on earth had he got into such an uproar over something so out of the question and which was set in stone in a contract?

"My artist deserves to give that guitar away! He's the king of country right now! It's absurd to choose those lunatics over him. It's an insult, and I won't stand for it!"

"Your artist is playing tonight," explained Ruby, again. "The guitar has to be given away on the last day of the festival. We negotiated what night your guy was going on and tonight is the night you wanted."

"We never discussed the guitar!"

"Because we didn't have to."

"I'm not saying this again."

"Good!"

Gordon stomped through the trailer door nearly colliding with the back of the angry manager.

"What are you doing in here?" he asked.

"Your staff is being very rude and uncompromising!" said the manager.

"I highly doubt that," said Gordon. He cast a wary eye to Ruby, who rolled both of hers.

"Oh, brother." Ruby sighed.

"You're talking to my right hand, Bingham," said Gordon. "She's the epitome of tact and diplomacy."

"She is keeping my artist from receiving the respect he deserves!"

"How is she doing that?" Gordon had to look three inches up to stare Bingham in the eye. Not many people required that of him.

"My artist should be giving away that guitar," said Bingham.

"Impossible. He's going on tonight as he agreed to do in his signed contract."

"You never mentioned the guitar."

"I didn't need to. I hired your artist to perform, not give away contest prizes."

"Burke is perfect for that and you know it," said Bingham.

"He's not perfect for it, because he's playing tonight and the guitar is going to be raffled on Sunday."

Bingham pulled up all his considerable weight and stepped a foot closer to Gordon. Ruby glanced at the bat mounted on the wall.

"Switch it or Burke doesn't go on tonight." An unfortunate drop of saliva landed on Gordon's forehead. Gordon grabbed Bingham by the shoulders and shoved him down into the straight-back wooden chair by Ruby's desk. Bingham tried to stand up but Gordon's hands kept him down.

"Okay," said Gordon, "Burke doesn't go on. I'll go out on that stage and make the announcement myself." Bingham jerked but could only stay seated. "I'll tell all those people who came to see him that Burke Boyde refuses to perform because he's having a tantrum over who gets to give away the raffle guitar."

The two men's eyes locked. The staring contest went on for twenty-two seconds, until Bingham looked away.

"But we have a contract," he muttered.

"Are we done here?" asked Gordon.

"He'll go on," said Bingham.

Gordon released Bingham's shoulders. He straightened and made room for the manager to leave the trailer. When the man had gone, Gordon and Ruby exchanged looks.

"Damn criminals," spat Gordon.

Ruby stood motionless. The adrenalin flooding her arms and legs began to subside. Gordon walked into his office and slammed the door. A few moments passed.

"Where's my hat?"

CHAPTER SIX

—≪≪•≫≫— —≪≪•≫≫— —≪≪•≫≫—

L ew awoke to the aroma of bacon, warm maple syrup, and cinnamon rolls. He took a moment to make sure he was indeed in a motel room. Surely that intoxicating smell was not from the motel's complimentary continental breakfast.

A knock on the door. Mitch.

"Mother Schroeder's brought us breakfast, Lew. It's in Gary's room. She wants to make sure we're all well-fed before our set, God bless her. Better hurry before Slim eats it all."

Lew threw on his plum satin dressing robe. He hoped none of the fellas would make fun of him for it. Cowboys didn't as a rule wear dressing robes.

Then again, perhaps gentlemen cowboys did. He tightened his belt and made his way to Gary's room. Slim sat at the writing desk with a warmed plate full of delectable breakfast morsels.

He looked up from his morning feast when Lew entered the room.

"Good morning, Lew. I've received word that we're going on fifteen minutes late today. They're making room for, well, you know, by moving us back and reducing the break after the gospel choir. Nancy says Mr. Morgan apologizes that Ann—that the *new act* is going on at all, but she is only getting ten minutes total to perform."

Lew helped himself to the food.

"I'm surprised that woman's singing at all, considering what happened yesterday," said Mr. Schroeder.

"Well, Nancy says Mr. Morgan is a man of his word," said Mrs. Schroeder. "If he told her she could sing, we can only expect he'd stand by his promise. I respect him for that. We'll all just have to lump it."

"Her band will be hard-pressed to get onstage, perform, and get out between the gospel choir and us," said Slim. "I think Mr. Gordon may be making sport of her. At least we won't have to trim our set."

"I propose we not talk about her," said Lew.

They ate silently for a few minutes.

"If we *were* talking about her though," said Lew, "I'd probably say that I wouldn't cry into my beer if she fell off the stage. If we were talking about her that is." He bit a smidgen of nail off his thumb.

Mrs. Schroeder topped up his coffee.

⋅⋅⋅⋅⋅⋅⋅⋅⋅⋅

While Ann-Dee sang her cover of "Stand by Your Man," Lew and the Gentlemen Cowboys readied themselves in a dressing-room trailer in between Artist Hospitality and the FallsFest office. Lew studied himself in a mirror. He turned to this side and that. What the—? He turned a little more; turned until he could see as much of his tweed suit jacket as possible. That was definitely the most hideous jacket crease he could remember seeing in all his born days. He checked the closet for an iron. None.

He knocked on the door of the room next to his.

"Any of you fellas see an iron in there?"

Slim came to the door.

"I told you to wear linen, Lew," said Slim. "People expect wrinkles in linen. And it has the added bonus of being cooler than your beloved wool blends. I don't know how you're going to play in this heat in that tweed. If you'd earned your chops in New Orleans like I did—"

"There's plenty of heat in Texas, thank you very much. Anyway, you were raised in Iowa right next to a cornfield, and you and I both know it."

"I can see why you're owly over that crease. It is most unsightly. I'd check the office trailer. They might have an iron. That Ms. Flynn seems to be prepared for most anything."

Lew strode next door. He walked in on Nancy swinging a Louisville slugger. She jumped at the sound of Lew's voice.

"Unexpected place for batting practice," he said.

"Oh, just getting used to the feel of it," said Nancy. She chuckled. "We each keep a bat on hand for security purposes." She stored the bat in the kneehole of her desk. "We have real security too, of course—trained personnel, off-duty cops—but Gordon likes us each to have access to our own bat, to help out, just in case. The major muscle isn't always in the exact spot you'd like when a fight breaks out. You'd be surprised how much respect a bat commands—even in the hands of someone like me—or Ruby. Well, especially in the hands of someone like Ruby." They each laughed.

"You wouldn't by chance have an iron down there by that weapon of yours, would you? My suit jacket is in a rather unfortunate condition."

"Oh dear," said Nancy. "Y'know, I'll bet Ruby has one." She nodded toward the next room. Lew followed the nod and found Ruby at Gordon's desk examining the Martin guitar.

"Ma'am," said Lew, "I have the most undistinguished crease in the back of my jacket. Would you by any chance have an iron on hand I could borrow?"

"Of course I do, Lewie." She opened a side desk drawer and extracted said iron. "Nancy!" Nancy popped into the doorway. "Press the crease out of Mr. Sinclair's jacket for him please. Do you have time?"

"Of course," said Nancy. She took the iron and waited for Lew to remove his jacket. "Where's the ironing board?"

"It's your desk. It's unfinished wood. Should work fine," said Ruby. Nancy took the jacket and iron to the other office. "She learns something new from me every day," she said to Lew. She handed him the guitar. "Take a look at this. Some lucky fan's going to win it. I'm sure it'll mean more to him or her if you sign it first. Here's a marker." Lew took the guitar and marker. "Raffle's on the last day of the festival. Everyone with a FallsFest ticket has a chance to win it. We're trying to get the TV stations to cover the drawing. Maybe get picked up by the cable channels."

Lew smiled and signed the guitar. It slowly dawned on him that he could hear Ann-Dee singing.

"Sorry about that," said Ruby. "You're hearing the monitor." She nodded to the TV. "It's how we keep tabs on the stage."

Lew was transfixed by Ann-Dee on the monitor. Her face filled the screen, blue eyes sparkling with fierce energy. Her fingertips rested at her throat, touching ever so gently the gem-encrusted brooch clasped to her scarf. Ann-Dee once told Lew the brooch was her signature.

She meant to wear it every time she performed, every time she was in the public eye. Lew had wondered why a woman as young as she chose such a baroque piece of jewelry for a signature. She'd said it was her grandmother's, and that her grandmother wore it to bingo for good luck and always won. Plus, it was versatile. She could wear it a dozen different ways. It would be fun for fans to look for it and keep track of it.

Ann-Dee's fingers moved to the brim of her pink straw hat. An antique red heart was painted on the crown. She swept off the hat. Sunlit tresses cascaded to her shoulders. *What a beautiful woman,* thought Lew. *What a beautiful voice.*

He was proud of her performance, then realized she was singing, "Stand by Your Man," and he remembered that beauty was sometimes only skin deep. Ann-Dee finished her song. John Turnbell was acting emcee for the day. He came up to her as her head stayed bowed for applause.

"Ladies and gentlemen, Miss Ann-Dee Phillips!"

Lew's face sagged. All the love and support of the band and the Schroeders had buoyed him up until now. Ruby walked to his side.

"Could have been worse," she said. "You could have married her. Her kind always finds a top-notch divorce lawyer."

⸻⸻⸻

Ann-Dee kept her head bowed. She took in the applause like oxygen.

"Ann-Dee Phillips, everybody!" said John Turnbell. "And now we have a special request! Would the gentleman with the special request please approach the stage?"

Ann-Dee raised her head. She scoured the audience for what the special request might be. Archie Grant strutted forward from behind a screen backstage. He knelt before her. Ann-Dee's stomach churned. She looked to John Turnbell who was recording the scene with his phone.

Many people in the audience began whipping out their own phones. An icy dread rose up Ann-Dee's spine.

"Ann-Dee," said Archie. "I have searched the world over for my soul mate."

Oh no, thought Ann-Dee. She wanted out of this blather tout de suite. Did he really think marrying someone like him would be good for her career?

"... for someone so beautiful, so kind, so ..."

Why in the world would he think she wanted to marry him? Especially after yesterday morning.

"I can only hope that you'll find it in your heart ..."

Then again, any publicity's good publicity, she thought. Maybe she could parlay it into even more press later with a messy breakup. She'd keep in touch with that John Turnbell. Where'd he say he was staying? The Schroeder Resort?

"Please, bestow upon me the honor ..."

Like this chump knows anything about honor, thought Ann-Dee.

"... of your hand in marriage. Will you, Ann-Dee? Will you be my bride and walk with me in eternity?"

Ann-Dee stared at him. He deserved to wait, pulling a stunt like this. It would play best if she hesitated. Her eyes scanned the stage while her head stayed still, so only he would know she wasn't looking at him. Wait for that teensy bit of sweat to form on his forehead. There it is.

"Archibald Grant, my answer is ..." A flash in the audience distracted Ann-Dee. She looked out at the crowd. "My answer is ..." Flash! A camera. A bodacious, laughing woman in sky-blue satin, looking not at Ann-Dee but at the jumbotron, took another photo of the giant screen, causing another flash. Ann-Dee looked to the jumbotron and saw her head and shoulders twenty feet wide and fifteen feet tall. Flash! Ann-Dee looked back to the woman in blue. There was someone beside her.

What the ... It couldn't be ... Flash!

Ann-Dee collapsed. The full weight of her body hit the stage with a definite thud.

It was clean, for an alley, but it was still an alley. The late-morning sun had risen over the buildings on each side. Its warm rays encouraged the release of an acrid bouquet from the dumpster's discarded foodstuffs. Last week's unsold coleslaw, rancid expired deli meat, onion skins. Ann-Dee could hear rats chattering in their hiding places.

She rested her forehead against the dumpster, making sure, despite her tremors, to find a spot without rust or flaking paint. She was tired down into her bones. Tired of rolling drunks. Tired of running from men who weren't drunk enough. Tired of working jobs that didn't ask for a Social Security number. Tired of leaving jobs when the threat of being reported inevitably came.

And she was especially tired of hanging out by this dumpster looking for expired food that the bodega owner threw out.

She gathered her resolve, stood, and lifted the dumpster lid. Thank goodness, the owner never locked it, probably because no one walked dogs in this neighborhood. The owner eventually caught on that she was going through his garbage. It took a pretty long time because there were no security cameras and Ann-Dee was a tidy forager. She'd seen bums foraging in other places and they left junk all over the alleys. Another reason some bodega owners put locks on their bins.

Ann-Dee didn't want to lose her claim, so she was careful. When this bodega owner caught on, he started separating the goods that were right on their expiration dates from the ancient ones. Ann-Dee kept the spot-on products and took the rest down to the Wallace overpass. She never went all the way down to the river or under the bridge. She left the bags close enough for the residents to find on their way home, ahead of the curve, before the descent, so no one would see her. And she didn't do it with regularity. She didn't want to be anticipated. It worked out for the bodega owner too. He didn't have to pay to have the dumpster emptied as often.

The dumpster smelled really foul today.

Ann-Dee held her breath. Squinching her eyes almost shut, she scouted out the latest haul. As the dumpster was almost full, it was easy to find. The dumpster would be emptied this week, probably tomorrow. Friday was the usual day Ann-Dee noticed garbage trucks driving around.

She retrieved the expired foodstuffs, replaced them with a parcel wrapped in a roomy used Walmart bag, then covered it up with debris. Still squinting, she lowered the dumpster lid.

She looked up and down the alley, waited a few minutes, then knocked a coded rhythm of raps on the back door. This told the bodega owner she was leaving. He respected her privacy and pride. He didn't like to surprise her while she was there.

She walked down the alley to the future. She was still shaking.

———

Lew and Ruby, their mouths slightly agape, watched the scene unfold on the stage monitor.

"What the hell was that?" Ruby asked. Lew gazed transfixed at the screen. "Sit down, Lewie." She guided him to a chair, found the remote control to the jumbotron monitor and muted it. Footsteps outside the trailer. "Cool down with this while I shoo the crowd away." She thrust a chilled bottle of water into his hands. "But don't spill it on your clothes. You still have to go on in ten minutes." Lew looked up at her. "We have sponsors who would wring your neck if you didn't go out there. Sorry, but you're show people. You smile when you're low. It's in your contract. I'll be back in ten minutes." She left Lew alone.

A clamor in the next room was followed by the appearance of Gary in the doorway. Mitch's head popped up behind his shoulder. The rhythm section parted as Slim proceeded into Gordon's office.

"Son, I can't kiss you or tell you you're handsome, but I've known you a lot longer than that woman has, and, well, you can always count on me. Same with these two behind me. We're your band. Let's go out onto that stage right now and set it on fire."

Nancy entered with Lew's now wrinkle-free coat. Slim winked at her.

"Since we're talking about setting things on fire, if you like, we can put a match to that red Mustang, or any other damn thing Archie owns—but later, after the show."

Lew nodded at Slim and donned the jacket. He straightened his tie with trembling fingers. Ruby entered the room with the white Stetson.

"May as well borrow this again. Gordy won't need it for a while; he's out in the audience already waiting for your set."

Lew put it on and adjusted its tilt just a tiny bit forward toward his right eye.

"C'mon, boys," said Lew.

Lew led the Gentlemen Cowboys out of the trailer and up the steps to the back of the stage. He looked out at the crowd. The audience was agitated. They'd just seen a marriage proposal blown up twenty times the size of human reality, followed by the lady's collapse, and the excitement of paramedics and an ambulance. It was a hard act to follow. Lew figured there was a number in attendance who'd heard of him. A few less who'd actually heard his music. And another contingent who'd never heard of him but wondered if someone would suffer a heart attack on stage or tear their clothes off and run amok through the fair. It wasn't out of the question. It was a sweltering day, the kind only mad dogs, Englishmen, and music festival fans went out in.

Lew searched the humanity before him. Medics and security were bringing liquid to some fans and escorting woozy others to shadier seats. The faces of the audience blurred into one big rainbow dot pattern. As their murmurs reached his ears, they once again separated into individuals and Lew spied Gordon Morgan. Gordon tapped his head and gave a thumbs-up. Lew tipped his hat to him. The Cowboys picked up their instruments and jumped into their show, a collection of songs of love and betrayal.

Lew baked in the sun. Slim was right about the tweed. It was deadly hot. Lew felt the sweat accumulate on his brow. The Cowboys reached the point in the set list to play "This Angel." Lew had written it for Ann-Dee. Why hadn't he taken it off the list? Because it was a damn good song, one of his best. It had hit potential. The band waited for his cue.

Lew waded slowly into the introduction. He felt his throat constrict a tiny bit. *Focus on the music, Lew*, he thought. *You're a pro. You can do this. There's no business like show business.* He floated further into the melody carried by the notes. Mitch and Gary glanced at each other. It was time for the lyrics to start. Could he do it?

Softly, Lew began the first verse. Each word broke free from his heart. He realized up there on that hot, cruel stage that he'd loved Ann-Dee or whomever he'd thought she was. And he still wanted to love that phantom woman—and be loved back. He sang his sweet lyrics to her, to that phantom, that angel. His trusty guitar led him through the song, spoke his heart for him. A fresh breeze wafted in, cooling and drying the drops on Lew's forehead. He closed his eyes and let the song flow from him.

When he opened his eyes after the final notes faded, he looked out into the crowd. A sturdy woman with white-blonde hair in the third row pointed her camera up away from the stage to her right. Funny, thought Lew, how people can be ten feet from an entertainer and still be drawn to the jumbotron. The power of TV. Well, it was jumbo, kind of hard to ignore. He followed her gaze to the screen, the scene of Archie's proposal. The scene of his lover's betrayal. He saw himself and the Gentlemen Cowboys. There were roadies and a stage manager behind them off to the sides. And there, upstage, at the back, lurked Ann-Dee and Archie. Who in the green, green grass of home let that pair onstage? Didn't they belong in a first-aid tent far, far away? The camera zoomed in tight on them. The crowd started talking. A few people cheered. One wag started singing "Here comes the bride." Ann-Dee handed Archie a plastic beer cup. Lew saw no love in her eyes. Archie looked down at the cup, then up at Ann-Dee. Fool looked drunk already. He grinned lazily and accepted the cup as if it were the precious Grail.

⋘•⟫⟫ ⋘•⟫⟫ ⋘•⟫⟫

Ruby stomped up the back steps with two beefy security guards. She touched Ann-Dee's forearm gently and guided Archie with her hand at his back. Archie looked from her to the security guards. He sipped his beer, then the pair left without fuss.

Lew waited dumbstruck to make sure they didn't reappear. The crowd fidgeted. They were eager for the next song. Lew still looked to where Archie and Ann-Dee had stood. The sturdy lady in the audience lowered her camera. Gary and Mitch looked to Slim. Slim started the introduction to "Ghost Riders in the Sky." Gary joined in with a foreboding bass line. Mitch snuck in his drums as soft and subtle as drums could be played. The music found its way into Lew's consciousness. He strummed a few notes, still looking back, not aware he was even playing, his fingers finding the right strings through muscle memory. Gradually, the vibrating strings brought his head forward, focused his eyes on his guitar.

The Cowboys played through all the verses. The grim lyrics warning restless wrongdoers not to join their drive jangled through Lew's brain. They arrived at the part of the song where Lew usually took a solo. His fingers moved, due to practice and instinct, independent of thought, into the serious waves of a dangerous guitar medley. Tension ebbed and built, crested, and built again. His hands grew hot. Heat radiated from the ground distorting the crowd into a mirage of oscillating, vibrating, colorful shapes. Lew remembered Archie kneeling before Ann-Dee. The music heaved with muscle, blood, and venom. Flashes of white burst in and out through Lew's brain. He saw Ann-Dee in his mind's eye. He saw her collapse. More flashes. The heat rose thick and damp around Lew's neck. He was in the song now, not on the stage but inside the notes and the rhythm and the flow. He saw Ann-Dee's graceful fingers lift a chalice to her lips, but she did not sip. She looked over the rim of the goblet, deep into Lew's eyes. Flash. The guitar strings snarled and howled. Heat rose from Lew's collar up past his eyes. Sweat beaded and dropped from his brow. He sensed the swaying colors of the audience again. Their shapes blurred into vague pulses of bobbing and sinking patterns. Surely good and evil struggled, mingled, thrummed through the crowd. The audience and music swirled into one figure, one sound, transfixed and controlled by the menacing guitar. It gathered up before him, giant and cruel. A vengeful undead monster. It circled Lew, sweeping around him ready to fight. Lew struggled for breath that was not to come. His tormentor swirled into a cyclone. Its heavy, damp heat rose from the earth and swelled over the stage. It took the audience, the shapes, the air. It tried to steal all of the life from the world, every soul.

But it couldn't master Lew. A drop of sweat fell from his forehead to his wrist. The air chilled it and broke the spell. Lew closed his eyes and sought out a breeze. He called back the music to his hands. Called the demon back from its ride. Commanded it return to the earth. The Cowboys faded out their part of the chorus. Lew plucked the last notes of the song, his fingers cool and sure.

He looked up at his face on the jumbotron. It filled the screen. Pure, icy pearls slipped from his brow. The breeze returned and brought him peace. The multitude before him were silent for several seconds, then they rose and roared with adoration. Lew bowed his head, closed his eyes, and listened.

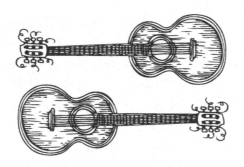

CHAPTER SEVEN

huck Nelson couldn't believe his ears. He'd been baptized—dunked in the river and hoisted straight back up alive, cold, and shivering on a ninety-degree day. The audience around him sat dead quiet, still. Chuck stood, reached his hands high above his head, and clapped with abandon. The crowd likewise came to and rose. Cheers and whistles and applause rang around the walls of the amphitheater.

"Ooh!" cried the sturdy woman in blue satin next to Chuck. "I can't wait to see these." She lifted her camera and grinned. "I took some real good pictures during that song. Flash didn't always go off though. I hope they all turn out."

Chuck looked to his shiny blue neighbor.

"I'm sure they'll be fine, ma'am," he said. He touched the brim of his cap out of instinct. "A flash isn't necessary when it's sunny like this."

"Oh, thanks hon," said Blue Lady.

"Not at all. My pleasure." Chuck touched his hat brim again.

Lew and the Cowboys played a strong set. And that "Ghost Riders" medley! How to top that? Lew and the band brought the crowd to their feet again with a rollicking cover of Hank Williams's "Move It On Over." Many couples took to dancing in the aisles while the entire sea of FallsFest humanity joined in on the chorus's call and response. Never before had so many enjoyed, and indeed celebrated, marital discord so heartily. At the end of the song, John Turnbell trotted to the front of the stage and placed his hand on Lew's shoulder.

"Lewis Sinclair and the Gentlemen Cowboys!" he called out. The crowd cheered and applauded. "Ladies and gentlemen, there's a meet and greet for Lew and the Cowboys, right now, behind the stage. Please line up along the velvet ropes. If you have a lanyard with a fan club sticker, you can line up in the VIP area."

"You wanna go? Sure! I'm game," said Blue Lady.

"Excuse me?" said Chuck. He assumed his new friend was talking to him.

"What, doll?" she asked Chuck.

"I'm sorry," he said. "I thought you were talking to me."

"Oh sweetie, you must think I'm such a flirt. You and your little beatnik whiskers." Chuck raised a hand to his soul patch. "Well, I am a flirt, and now I've made you blush. No, I was speaking to my friend Magda." She gestured to a small, aged woman in a tan sundress and men's white dress shirt.

The tiny woman peered up at Chuck and muttered, "Pleased to meet you." Or something like that. Chuck wasn't sure, she spoke so softly and with some kind of European accent. She tugged on Blue Lady's sleeve. "We must get in line! We must go!" She pulled Blue Lady away.

"I'm Charla by the way," called Blue Lady over her shoulder. "We're gonna go to the meet and greet. You can come with if you want. C'mon!"

Chuck caught up with Charla and Magda as they made their way through the lively and omnidirectional crowd. Magda's head jerked in various directions, her keen eyes scanning her surroundings like a small bird of prey.

—《《◈》》—《《◈》》—《《◈》》—

Young Magda tiptoed through the chicken coop, Frau Holthaus's sturdy ochre basket on her arm. Frau Holthaus had woven the basket in her own sturdier days. Now she relied on Magda to collect the eggs, milk the cow, churn the butter, weed the garden, and can the fruit and vegetables. At least there was the child Gertrude to help now. And an extra person was welcome when moving Frau Holthaus from her bed to her bath chair.

Magda gathered one egg after the other, enough to make a birthday cake! She had only a vague idea of when her actual birthday was. Her mother had burned all records of their identity after the Soviets smashed her father's violin and dragged him away. They sought refuge at Hohenfels Displacement Camp.

Now Magda lived on Frau Holthaus's farm doing the chores the frail woman could no longer do. This allowed Magda to eat better than the average refugee, to walk on green grass, to touch the soft nose of the cow and the warm feathers of the chickens.

Magda, for all the sadness that befell her, thought herself lucky. She didn't assume her position was normal. She didn't assume anything in this world was normal.

Magda stroked the feathers on Schatzi, her favorite hen. There was little use for a rooster with the feisty Schatzi on watch. Her cyclone of wings and talons did much to deter predators.

"Good girl." She soothed the hen. "You keep us all safe now." Magda stepped out of the coop and blinked, adjusting her eyes to the sunlight. Two figures approached from the grove at the far end of the farm. The one on the left was taller, but the one on the right was wider. As they drew closer,

Magda could see that the tall one was a soldier, one of those Americans stationed at Hohenfels. The Americans were so full of life. Such good teeth! And they had treasures, like chocolate, that were hard to come by in this land starved by war.

The shorter figure turned out to be a child—a sturdy child—perhaps large for his age.

"Does this young guy live here?" asked the tall one in English. Like most of the locals since the Americans transformed Hohenfels into their military base, she and Frau Holthaus now spoke some English.

"Zuhause?" He pointed to the boy, then to the house.

Magda admired the soldier's broad shoulders and sparkling black eyes. She slowly shook her head.

The tall soldier eyed her. Perhaps he thought she was mute. "Found him wandering on the other side of these woods," he said. "Thought maybe he belonged here."

Magda noticed the lost, frightened look on the boy's face. She knew that look. She wore it herself before she came to live with Frau Holthaus. Magda studied the boy's wide frame. With some farm meals in him he could become strong enough to guide the plough behind the funny little donkey, strong enough to help young Gertrude move Frau Holthaus from her bed to her bath chair.

Magda turned her gaze to the tall soldier and his fascinating dark eyes. What would they look like if he smiled?

"He can be here," averred Magda in her meager English. She did not want the soldier to leave. "You come check on him. Yes?" The soldier cocked his head. He nodded. He patted the boy on the shoulder.

"Du lebst hier. Besser als Wald." He pushed the child gently toward Magda and turned to go.

"You like kuchen?" gasped Magda. "Cake? I make cake today."

The soldier evidently did like kuchen. Magda learned what his eyes looked like when he smiled. Her heart was lost.

And it was found.

Chuck, Charla, and Magda arrived at the VIP gate, where they came face-to-face with Ruby. Charla and Magda raised their blue-stickered lanyards for her to inspect.

"We're here for the meet and greet," said Charla. "Maynard Krebs here is with us. He don't have the blue sticker, but that cute little beardy thing on his chin should count for something." Ruby raised her eyebrows at Chuck and nodded the trio into the roped-off maze. They reached a point in line close to Lew in front of the opening to the Artist Hospitality tent. Chuck noticed the lady who'd fainted onstage and her swain were in there.

"Ooh look!" cried Charla. "It's the gal who sang 'Stand by Your Man!' I do love that song. Sang it at my poor old sister's wedding." She then launched into a rendition that rivaled the original, not to mention that of the fainting lady.

Despite her friend's performance, Magda seemed more interested in the Artist Hospitality tent. Probably looking for stars, thought Chuck, but the only performer in there at the moment was Fainting Lady, and she only sang the one song. Fainting Lady threw some major stink eye in his direction. He couldn't think why she might look at him that way, but it shook his nerves just the same. Her gaze then shifted just enough to excuse him from her sightline. He felt a great relief. The line advanced and he was now so close to the tent he could hear the swain yammering. He was talking about baseball. Chuck could just make out the word *bat*. Chuck wished the line would move a little faster. Proposal Man leaned in to kiss Fainting Lady but she turned her head and he got a face full of Aqua Net Super Hold. Chuck briskly looked away.

"Ooh, I've just gotta get a panorama of this," boomed Charla. She began snapping away, turning fifteen degrees, then snapping some more. This time the flash worked consistently, once again gathering the sharp attention of Fainting Lady. Proposal Man slurped what looked like a margarita and talked incessantly, but Fainting Lady just stared into the meet-and-greet line.

"I just love panorama shots," said Charla. "I like to tape them all together at home. Sends me right back to where I took 'em. Sometimes I send 'em off to get made into a jigsaw." She pulled three cans of ginger ale out of a voluminous crocheted purse. "You thirsty, Maynard?" she asked in a loud voice, like someone used to speaking with the hard of hearing. "It's just soda pop, but that's all for the best after that sun we got at the concert. Here, Magda." Blue Lady handed a can each to her small friend and to Chuck.

"It's cold!" said Chuck. "How did you keep three cans of pop cold in—"

"Drink up, Maynard," said Charla. "You have to stay hydrated in this heat."

"My name's actually Chuck." He laughed and offered his hand. Charla took it and shook it enthusiastically. Then he and Magda shook hands. He expected her small pale hand to be damp and frail, but it was dry and firm enough. The look in her eye was pure steel.

"This is my first time at FallsFest," said Chuck. "I hope it's all as good as Lewis Sinclair and the Gentlemen Cowboys. And I hope all the fans are as good company as you two ladies."

"Oh Maynard! I mean Chuck." Charla laughed and waved away his compliments. "FallsFest's a good time. I like coming here. This is Magda's first time here too. I go to all kinds of fairs and festivals and things. Not just country ones. Sometimes I'll go to craft fairs—or polka fests. I just like to get out and meet people. That's why I wear bright colors, like this satin jumpsuit. It's easier to meet people when you're easy to see. Magda here has a harder time. Always in beige. Magda, I tell you, you can wear colors. They'd look good on you. Sometimes Magda comes to the fairs with me. We've been friends, neighbors actually, a long time. I live in her apartment building. We help each other out. Like with Strudel. That's my dog. Magda loves to take Strudel for his walks, which is a blessing, let me tell you, because I don't always feel like taking the curly little fella out. He's a poodle. That's when Magda smiles the most, when she's with Strudel. Sorry, Magda, I'm talking about you like you're not here. How's your soda pop, darlin'? Okay?"

Magda seemed distracted. Her eyes darted here and there, looking at the hospitality tent, then back at Charla, sometimes at Chuck. She'd smile sweetly at them, then resume looking around.

"Magda don't always talk much, but she sure takes it all in. We're good friends. And she's real good with Strudel. Of course, Strudel's a good dog, not to take away from Magda's handling skills or anything." Charla paused. Chuck took a deep breath. "Yes, so Strudel, you always can tell where he's gonna pee. No wandering around for hours waiting for him to do his business. Just find an apple tree if you can. Dang, that dog loves an apple tree. We got lucky. There's only one in the campground as far as I can tell and it's close by our site. I sure hope no lovers decide to sit under *that* apple tree— or canoodle. 'Cause Strudel the poodle done nixed that canoodle! Ha!"

Charla and Chuck laughed and laughed. It was easy to laugh around Charla. The line finally moved and the trio stood in front of Lew and the Cowboys.

"Oh, Mr. Saint Clair! I'm such a fan. Let me get a picture of you and Magda together." Lew smiled politely with his arm around Magda's shoulders.

"It's *Sin*clair, ma'am," said Lew. "Used to be 'saint,' but I fell from grace."

"Ooh, that's a good one!" Charla laughed. "Now, Chuck, take a picture of me and Mr. Saint Clair. *Sin*clair. Sorry, but I guess I just think you're an angel anyway."

"Thank you, ma'am." He posed with Charla.

"Now this young man here looks like a beatnik, but his name's not Maynard G. Krebs, it's Chuck," said Charla, gathering Chuck closer to Lew with a multi-ringed hand.

"That was amazing," said Chuck. "Every bit of it. That extended version of 'Ghost Riders in the Sky,' though, truly, truly blew my mind. My mom had the sheet music for that song. We used to play it as kids. I've never heard it performed—not that way, anyway. Brilliant!"

"Are you by any chance here with John Turnbell?" asked Lew.

"Um, yes!" said Chuck. "We worked together at the *Twin Cities Record*. We drove up together."

"Oh my," said Charla. "You didn't say you were in the media."

"Why ma'am," said Lew, "it's rumored that Chuck here has a camera in his hat that shows up on his website twenty-four hours a day."

"Not when I'm in the bathroom," said Chuck. He was sure that would alarm the ladies.

"Oh, dear," said Charla. "How's my lipstick? If I'd had any idea—"

"You look swell, Miss Charla," said Chuck. "You've been a perfect lady. If I'd sensed you were going off into an area you didn't want transmitted, I'd have stopped you. It just wasn't necessary. You're such a perfect lady."

Charla patted her hair and exhaled a sigh.

"You're a skunk, you are. But like that suave Frenchy cartoon skunk. I can't get mad at you, you little stinker. Here, let me get a picture of you and Mr. Sinclair. The beatnik and the angel!"

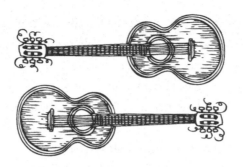

CHAPTER EIGHT

ew, Slim, and Mitch made their way to the Artist Hospitality tent. They'd just finished with the interviews Ruby'd set up for them after their meet and greet. The last one was with none other than Chuck Nelson. Chuck and Mitch became instant pals. Mitch was still full of adrenaline from performing. It could take hours for him to settle down, and his enthusiasm was infectious. He and Chuck bounded ahead of the sauntering Lew and Slim. They reached the bar and crowed their orders to the bartender. Their whoops and laughter served as a warning shot to Archie and Ann-Dee, who quickly put down their beverages and scattered from the tent. Their quick departure caught Lew's attention from afar. Slim leaned close to his friend.

"I wish I'd known earlier it was that easy to chase away Archie. I'd have set Mitch after him long ago."

Mitch and Chuck scampered to the table Archie and Ann-Dee had vacated. Mitch cleared away everything they'd touched. He took the used glassware to the end of the bar. By the time Lew and Slim arrived there was bourbon and ginger ale set up for them. Slim slid his shot over to Lew.

"Just the ginger ale for me today," he said.

Lew nodded and popped back his glass of bourbon. It was a welcome swallow.

Slim paused, his hand on his glass of soda.

"On second thought, maybe I will partake after all. It's been such an eventful day."

He reached for the shot glass.

"Oh no you don't," said Lew. He swiped the bourbon away from Slim and quickly tossed it back. "I know what that's about. You think you're gonna cancel your gastronomic getaway so poor, poor Lew can cry on your shoulder. Well, it ain't gonna happen, old buddy. Ain't gonna happen. You drive that old van straight to the Twin Cities right now. I'll be just fine."

"Well, it's just a dickens of a time for me to drive off and leave, I must say," said Slim. "A good Thai curry is of little value to me compared to your well-being and our friendship."

"I'm not exactly alone here. There's Mitchell and the Schroeders . . ." Lew gestured to the world outside the tent. "Not to mention several thousand of my closest friends here to keep me company."

Slim put an arm around Lew's shoulders.

"Besides," continued Lew, "I hear that Thai place has a way with basil. I'd hate for you to miss out on that because of me."

"Perhaps you'd like to join me," said Slim. "I'm told there are some good little jazz clubs in both Minneapolis and Saint Paul."

"Truth be told, I'm looking forward to some solitude and Mother Nature. We've been in cities pretty much our whole tour. I intend to take advantage of this country elbow room and be a simple tiny speck under a vast, uninterrupted sky."

Slim patted Lew's shoulder.

"Give me a call if you need a different ear than Ma Nature's," he said. "If not, I'll meet you back here in a couple of days for the trip back."

"Good enough," said Lew. "Bring the van back in one piece." The two smiled. Slim said his good-byes to Mitch. It was at that point that Gary exited the FallsFest office trailer and arrived at Lew's table.

"Nancy has to stay and work, so I'm heading back to the resort with Mom and Dad," said Gary. He clapped Lew on the back. "Come with us. You'd be doing me a favor. If we don't have any company, Mom'll force me to spend the whole night with her, planning Nancy's and my wedding."

"You two set a date yet?" asked Lew.

"No," said Gary. "We haven't even officially said we're getting married, but you know Mom."

"I thought I'd remember such a thing if I'd been told."

"We've been on tour for as long as I can remember," said Gary. "I haven't had a lot of time alone with Nancy to get down on one knee and pop the question."

Lew remembered Archie's proposal and tried not to wince.

"Well, if I'd known I was obstructing the path of true love, I'd have called the tour off three months ago."

"No way. We've been building up to this. These are the days to focus on our careers. Full head of steam all the way."

"True enough," said Lew. "And there was that break last February. Didn't you have plenty of chances to propose to Nancy when you were in Galveston?"

Gary took a sip of the gin and tonic that had been placed in front of him. The skin over his jaw muscles turned white.

"I hit a nerve, son?" asked Lew. "Sunshine, beaches, and Nancy. Never would have figured those to be sore spots."

"I just remembered something that happened there. Stupid. Nothing."

Several tense, silent moments passed.

"Food poisoning?" asked Lew.

"Yeah," said Gary. "I got hold of a bad conch fritter."

The kind of clouds that were roiling in Gary's eyes didn't seem like the kind caused by memories of bad seafood. The two musicians sat in silence.

"It's good we're rid of Archie," said Gary. He drained his drink and plonked the glass down on the table. "Now the band can move forward."

"I agree," said Lew. "I would have been happier finding a different route to that decision, but maybe what happens has to happen."

"'Men at some time are masters of their fate,'" quoted Gary. "'The fault, dear Brutus, lies not in our stars but in ourselves, that we are underlings.'"

Lew raised his eyebrows. This gig was one surprise after another.

"I don't believe in fate," said Gary. "We make our fate. We do what we have to do to get things done."

"I think you need a night with your mother planning weddings is what I think," said Lew.

"I'm sorry," said Gary. "You're the one who should be upset, not me. I mean . . ."

"I just need a little time to myself is all," said Lew. "We've been on the road a long time. I've been craving some peace and quiet since Cleveland."

Gary straightened up. He smiled his half smile, which was affectionate for Gary, and laid a hand on Lew's shoulder.

"Give me a call if you change your mind. We'd all be more than happy to have you around. There's plenty of room at the resort. It's the best place in the world when you need a little space—as long as your mother isn't planning your nuptials."

"I'll keep that in mind," said Lew. "But for now, I think I'll just go for a walk around the festival grounds."

"Suit yourself," said Gary. "But, seriously, think about joining me and Dad out on the boat tomorrow—or the next day. You won't get better fishing than on our lake."

"I'll do that," said Lew. He spied Mr. and Mrs. Schroeder advancing toward the tent. "Looks like your ride's here."

"Ha! Wedding plans or no, I have missed them." A broad smile now creased Gary's face. These were special circumstances. "Hope I see you later."

"Sometime," said Lew. "I guarantee it." He patted Gary on the back as the bassist departed. Gary walked out of the tent past the end of the bar and the glasses Mitch had bussed there. A familiar shade of rose on one of the glasses caught Lew's eye. Ann-Dee's lipstick. The signature color she wore when performing, a brighter, richer pigment than she used offstage. Lew thought about the lipstick on the glass and the discarded drink it contained. He thought of Jerry Chesnut's "A Good Year for the Roses" and all the other woebegone songs of lost love and longing. He pocketed the glass and the one last kiss it conjured. Love, oh love, oh careless love.

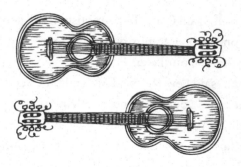

CHAPTER NINE

R uby burst into the FallsFest trailer, banging the door against
the wall. Nancy, at her desk, slammed her laptop shut.

"What's got into you?" asked Ruby. "Archie Casanova ask
you to marry him? That'd scare me." Ruby started to laugh at her
joke, then stopped short. "You're pale. You sick?"

Nancy shook her head.

"You sure? You look like someone just walked over your grave."

"I'm okay."

"All right. It's sticky in here. Better turn on the air." She moved to
the wall unit and dialed it up. "Say, did Lewie Sinclair return Gordy's
hat?"

"Yes. It's on his desk." Nancy sat up straighter and wiggled an
index finger toward Gordon's office.

"Good. I better get it back in the file cabinet." Ruby went into
Gordon's office and shut the door. She pondered Nancy's behavior with the laptop. What was that about? She was usually a cool

cucumber. Ruby let a minute pass, then eased the door open. Nancy's back was to her. The laptop was open again. She noted the rumbling air conditioner. It might mask the sound of her footfalls. Ruby crept toward Nancy on little cat feet and peeked over her shoulder at the screen.

She kind of wished she hadn't.

A gust of air pushed through the air conditioner, startling Nancy. She quit the browser. Ruby hopped backward. Nancy turned around with a jerk and saw her.

"Gordy's hat looked good on Lewie, don't you think?" Ruby pretended everything was fine.

"Yes," said Nancy. She cleared her throat. "It was a good idea to lend it to him."

"I thought so," said Ruby. "I can't believe he didn't have one of his own."

"He did," said Nancy. "But his manager sat on it."

"That's right. What a piece of work that guy is. I think his days are numbered, not just with Lewie and the Cowboys but in the whole business."

Nancy looked at Ruby. "You really think so?" Was that relief in her voice?

"I don't have to think. Lewie Sinclair's fist told me all about it. That sort of thing gets around the industry fast. You hear a juicy tidbit like that and it doesn't take two shakes of a lamb's tail to figure out that Grant is no one's idea of a manager. He's lazy and he's no good at hiding it." Ruby chuckled. "He's too lazy to cover up his laziness."

"I don't care for him," said Nancy. She glanced back at her computer screen.

"I doubt many people do," said Ruby. "He thinks he's got something with that blonde he's fronting, but he's got a surprise coming there. She's playing him like a deck of marked cards."

"Really? How long do you think it'll last?"

"Two weeks is my guess. He got her in here, and that's about all he's good for. She's not going to waste any time looking for the next stepping-stone."

"Even with the marriage proposal?"

"Especially with that," said Ruby. "If she's smart, and I think she is, she'll wrangle some publicity out of it. Then she'll wrangle some more when she drops him." Ruby spread the headline out before her with her hands. "FallsFest Lovers Break Up. Fainting Fiancée Flees." A good breath of laughter escaped her.

"It'll serve him right," grumbled Nancy.

"What's Gary say?"

Nancy shivered. "We don't talk about Archie Grant."

Ruby accepted this and went into Gordon's office. After a few beats, she reappeared in the doorway.

"Now didn't you say just last week that Gary . . ." But Ruby's audience was gone. She shrugged her shoulders and closed the door. Time to take another look at that website.

Gordon walked down the steps from backstage and strode toward the office trailer. Was that Nancy smoking outside of it? Nancy? Smoking?

"Nancy!"

Nancy flung her cigarette to the ground by a parked golf cart. She jumped and turned toward Gordon.

"I'm sorry," he said. "I didn't mean to scare you. I was just so surprised to see you smoking. I didn't know you did."

"I don't." She scurried to the golf cart, dug a hole in the ground with her toe and buried the cigarette. "I smoked in college. I don't know what happened. Somebody just gave me these." She gestured with the pack in her hand. "I think they'd just relapsed, themselves, and were getting rid of the temptation before they started up again. I don't know why they didn't just toss 'em in the trash. Don't know why I didn't."

"I've seen people throw their cigarettes into the garbage with remorse and dig them back up later in a panic. Maybe they'd been through it before and handing them to you seemed more effective."

"Stupid of me after all this time. I mean, I really haven't smoked since college. Well, okay. I smoked yesterday. But before that it was college. And I can't believe how rewarding it still is after such a long time. Well, actually, my throat hurts and I'm nauseous. Other than that it's rewarding. Maybe it just reminds me of my college days."

"When everything was simpler," said Gordon. "That's when I first started smoking. It was summer. I was right out of high school and I'd just got my social security card. I was in Memphis, at Uncle Morty's club. He gave me a cigar to celebrate joining the working masses. To him, it was a milestone. Plus, he could take my wages off his taxes. So we smoked cigars together." He smiled and held out an open hand. "Here, give them to me. I'll dispose of them where you'll never find them."

"Sure. Thanks." Nancy placed the pack in Gordon's grasp. She watched him pocket the smokes.

"I'm taking one of the golf carts to the StarWalk. Tell Ruby for me, would you?"

Gordon hopped in and started up the golf cart. Nancy waved good-bye as Gordon and her cigarettes drove off toward the Star-Walk hill.

<hr />

It was windy up by the StarWalk. Gordon stood before the scaffolding and surveyed the festival below. He felt like he was at Stonehenge. The place had the same eerie feeling. Only wisps of sound from the amphitheater could be heard. The rest was swept away by the wind before it could ascend to the top of the hill. Gordon looked out upon the festival: the vast expanse of land, the revelers, the wind blowing the banners like sails on a ship. It felt primeval. Was that the right word? He wanted it to be. Here he stood, the high priest of FallsFest. The concertgoers below weren't building any monuments today, but they were taking part in a ritual. It was a ritual that extended back to Stonehenge and beyond, people gathering together for music and dancing—and some imbibing too. But the imbibing wasn't necessary to the ritual. The music was. People came here to be part of the music, to celebrate something they'd always been part of, something that was inside them and outside them and ran through them and through everything they did.

It was his uncle Morty who first taught him about that. He taught him that music could be sacred and profane at the same time. He taught him that this strange combination was what made life great and beautiful. He taught him that he and Gordon were entrusted with this glorious mission to bring music to people.

Gordon turned his head and looked over at the campgrounds. He pulled the pack of cigarettes from his pocket. Were there matches? Yes. They were tucked into the cellophane. He chuckled. Why not? He pulled out a smoke and stuck it between his lips. He leaned into a sheltered spot in the scaffolding, cupped the matches and the end of the cigarette and lit up. The smoke filled his lungs and his brain. His head swam. What a fool. What's the point of building your body up like a temple and then polluting it with something as silly as cigarette smoke?

Oh, to hell with it, he thought. He took another drag. He was immortal today. Standing here at the top of the hill, watching thousands of people enjoying the music that he'd brought to them. *To heck with the autonomous collective*, he thought, *I am the King of Falls-Fest.* He laughed. Uncle Morty would have laughed too.

I wish Uncle Morty could see this, he thought. *This is all because of you, Morty.* Gordon smiled, took another puff. He remembered sharing a smoke and whiskey with Uncle Morty at the end of the night at his club, after the band had packed up and left, after the bartenders had wiped down the bar and put away the last steamed glass.

Uncle Morty had built a nice bar. It was a good place to hear music and to kick up one's heels. Gordon's uncle liked to complain, but he'd have a wide grin on his face as he did it. Gordon got the feeling that whatever caused the complaint was inconsequential compared to what Morty got back from running that place.

Like a lot of good things, however, there was always someone who wanted to muscle in on it. In this case that someone didn't care at all about the music. Their drive came from a primal place, just as Gordon's and Morty's did, but from a much lower chakra. Their motivation came from a desire to dominate. They wanted territory, all the better if it actually belonged to somebody else first. They were base creatures barely out of the mud. If they saw something in someone else's possession, they wanted it, even if they didn't know what it was.

Uncle Morty held his own against the hoodlums who leaned on him. His club thrived for decades. It helped when Gordon came on board. Morty loved having a protégé and Gordon loved being one. That made it all the more bitter when the thugs brought the club to an end. Gordon remembered that last visit from the trio of musclemen—including that punk Grant. Not even the Louisville Slugger could protect them. It was the straw that broke the camel's back. Uncle Morty kept his smile though, even as he sold the business. He gave the profits to Gordon and told him to start his own place of music somewhere new. That somewhere new was Big Pearly Falls. Uncle Morty joined him and helped him start the thing up. He died a couple of years ago, but not before FallsFest was well on its way to being the premier country festival in the nation.

Gordon gazed down at the amphitheater. He watched the patrons flow around the stage. The act was in high gear. The audience danced, natural ripples in the current.

"Look what we made, Uncle Mort." Gordon lit another cigarette and grinned, just like Uncle Morty used to grin. Yeah, he felt immortal.

⋙—⋙—⋙

As Gordon lit his third cigarette—it was unlikely he'd smoke again after today, so he decided for the moment to do it thoroughly—one drop from the ripple of humanity was breaking away and advancing up the hill to the StarWalk.

"There's the man!" Gordon called out as the drop drew closer. Lew Sinclair looked up and grinned when he recognized his host. "Come to see your handiwork?" asked Gordon. Lew chuckled.

"I told myself I just wanted to stretch my legs and get a little perspective on the festival," said Lew, "but somehow I arrived at the StarWalk to do it. I can't imagine why."

"I take that as a compliment to FallsFest. Thank you." Gordon offered the pack of cigarettes to Lew. "Smoke?"

Lew chuckled some more. "One habit I never took up."

"Good man," said Gordon. "Here, take these from me. I quit years ago, but I'm having a losing battle with temptation today. I'll finish the pack if you don't get them out of my sight."

"Easy enough favor to do," said Lew. He stowed the cigarettes in his inside jacket pocket.

"Have any ideas for a new manager?" asked Gordon. "It's soon, I know, but I think you're going to get a lot of buzz after today. Be ready to get the next year lined up."

"I made a hasty decision when I hired Archie. I'm a bit shy to move quickly a second time."

"Understandable," said Gordon. "Nancy's pretty savvy. She could help you out. I understand she kicked around Berklee for a while. Took some classes at McNally Smith too. I have some other names I could give you if you're interested. Let me know."

"Much appreciated," said Lew.

"Hey! My lawyer's headed this way tomorrow. Thurgood Buchwald. He's a jazz cat, but he always takes in a day or two of the festival. I'll introduce you. You going to be around?"

"I thought I'd check out some music while I'm here. You've always got a good lineup. This year's no exception."

"Yeah, I'm pleased with it. Listen, hang out wherever you want. There are extra chairs in the onstage VIP area. You're welcome to watch the acts from there. We always keep some extra space open for guests."

"Thank you. I'll check it out."

"You like Hicks and Hampton?"

"They're entertaining," replied Lew.

Gordon laughed.

"That they are. They're playing the last day. Big finale. They're flying here in a hot-air balloon. It's part of their show. You can imagine how happy Thurgood is about that." Gordon dropped his cigarette and ground it under his boot. He frowned at the small pile of debris he'd accumulated at the foot of his cathedral.

"I've heard they're crazy," said Lew.

"Oh yes," said Gordon. "No talking them out of a stunt once they've thought it up either. But that's okay. The fans love it. We'll get some national media out of that balloon I'm sure."

"No crime in that," said Lew.

"Not at all. Not at all," replied Gordon. "In fact, we got a Martin for them to raffle off once their feet hit the stage. We hired a local artist to paint the FallsFest logo on the guitar. Got all the acts to sign it." Gordon looked at Lew. "Oh wait, you've signed it, right?"

"Yes indeed," said Lew. "Ms. Flynn bestowed that honor on me before we went on. I had a crease in my jacket and went to your offices to see if they had an iron."

"Gotta look sharp. Part of the job."

"Indeed," said Lew. "Gotta keep up appearances."

"Don't I know it." Gordon bent down and collected the cigarette butts. He straightened up. "I'll give you a call once Thurgood's here."

"I look forward to meeting him."

"Hey, you want to borrow the golf cart? They're kind of fun to zip around in. Just drop it off at the office when you're done with it."

"Why thank you. I'll take you up on that."

"Just leave the keys in the ignition. Fans aren't allowed in the backstage area except during meet and greets. It'll be okay. And, FYI, I don't do this sort of thing for everybody, so don't spread it around. I don't want people getting the idea I'm a nice guy. Gotta keep my edge with the managers. Know what I mean?"

Lew grinned and nodded.

"C'mon," said Gordon. "Let's look at your prints." They went inside the StarWalk. Lew's block was close by Willie Nelson's. "See there? Same thumb-to-index-finger ratio as Willie."

"Well, I'll be," said Lew. He shook his head.

"How does it feel?" asked Gordon.

Lew put his hand to his mouth and broke into a deep smile. "Truth be told, it feels just a little bit like I'm immortal." He laughed. "I wish my drummer was here with his pipes. I'd dance a jig."

Gordon laughed too. "Hey, as long as we're immortal, how about one more cigarette for the road?"

Lew retrieved the pack from his pocket and Gordon drew out a cigarette. Lew looked down at the pack. Gordon raised an eyebrow.

"Why not?" said Lew. "Gotta try everything once." He took one, lit it, and inhaled. The smoke choked him. He hacked and gasped for a minute straight. "So much for immortality," he said.

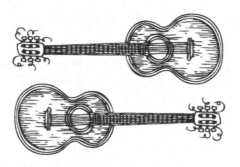

CHAPTER TEN

T he telephone woke Lew. He let it ring. Having drunk a bit of bourbon the night before—and, well, if that wasn't a night for bourbon, he didn't know one that was—his head was just a little bit fuzzier than it normally would be at 7:00 a.m. Now, understand, Lew hadn't drunk so much that he was hung over, just enough to find a wake-up call a mite unwelcome. He forgot for a moment where he was or what had happened. The telephone stopped ringing and his head dragged itself into the present.

Oh, yes. FallsFest. Breakup with Ann-Dee. Archie betrayal. Killer set. Lew was thankful Ruby had set up all the media for directly after their show. They'd all—the band, and especially Lew—been flush with the joy of a great performance and the boost of energy from their audience. He wasn't so sure he'd be as upbeat or interesting today.

Today his breakup with Ann-Dee felt a little more potent than it had yesterday. Yesterday was drama. Today was loss, cold and final.

He'd thought he was fine with it last night. The crowd's response to his music reminded him that his life was much more than a stepping-stone for a sidewinding Salome. He just needed some alone time. That's what he'd told Slim in the Artist Hospitality tent. Lew told him he was fine last night and he'd meant it. He still meant it.

Of course, he had taken a drive for an hour or so in one of the FallsFest golf carts that Gordon lent him, just to make peace with everything. He'd driven real slow through the retrofitted pastures along the fence line, taking in the sky and the lake. By the time the stars came out he was serene and able to enjoy the velvet expanse of universe above him. He once again believed in his place in the scheme of things; and as he'd told Slim, he was fine with it.

The motel-room phone rang again. One of the reasons Lew had enjoyed his ride so much was because he'd turned the ringer on his cell phone off. The various Cowboys and their relatives had called him nonstop, checking in on how he was doing. In fact, they'd gotten downright pesky about it. Now, he understood and appreciated their concern, but what he truly needed was that sky, and so he'd muted his phone. Having successfully avoided their concern for an entire night, he decided he may as well heed the call and let his loved ones back into his ear, if not necessarily his head.

"Morning." Lew picked up the phone. "This is Lew."

"Lewie, this is Ruby Flynn."

"Good morning, Ms. Flynn." Lew shook himself awake.

"Lewie, I'm not sure how to tell you this, so I'm going to be direct. Archie Grant's been murdered. The police just left our office."

"Murdered!?! Well, how do they—I mean, dead—holy cats— but—murdered!" Lew sat up, his spine stick straight. He reached for his flat Stetson.

"Again, I have to be direct. It's just too weird to put delicately. His head was encased in cement. Fully set. At the StarWalk. Hard to explain it as an accident."

"Mercy," said Lew.

"Do you have a lawyer?"

"Do the police suspect me?"

"You fired the victim two days ago and yesterday he proposed to your girlfriend. They're bound to look at you at some point."

Lew considered his new world—one as upside down as his stomach now felt.

"Lewie, Gordy has a real good lawyer in the Cities. He's already on his way here, but he won't arrive for a couple of hours, so make yourself scarce. Don't say anything to the police yet. Wait for this lawyer. His name's Thurgood Buchwald. Gordon thinks very highly of him. Make sure your cell phone's handy. I'll call you when he gets here."

"Yes ma'am."

"You didn't do it, did you?"

"What?"

"I know you didn't do it. Don't worry. I meet all kinds in this business. I can tell who's shady and who's on the up and up. But I thought I should ask. I have to go now, Lewie. Bye."

Ruby hung up. Lew put the receiver down on his knee. He sat thus until the telephone griped a series of annoying beeps. Even then he merely restored the receiver to its cradle.

How had it come to be that Archie was dead? Could it be true? It merely felt like a story to Lew, some piece of fiction that had been read to him. His mother would have gasped if she'd been told such a thing.

It was true. Archie was dead. Why would Ruby tell him so if it wasn't real?

Lew shook his head, tried to clear it, tried to free it from the vacuum-sealed finality of Death. He yearned to turn the clock backward, to turn back the shock. Time doesn't move that way though. Archie's body lay in a morgue; his life lay in the past. No turning around and reaching for it could move it anywhere else. There was no act of atonement, no gesture of kindness that Lew could perform that could scrub away Death. It was permanent and it moved in one direction. Lew wasn't thinking about Archie anymore. He was thinking about his folks. At the time they died, he'd thought of them as old, but they were hardly much older than he was now. Just then, Lew felt he was very, very old and his parents very, very young.

Lew rested his head in the cradle of his hand and wept. Death had no right to move only forward. Death didn't care. It was oblivious.

Lew stood and walked to the closet. Then he turned and walked back to the bed, looked around, saw his suitcase upright by the wall mirror. He rolled the case over to the bedside, then collapsed, leaden, on the comforter. He stretched out a hand and found his Stetson. A sad crumpled mess it was too. Would Lew's last memory of Archie be his butt on this hat? No, no. That's not right. There were surely other, more recent memories.

Lew's fist in Archie's soft stomach. It had felt like his hand going into a pillow whose stuffing was collected into lumps but still soft. There had been so much give to it. Lew remembered feeling relieved that there'd be no swelling in his hand. He hadn't thought of Archie's well-being at all.

But that wasn't the last memory either. There was Archie on one knee proposing to Ann-Dee. Heat rose into Lew's ears. That lowlife hound! She was Lew's girl. Had been anyway, right up to the day before. Archie was so callous, so oblivious to the feelings of others.

No, even that wasn't the last of it. Archie had had the gall to go backstage during Lew and the Cowboys' performance. He layered insult and spite over and over onto itself like a malicious baklava. Well, he got what was coming to him.

Lew caught a glimpse of himself in a mirror. Oh Lew, Archie didn't deserve to die. He didn't deserve to be murdered. Archie, no matter his and Lew's differences, was a human being. He'd had feelings and goals and loved ones. Lew paused. He tried to remember Archie ever talking about anyone other than himself. If Lew thought about his own self or any of the Cowboys, he could recount copious stories told about family, romantic partners, school chums, friends. Slim even spoke at length about pen pals who evidently led fascinating and charming lives.

But Archie?

He only spoke of his hairline or Botox or potential conquests, never people he was actually involved with.

Lew felt his blood pulsing through his ears. He sat still. Should he take Ruby's advice? What else could he do? He sure didn't want to sit around in his motel room waiting for the police, or for the vacuum to overtake him, or for the blood to pound a tattoo in his cranium. For now, he'd get back out under that sky. He dressed, called the front desk, then took the FallsFest shuttle to a place with plenty of blue up above and lots and lots of people below it.

Tap, tap, tap . . .

Chuck peered in through the sliding door at John Turnbell asleep on the couch. He rapped on the glass again.

Tap, tap, tap . . .

John scowled.

Tap, tap, tap . . .

Get up, John, thought Chuck. *I don't want to wake the entire resort.*

John's eyelids parted just a crack.

"John! Come to the deck," whispered Chuck, as loud as he could with it still being a whisper. "It's Chuck."

John slowly pulled himself upright.

Chuck rapped again, softly.

John rotated his head in the direction of the door. His eyes followed on a five-second delay. He was obviously still half asleep.

C'mon dude, it's important!

"Chuck?" John rose and stumbled over to the sliding glass door. He undid the lock and pulled, but the door didn't slide open. Chuck pointed toward John's feet. John rubbed his scalp and looked down. A safety bar kept the door in place. John removed the guardian and opened the door to his comrade. Chuck bustled into the room. John trudged over to the coffeemaker in the kitchenette and plopped a filter into the basket.

"This better be good, Chuck. I need my beauty sleep."

"Lewis Sinclair's manager's been murdered!" He was so relieved to finally have this information out of him.

John turned around looking very much awake.

"I found the body," said Chuck. Words tumbled out of his mouth. "At the StarWalk. Wrapped up in sheets. In cement. His head—not the sheets. I'm pretty sure it was him."

"When was this?" asked John.

Chuck perched on a tall four-legged stool near the coffeemaker. He looked at the empty carafe and wished it were full.

"Just now. Or half an hour ago maybe . . . okay, an hour. I called the cops and split for Ruby's trailer. I told them where I was going. One of the detectives talked to me there. I came here as soon as we were done."

John grabbed the pen and notebook next to his laptop on the dining table. "You're sure it was Archie Grant, the manager of the Gentlemen Cowboys?"

"Pretty sure. I recognized his clothes. Same build, hair, bald spot. He's the guy that proposed to the blonde lady. They were in the Artist Hospitality tent together. Mitch told me who he was."

"And what time did you find him?"

"About six o'clock."

"Six a.m. . . . p.m.?"

"This morning."

Chuck filled John in on the details of the crime scene.

"I came here right after the detectives questioned me," said Chuck. "I wanted you to have the mainstream scoop."

"A scoop! A murder scoop!" said John. He ripped a paper towel from the roll above the sink and blotted his brow. He then flipped open the notebook and began scrawling. "This could make a book. I've been thinking of starting one on Lewis Sinclair, or maybe Falls-Fest. It's been eleven years since my last one came out. But this, this is everything rolled up into a big bouncy blockbuster!"

Chuck smiled. It was good to see his mentor back in form. It had been a while. He slid off the stool and gestured to the coffeemaker. "Where's your coffee? I'm about to fall asleep standing up." John pointed to the corresponding cupboard. Chuck set about making a pot of brew. Once the drip started, he turned around and saw John at his laptop.

Damn, thought Chuck. *Please don't be looking at my blog.* There'd been thirty-two likes and fifteen shares last time he'd checked it. The numbers were probably six times that by now.

"Sorry, mate," said Chuck, assuming a Cockney accent in hopes of lightening the situation. "I had a bit of time on my hands while I waited for the old coppers, see." He dropped the accent. "You've got the print exclusive though, I'm pretty sure."

John's shoulders slumped.

"You can still write that book," offered Chuck. "I'd read it."

⫷⫸⫷⫸⫷⫸

"Gordy . . ." Ruby stood beside Gordon in front of the television in his office watching the coverage of the stage. "Why cement? Is that a Mafia thing?"

"How would I know?"

"You know Mafia people, right?"

"No!" Gordon stared hard at Ruby. "I have never met a mobster in my life. Never."

"You're in the music business. Of course you have."

"If I did I didn't know it. It wasn't on their business card."

"So, did . . ."

"Why are you grilling me?"

"I'm not. We're brainstorming."

"Brainstorm quietly to yourself."

"Gordy, aren't you interested? Someone was murdered on your property."

"The less I know about it the better."

"So, you do think it was the Mob?"

"I think nothing of the sort. As long as whoever it was isn't after me, or you, or the staff, I don't care."

"What about the acts? Don't you think they'll be scared? What about their safety?"

"I don't know how we can make them any safer. We've got flawless security."

"Not flawless enough for Grant."

"Ruby, you know this murder had everything to do with Archie Grant and nothing to do with FallsFest. But, if you're thinking about it, then the artists probably are too. Go speak to their management, or the artists if they want, and tell them that this is not a safety issue. This is not a random act of violence. It was not the act of a stalker."

"We don't know that."

"Of course we do."

"It would be better if we had an idea who killed him," said Ruby. She began counting on her fingers. Finger one. "Lewie. No way. Not the type." Finger two. She paused and stared at that finger, then fingers three, four, and the thumb.

"That's a lot of fingers," said Gordon.

"The blonde floozy's worth three if you ask me." Ruby shook her hand and shoved it into a pocket.

"Go tell the acts that Archie Grant was a man with many enemies—enemies he made all by himself. I'm sure he went out of his way to attract and then tick off whoever it was that killed him. Tell the managers that."

"Isn't that slander?"

"You can't slander the dead."

"Really?"

"Really."

"How do you know that?"

"How does anyone know anything? Game shows, probably. Have Nancy see what extra security she can hire."

"Maybe not Nancy," said Ruby. Gordon canted his head. "Her boyfriend's in the band that fired Grant."

"But she's so reliable."

"It wouldn't be a fair job to put on her. I think we should be careful about what we assign her the next couple days. Maybe she should just take it easy out at the Schroeder resort."

"Hmm. Maybe. I'll think about it. For now, I guess, you'll have to hire the security."

"Brad can do that."

"Brad . . . okay. Put Brad on that and talk to the acts. Make sure they know we're increasing security but that we think this was purely a matter of one crooked guy catching up with another crooked guy."

"A sloppy crooked guy," said Ruby. "He spilled my gorgeous FallsFest blue all over the StarWalk. You can't just pick that up off the shelf you know. They mixed it to match a PMS chip I took to the store. It's in our logo. Some people have no respect for nice things."

"Order up some more FallsFest blue then too. You'll enjoy that."

It was true. Ruby would enjoy that. Perked up by the idea of a newly mixed can of customized paint, she moved toward the door. She stopped and turned toward Gordon.

"Who do you think did it?" she asked.

"You're back to grilling me again."

"It's an episode of *Kojak* dropped right in our laps!"

"Put that criminal mind to work *for* me, okay? Get out there. Talk to people. Be my eyes and ears. You'll dig up a lot more information out there than in here. Now, go!"

Ruby's eyes lit up.

"Who loves ya, baby?" she poked Gordon in the ribs, then flew out the door to ramp up her investigation.

⊰⊱⊰⊱⊰⊱

They were just kids, years earlier, when they started FallsFest. They grew up in the same neighborhood, went to the same schools. Oh, but they were young. Where had they found the nerve? It never occurred to them that they couldn't conquer the world, so starting up a music festival was easy— kids' stuff.

Ruby and Gordon zipped to the top of the hill in the brand-new Falls-Fest golf cart and lurched to a stop. Gordon leaped from the cart and surveyed the valley below like the prince of a grand kingdom. He began pacing off the foundation of something.

Ruby fretted. She looked down the hill toward their office trailer. She was waiting for a call from their temperamental headliner. It wouldn't do to miss it.

"Gordy, let's head back. I can't miss that call."

"Morty'll radio us if they call."

"Like hell he will. If Morty takes that call, he'll do his wheeler-dealer thing, and Hicks and Hampton will fly the coop."

"Morty can handle it."

"It's my job! Morty doesn't know a thing about local media."

"Neither do you," said Gordon.

"I have better manners than Morty," said Ruby. "These things require tact and diplomacy."

"I didn't hire you because I thought you had those qualities," said Gordon. "Just the opposite. Sometimes tact and diplomacy are exactly what you don't need in the music business. I hired you because you're a straight shooter and you're tough."

"So let me do my job."

"Morty promised me he'd respect your turf. If Hicks and Hampton call, he'll radio us."

"Sure," said Ruby. "I can see it now. Hicks and Hampton, happy as clams, singing rounds to pass the time while they wait for you and me to dally down the mountain in our put-put."

"Well, I doubt that will happen," said Gordon. "It'll probably be their manager who calls, and singing rounds isn't much fun for just one person alone."

"This isn't how the big leagues work, Gordy. FallsFest will be over before it's even started."

"Ha! If I remember correctly, you were always the 'anything goes' member of our gang. Some of our least responsible behavior was your idea. Since when did you start worrying about anything?" He continued to pace.

"Since my daughter was born," said Ruby. "If you had kids, you'd worry too."

"This is my baby."

"Oh, brother."

"Oh come on, Ruby. Look at this place. Isn't it great?"

Ruby studied the valley. Looked like a pasture to her. Smelled like one too. How were the ticketholders going to react to that?

"So, what is so important for me to risk missing our headliner's call?" asked Ruby. "What are you doing? Captain, May I?"

"This is where the StarWalk is going," Gordon blurted out. "We're going to have all the big names who play FallsFest put their hands in cement, like at Grauman's."

"That's smart," said Ruby. "Now, if you want Hicks and Hampton to dip their pinkies in, we should head back to the office toot sweet."

"It was Uncle Morty's idea. He always wanted to do something like this at his club, but there wasn't enough room. He had them sign a wall. Couldn't get them to do handprints though. Musicians are like cats sometimes. They don't like to get their hands messy."

"I've heard your stories about that place. They probably didn't want their fingerprints documented."

Gordon said nothing.

"Well," said Ruby, "I'm glad you're here now. I saw the pictures of you after those criminals trashed Morty's bar."

"That will not happen here," said Gordon. He walked around looking at the ground, looking down the hill, seeing things Ruby didn't see.

She eased off. There was no rushing him. She knew when pushing him was futile, when it would indeed bring the opposite result she wanted. See? Tact and diplomacy are important. May as well let him enjoy himself. She still didn't get why he'd brought her here at the risk of ticking off their headliner though. Gordon gave a little hop as if landing on home plate.

"Here it is!"

"What?"

Gordon strode to the golf cart. He removed a tarp from the back.

"What are you doing?"

Gordon heaved a bag of cement to his shoulder and looped his arm through three makeshift wooden frames.

"We'll be the first ones," he said.

"Don't you need water for that?" asked Ruby.

"Yep. Here comes Morty with it now." Another golf cart ascended the hill.

"Morty!" cried Ruby. "Now who's going to answer the phone?"

"Brad, I think."

"Oh, brother."

Uncle Morty tooled on up and parked beside Ruby.

"Ruby!" chided Uncle Morty. "What are you doing here? Hicks and Hampton could call at any minute. Don't you take this job seriously?" He and Gordon burst into laughter.

"What did I get myself into?" said Ruby, but she laughed along with them.

"I got the water right here, Gordy," said Morty.

Gordon fetched it and set up the ingredients over at home plate. He mixed it all up with the biggest, toothiest grin Ruby'd ever seen on him.

"All right," said Gordon. "Morty, I think that should be your side. You'll face the stage. Ruby, as my number-one general, you'll put your hands there. You'll face the office trailer. I'll go in between. Ready? Here we go!"

The three put their hands in the cement. They laughed and laughed. Each one signed their name. They were now immortal. They capered down the hill to the trailer. Ruby got back to her desk just in time to answer the ringing telephone.

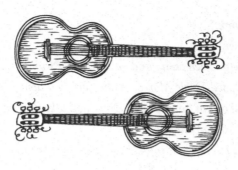

CHAPTER ELEVEN

L ew stood on the crest of FallsFest pasture, which was popu-
lated by food and souvenir stands. The angle of the sun was
harsh on his face and particularly to his eyes, so he purchased
a replica of the dark Nudie hat worn by Clint Eastwood in *Joe Kidd*. It
both shielded his face from UV rays and returned to him a sense of
bravado that Ruby's phone call and the news it brought had knocked
out of him.

He wanted to snoop around incognito and find out what he
could about the festival, about where Archie spent his last hours;
and yes, maybe a little bit, how Ann-Dee was reacting to everything.
He just hoped he didn't look too foolish. It wasn't the sort of hat he
normally wore.

Fans assembled down in the amphitheater for the Brenda Murphy concert. Lew intended to listen in. He could use some healing
music, and Brenda's brook-like voice and gospel tunes fit the bill.
He'd make a few calls while he waited for her show to begin.

He automatically scrolled to Slim's number, then paused. He'd already left a few voice mails for him to call back. Maybe he should let the man get a few more good meals in him before finding out about Archie.

Lew called Gary.

"Lew! Finally. How are you?" said Gary. "Did you hear about Archie?"

"Yes. Terrible."

"I don't know if I'd call it that, but it sure is weird. I hope it doesn't hurt FallsFest."

"Gary . . ."

"Lew, insomuch as Archie was a human being, I'm distressed that he didn't leave the earth naturally. But as far as being upset that he's gone, I'm not. He was a jerk. I'm not going to pretend the world isn't a better place without him."

"I'd tune that opinion to a sweeter key if the police talk to you. Just a little advice."

"I'm not worried," said Gary. "I have an alibi."

"They know when Archie was killed?"

"Not that I know of. It's just I haven't been alone for one second since we got to Big Pearly. In fact, I'm really looking forward to the next couple hours of being out on the lake with just Dad. Most peace I'll have had in months. You can join us if you promise not to talk much. I think that's a promise you could keep." He chuckled. "Be good for you. What do you say?"

"I surely would like that, Gary, but I think maybe I'll poke around FallsFest for a while, see what I can find out. You know I like a good puzzle . . . not that I wouldn't prefer that Archie still be alive."

"Tell you what. If you change your mind, just come out to the lake and wave at the blue boat with two lazy Germans in it. Dad and I'll cruise to shore to get you."

"Good enough."

"But don't call. I'm muting my phone once we get out on the water. Listen, whatever you do, come to Mom and Dad's house tonight. We're sure to have a fresh catch. You'll love how Mom fries up fish."

Lew no longer needed proof of Mother Schroeder's culinary magic. He was now deeply convinced that even if Gary weren't a superb bass player, his mother's kitchen skills were just as good job insurance as Mitch's uilleann pipes.

"You don't have a car, do you?" asked Gary.

"It looked to me like the resort was in walking distance from the FallsFest stage," said Lew.

"Yeah," said Gary, "but it's a long walk. Call Mom when you need a ride. One of us can come pick you up."

"If I'm not arrested, I'll be there."

"Don't joke. That would be horrible."

"Of course it would be horrible. Do you think . . ."

"Oh, I don't think you did it," said Gary, "but I'm not the police. Do you think we should find lawyers?"

"Ms. Flynn and Gordon are bringing someone in late this afternoon. They want me to speak with him. In fact, they don't think I should talk to the police until after the lawyer's here."

"Bring the lawyer to the fish fry. Maybe we can get a group rate. I gotta go now. Dad's giving me the eyeball. See you later."

"Bye, Gary."

⸭⸭⸭ ⸭⸭⸭ ⸭⸭⸭

Gary and Lew compared notes in the recording studio. They sipped sweet tea and Cokes. Well, Lew sipped sweet tea. He stayed away from the fizzy stuff when his vocal cords were on duty. The comely receptionist had offered them stronger beverages, but it was the unspoken law of the Gentlemen Cowboys to play under no other influence than that of Euterpe's call.

Slim and Mitch had left the room. Slim said he was in need of a snack; Mitch was more interested in the comely receptionist. Lew had confidence in their instinct to return at the exact moment they were needed. How they knew that was a band mystery. The record was finished, but there was time left in the booking, so Lew and Gary decided to noodle with a new song Gary'd been working on. They were presently sorting out the bridge.

Gary played the bass line and hummed the melody. Lew plucked out a few notes on top.

"I think you have it there, Gary," said Lew. "Don't think about it so much."

Gary scowled, not at Lew, but at his blocked tune.

"I did have it," said Gary. "But it's not working now."

"A disturbance in the force." Lew chuckled. Gary looked up at him. "Star Wars," said Lew.

Gary's brow creased. He looked back down at his fingers on the strings.

The door to the studio slammed open, startling Lew. He turned around to scold Mitch, but instead in breezed Ann-Dee and a tall scruffy chap with a guitar slung on his back.

"Hey sugar," cooed Ann-Dee, "how's the session going?" She strode over to Lew and wrapped her hands behind his neck.

"Bit of a tender patch right now," Lew whispered.

Ann-Dee looked over at Gary and frowned.

"I brought a friend by," said Ann-Dee. "Lew, this is Dale. We go way back. Dale plays guitar and bass." Dale gave them a generous grin. It revealed his sweet, trusting nature and a mouth full of rotten teeth. He appeared to remember his dental failings all of a sudden and quickly clamped his mouth down shut, pursing his lips tight together and hiding the ghastly choppers. "Maybe Dale could help you out here," said Ann-Dee, "if Gary's having problems."

Gary looked up at Lew, then at Ann-Dee. He stared long and hard at her.

"I'm sure you're a fine musician," said Lew to Dale. He bestowed on him the honor of a small nod. "But I have a bass player—Gary here. We're a band. No offense."

"None taken," said Dale. He broke into a big smile, remembered his teeth, and pinched his lips back together.

"You writing a song for me?" asked Ann-Dee. She cuddled closer to Lew and smiled.

"This is Gary's song," said Lew. He received Ann-Dee's sweet smile and reciprocated.

"Hmm," said Ann-Dee. She scowled at Gary. "How long you figure on being here? Dale and I wondered if maybe we could sneak in and take up just a teensy bit of your time. I've got a song I think's ready to lay down and—"

A clamor of metal falling on metal arose from the corner of the studio. Dale had knocked over one of Mitch's cymbals and at least one mic stand. Just then, Mitch walked in through the studio door. Mitch saw the disturbed kit and ran over to it and Dale. Lew sprang up and over to the chaos. He helped pick up the cymbal and guided both young men out the door and into Slim's care in the kitchen down the hall. When he returned, the drum kit and microphones were restored to order. There was no sign of Ann-Dee. Gary picked out an intricate melody on an acoustic guitar. He looked up at Lew with a beatific smile and half-lidded eyes. Lew listened to him play the tune through one more time, then picked up Gary's bass.

Lew walked down to the amphitheater. Ms. Murphy's people were still swapping out guitars and testing mics. A big act like Brenda Murphy got more set-up time than someone like the Cowboys did. Lew decided to amble over to the Artist Hospitality tent to see if it conjured up any clues as to what happened to Archie. He walked to a gap in the fence next to the stage and showed his artist lanyard to security. On the way to the tent his eyes traced up the backstage steps to the spot where Ann-Dee and Archie had stood before the Cowboys' set. He shook his head. The audacity. He wouldn't have believed it if he hadn't seen it with his own two turtledove eyes. The look on Ann-Dee's face. He remembered it as sorrow. Could that be right? What was on Archie's face? Lew couldn't remember. Only Ann-Dee's expression—or maybe what he hoped was her expression—remained in his memory.

Lew took off his hat and mopped his brow with his sleeve. That damned Archie. Lew couldn't shake the feeling that this was all the careless manager's fault. Every bit of it. Then Lew felt guilty. He remembered the feelings of anguish and anger that enveloped him onstage during his "Ghost Riders" solo. He wasn't proud of those feelings, even if they did result in a standout performance. He wiped his palms on his jeans, leaving damp spots on them. Lew fanned himself with his hat and made haste to Artist Hospitality. He sat where he and Gary had sat, where Ann-Dee and Archie had sat before scampering away with their metaphorical tails between their legs.

Waitstaff came over to get his request. He wished for something potent after all he'd learned and felt this morning but asked for ginger ale, Vernors if they had it. He put his hat back on and cast his eyes about in search of memory—in search of clues.

Ruby Flynn marched out of the office trailer. Lew envisioned her pacing on a tall ship, master and commander of all she surveyed. She pointed and waved her arms. Festival staff responded by setting up a maze of stanchions and ropes. Must be a meet and greet soon. Who played before Brenda Murphy? Fans began filtering in under the watchful eye of security. They filled in the maze in a matter of minutes. A clear laugh and a gleam of scarlet brought Lew's attention to a line of fans several feet away.

"Mercy, Magda. I never knowed you to be so persistent about anything the whole time we been friends. I swear you ain't said more'n seven words in seven years, and now—" Charla's face lit up. She waved and flashed a brilliant smile at Lew. Lew removed his hat and smiled and nodded to Charla. Charla elbowed Magda, who turned around and shaded her eyes with a petite hand. She stared into the tent, turning her head this way and that. Lew nodded and smiled. Magda continued to peer into the tent for a few moments, waved feebly and turned back around.

The meet and greet line moved on and Charla and Magda with it. Their backs were now to Lew, but Charla craned her neck now and again to get another peek at her favorite fallen saint.

Lew sighed. He looked down at his hands on the oilcloth-covered table. Was it worth it to look for clues here? Might Archie have left something telling behind? There was a napkin and a swizzle straw, but that was most likely from earlier today. Waitstaff came over, removed the debris, and swabbed the table with a sponge full of strong-smelling disinfectant.

"I'll be right back with that ginger ale," said the waiter.

That's when Lew noticed a small rip in the oilcloth. Was there something under it? He folded back the cloth and found half an empty pill capsule. Lew'd seen one like this before. Where or when was that? He sat back and thought. Then he spied something similar—the capsule's other half?—in the grass below the table. He got down on his knees and looked closer. He remembered where he'd seen it—in his own house. Ann-Dee suffered from allergies something terrible in the fall and spring, just like Lew did. She took an antihistamine when certain trees were in bud or when the leaf mold got bad. She gave a bottle to Lew for when the maple trees were being particularly cruel. Lew pocketed the two halves of the capsule. No sense in leaving litter. Waiter's got enough to do. He stood up, straightening his knees and back with a bit of complaint and relief. The notes of Brenda Murphy's first big hit "You Know Me Now" reached Lew's ears. The waiter returned with the ginger ale. Lew swallowed it down, re-donned his chapeau, and walked out front to catch the show. He stayed for the whole set, bathing in the redemption of her beautiful voice. Her final number brought cheers from the crowd and tears to Lew's eyes. He breathed deep and applauded. Then, full of goodness and human spirit, he turned and looked over the crowd and up the hill. Now would be a good time to face the Star-Walk. It would be his third visit in as many days. This time wouldn't be so joyful as the previous two.

Lew trudged away from the amphitheater crowd and ascended the hill. It was probably closed off, being a crime scene and all. He could see the yellow police tape now. He removed his hat and slowed his pace. At twenty feet away from the site he paused. The flapping tarp now reminded him of a pirate ship—or maybe a ghost ship. Would he have thought such a thing if he'd no knowledge of recent events? He heard the wind whipping through the plastic, slapping tarp against tarp, plastic against metal scaffolding. The wind wheezed and whistled. It was not to be toyed with.

Lew turned around and looked down toward the amphitheater. The audience for Brenda Murphy was dispersing, some to the beer tent, some meandering uphill toward the vendors and campgrounds. Some were going around backstage for a meet and greet. None were heading for the StarWalk. Lew would have the place to himself. He turned back around and resumed his advance toward the flapping structure.

Lew was a law-abiding man. He was not the sort to duck under police tape to snoop around. He did, however, have a keen imagination and sense of curiosity, and he owned the proper tools to have a go at investigating from outside the tape. He didn't actually own a deerstalker cap and pipe, but he did have a plastic magnifying square that his mother used to carry in her purse for reading menus and store receipts and such. It was small and flat and at present was in the back pocket of Lew's jeans.

He was also in possession of what he called his spyglass, a two- to three-inch monocular he used for birdwatching and general nature viewing when he was out on a walk. It was buttoned inside the chest pocket of his Columbia Tamiami shirt. (The shirt's sun protection came in handy for both outdoor festivals and fishing.) These tools helped him set aside his artist's sensibility and assume a more scientific surveillance of the scene.

Lew walked around the perimeter of the StarWalk. He checked the tarp for openings and was rewarded by a gap where the plastic had broken loose, most likely due to the wind that had worked itself up that morning. Its grommets struck the scaffold pipes. *Clang! Clang! Clang!* It made a much louder noise than it had any right to.

Clang! Clang! Clang!

Lew tucked his right hand into the cuff of his shirt and moved the flapping plastic aside. He held it in place with his sheathed forearm, thankful for the metallic percussion to cease. He scanned the inside of the StarWalk as much as he could from his vantage point. There were a few small paper tents with numbers here and there along the ground. One or two had toppled over from the wind, despite the shelter of the tarp. Then Lew's eyes fell upon the outline.

Lew gasped. His heart stopped beating just long enough for him to notice. The outline spread over the sidewalk and square just to the right of Lew's handprints. He unbuttoned a pocket and removed the monocular. Putting it up to one eye, he could see that the outline didn't overlap his square.

He was relieved. He felt guilty to feel relieved, but he had to be honest about it. He traced the site through the monocular. There were some tire ruts, not wide, not much of a trough; two, maybe three or four matching divots spaced to where he imagined four golf cart wheels might align. A smattering of small—concrete?—lumps nestled in the grass near them. Perhaps the murderer spilled water there while mixing the concrete, the moisture allowing the tires to sink in.

Farther down, the sidewalk and grass were blue. He recalled seeing that color elsewhere. Yes. On the sign over the StarWalk. He tilted his head up and could make out a corner of the FallsFest logo on an archway that christened the site.

That was the blue all right.

Laughter and shouting drew Lew's attention from the crime scene. Festivalgoers were coming up the hill. Males. It wasn't friendly laughter, and shouting rarely sounds pleasant. It was the sound of men testing each other's egos, vying for status. Lew brought his phone out of one of his pockets, found Ruby's number and called. The voices of the interlopers grew closer.

"C'mon, it's a murder scene," yelled one of them. "We gotta look at it. You scared?"

"Not scared," said another. "But we're gonna be late. Let's just go to the saloon."

"We're already here. Chicken."

Ruby answered her phone.

"Yes, Ms. Flynn," said Lew, assuming his best "security" voice, "I'm standing watch at the StarWalk. I'll keep you posted."

The owners of the voices rounded the corner of the scaffolding. They were pushing each other, jostling. They saw Lew and stopped. One of them met Lew's eye, then looked down, his lips pressed tight together. Lew thought he looked familiar.

"What is it, Lewie?" asked Ruby. "Should I send Brad?"

"Yes, ma'am," said Lew. "I'll stay here until backup arrives."

"I'm on it," said Ruby. "Leave if it's not safe."

"Yes, ma'am."

The pack of males eyeballed Lew. Would they press on with their advance? Who would back down first? Lew stared back at them with a steely-eyed stillness that rivaled Gary in his dourest mood. One or two of the interlopers flinched. One slowly stepped backward, hoping no one would notice if he exited gradually.

"Um, yeah," said the one closest to Lew. "We're looking for the saloon."

Lew nodded in the saloon's direction.

"Right. Thanks."

"I told you it was over there," said one of the betas.

"Sure, Dale." One of the men laughed and shoved the beta's shoulder. The beta yelped in pain.

"Let's get out of here then," said the shover. "Shots aren't going to drink themselves."

The pack scurried away, calling to mind puppies now instead of wolves. Their voices grew distant as they moved down the hill.

"Bonehead! What a bonehead idea."

"Wasn't my idea."

"Well, it wasn't mine."

While Lew waited for Brad, he noticed some strands of hair caught on a stray thistle growing near the scaffold. The strands were blonde and they were long. The moisture on Lew's face dried cold. Now, there were possibly forty thousand people at FallsFest, half of which were probably female, and half of them most likely blonde. The hair could have been there for days. Maybe it was Nancy's. Even if it was Ann-Dee's, she'd been there the day Lew put his prints in cement.

It could have caught then.

He heard the motor of an approaching golf cart. That was enough sleuthing for now. Lew needed more music and maybe some food. He tipped his hat to Brad, told him about the wolf pack and departed for the vendor tents and some semblance of normal civilization.

Once again, a flash of scarlet caught his attention. Charla? No, this figure looked more like a 1930s movie cowboy. Its vermillion shirt had a vee of white fringe across the chest and lariats embroidered on either side of the collarbone. Gene Autry by way of Bob Mackie.

His crowning touch was a brilliant white cowboy hat. It wasn't large enough to be comical, but was tall enough to be notable. This singular creature was heading straight for Lew. Lew pulled his hat down on his forehead as far as it would go. Cowboy Red strode right up to Lew, released a grand guffaw and slapped him on the back.

"Howdy, pardner!" This cowpoke had an Irish brogue.

"Mitchell?"

"Aw Lew, how'd you know it was me?"

"Because, neither Smiley Burnett nor Cher has an Irish accent. Decided to keep a low profile, I see."

"It's a mighty plan. Nobody expects a fella in a shiny red cowboy shirt has anything to hide." Mitch's face turned ashen, then red as his shirt. "I'm assuming you heard. You did hear, yeah?"

Lew nodded.

"I don't imagine I'm a suspect, so," said Mitch, "but it's best to take precautions."

"Ruby call you?"

"No, Gary did. Nancy told him. Disturbing. I'm not the better of it yet. I wonder if the police are looking for us."

"They haven't sought me out," said Lew. "I do feel kind of dodgy not giving them a call myself."

"Oh, I expect they'll find you soon enough," said Mitch. Lew swallowed harder than he expected. "Despite our worries, I wouldn't mind a bite to eat. Have you ever had a Norwegian taco?"

"Can't say that I have."

"I've been wondering what they are since we got here. Let's get a couple then."

Lew's mother hadn't been the best cook in Texas. This was both a blessing and a curse. On the plus side, Lew thought everything he ate tasted good. On the negative side, he seemed to be eternally hungry. After Lew's mother passed away, his stomach never forgot he was an orphan and just never seemed able to be filled. Hence, taco-seasoned ground beef on hot fry bread under a summer sun held no qualms for Lew.

While Mitch and Lew waited in line to order their "tacos," a stranger walked up to Lew and tapped him on the shoulder.

"Excuse me, aren't you . . ."

Lew started, then mumbled, "Well, yes, I . . ."

"The power outlet in my site isn't working. Can you take a look at it? Or can I move to a different spot? I think the pop-up in twenty-seven is leaving and . . ."

"I'm sorry, I'm not who—"

"Aren't you the campground host?"

"No."

"Then why'd you say you were?"

"I didn't really."

"You sure did!"

"Arthur," drawled Mitch, patting Lew on his other shoulder, "how many of these here tacos do you reckon you want?" The agitated camper wandered off in search of the real campground host.

"Make it three, Leroy."

"That's the spirit."

Lew and Mitch took their tacos to a clear spot of grass and sat down. Mitch extracted a large cloth napkin from his hat, tied it around his neck for a bib, and returned the hat to his head.

Lew eyed his tacos. They were larger than he anticipated. Three was gonna be quite a meal.

"These look like funnel cakes," said Mitch. "Are we supposed to put icing sugar on them?" Even Lew with his orphaned stomach couldn't wrap his head around that idea.

"I don't think so. Hot sauce maybe, but not sugar."

A strong rush of wind stirred up a whirl of dirt and chaff. Mitch protected the tacos with his extravagant napkin, which now seemed rather practical if not downright ingenious. What else about Mitch had Lew thought outrageous that would someday reveal itself as beneficial?

Some residual dust caused Lew to sneeze.

"Bless you, Lew." Mitch leaned back and checked behind his dining companion. Lew craned his neck to see if there was any more chaff on his shirt. "No worries," said Mitch. "You're clean. They say when you sneeze, your heart stops for just a moment and the devil stands behind you waiting to snap up your soul. That's why we say 'bless you.' Did you know that?"

"No," said Lew. "Thank you. Gives another angle to the phrase 'watching someone's back.'"

"I always wear a cross in tree-pollen season," said Mitch.

Lew remembered with regret the capsules in his pocket.

Mitch furrowed his brow. "Lew, since the police have talked to neither of us, maybe we should tell them we were together."

"Do you need an alibi, son?" asked Lew.

"Depends on when Archie died," said Mitch. He looked down at his taco and shook his head. "So strange." He looked back up at Lew. "I was with Charles—the blogger? —pretty late into the night, morning really. But I was alone in my room after that. Would our hotel have a record of our key cards?"

"Hmm," said Lew. "That's a good question. Worth checking into."

"Police on the telly are always arresting the wrong person first," said Mitch. "That's why we should make up an alibi for the both of us right now. Save us a lot of bother."

"This isn't television."

"No." Mitch cleared his throat. "If they send you to the big house I could lose my green card." He looked down at the fry bread again. He'd eaten all the toppings off of it. "I'd do it anyway, green card or no. We're a band."

"I'm sorry, Mitchell. It's just too easy to get caught in a lie."

"We could keep it simple."

"Oh, you'd embellish it, Mitchell. It's in your nature. I'd say we were watching a movie in your motel room. And you'd say it was some phantasmagorical story about swans. Then we'd get caught. Best just to tell the truth."

"Well, if you change your mind, let me know. I'll back you up on that swan story."

"All right, but for the time being, let's just say we're going with the truth."

"Lucky Slim," said Mitch, "being out of town during all this."

"Yeah, I hope he made it there okay. I've called him a couple times since Ruby told me the news. Went to voice mail every time."

"He got a new phone," said Mitch. "Maybe he's not acquainted with it yet." His attention was diverted. "Y'know, I do think these tacos might be improved by a spot of icing sugar after all."

"Did you see that lady Charla at the meet and greet? Woman dressed in blue satin?"

"A sweetie. Full of life, that one."

"I thought maybe she was your mother. You've got the same taste in clothes."

Mitch laughed. "Yeah. It's called fashion sense."

A gaggle of shirtless young men began forming a human pyramid next to Lew and Mitch. They stacked themselves up to an impressive height, but soon threatened to topple onto the two Cowboys.

"C'mon Leroy. Let's get out of the sun, head up to that saloon over there."

"Sure thing, Arthur. I wish we had one of those golf carts."

"Nah. You might get grease on that satin."

"Are you sure you don't want to make up an alibi? I always thought you'd be more creative in a situation such as this."

"Have you actually imagined me in a situation like this?"

"Oh sure. I have a lot of time on my hands when we're not playing. I might need a hobby, I think."

Lew and Mitch entered the saloon. They stood dazed as their eyes adjusted to the dark. The smell of stale beer and whiskey both offended their senses and welcomed them home. They made their livings in rooms that smelled like this. Lew tamped his foot on the floor. Yep. Just a little bit tacky. His foot and the floor sang a crinkly duet.

"Excuse me," said a woman to Lew's right, "are you . . ."

"Oh, well, I . . ." replied Lew.

"We'll have two Grainy longnecks and a Windsor Seven."

"Oh no ma'am, I'm not your waiter."

"Then why'd you . . ."

Mitch dragged Lew to a free space ten feet away.

"Maybe you need a different hat, Lew. People seem drawn to it. That woman couldn't take her eyes off of it. Do you want to switch—" Mitch's attention turned in the direction of the saloon's stage. "Ah, for the love of . . . We'd best be off now, Lew, go get you a new hat." Mitch grasped Lew's shoulders and tried to steer him toward the entrance.

Lew looked over Mitch's shoulder. Ann-Dee stood behind a microphone chatting up what appeared to be the bartender. She gave him a kiss on the cheek.

He moved to the microphone and spoke.

"Ladies and gentlemen, we've got a real fine treat for you this morning. All the way from Louisiana, America's next top idol, Miss Ann-Dee Phillips. Let's give her a big hand." A smattering of applause, as much as you're going to get before noon in a saloon, was granted.

"Thanks folks. I'm going to sing a song that's real important to me right now. The great Tammy Wynette's 'Stand by Your Man.'"

"Mercy," said Lew.

"What nerve, huh Lew?" said Mitch.

It was all so confusing to Lew. Ann-Dee wasn't like this, at least not to him. And Mitchell had always appeared to get along fine with her. (Of course, in the carnival whirlwind that surrounded the young Irishman, everyone was pretty happy—unless you messed with his drum kit or pipes.) Slim or Gary, however, was another story. Those three had more of an oil-and-water thing going on. The trusted and easygoing Slim even once hinted that Ann-Dee was a gold digger. True, seemingly everything she did resulted in her moving one step up the ladder of success, but she treated Lew with genuine tenderness. He wasn't stupid. He knew what tenderness was.

◦◦◦◦◦◦◦◦◦

Ann-Dee brushed the backs of her fingers against Lew's cheek. She looked so deeply into his eyes, he figured she could see all the way back to his childhood.

"You sweet, sweet man," she said. "How did I ever get lucky enough to find you?"

Lew blushed. He would gladly listen to her coo such niceties nonstop on into eternity, but some nettlesome Texas prairie modesty caused him to fidget and glance down at the barbecue sauce in the picnic basket.

"Here, sug," she said. She spooned a peppery teaspoon of some kind of Memphis/Asian barbecue hybrid onto a slice of chilled chicken breast. "Eat this up while it's cold. It'll go bad once it's warm."

"You sure do know how to cook," said Lew, accepting the treat. "Your mama teach you?"

Ann-Dee's eyes narrowed. Her gaze hardened like ice for just a second, then thawed. One side of her mouth crinkled up and she gave her head several minute shakes no.

"Oh Lew," she said, "you're not a silly man, and you're not a stupid man, but you certainly are wide open to the possible goodness in just about everything." She made herself up a barbecue treat as well. "My mama and

daddy pretty much just taught me how not to do things. No, I take that back. They taught me to do things I never want to do again." She took a bite of chicken. *"I can skin a rabbit and hang a deer from a tree, but unless it's pemmican or in a Dutch oven, I can't much cook it. And I promise you, you are never ever gonna see me next to a campfire again for the rest of my life."*

Lew put his chicken down and toyed with the fork on his plate.

"I didn't mean to dredge up bad feelings," said Lew. "Sounds like you were raised rough. I was lucky myself. I can't complain one lick about anything in my childhood."

"Can't or won't?" asked Ann-Dee. "That's the difference love makes." *She took the fork out of Lew's hand and placed it out of the way on her plate. She once again brushed her fingers against Lew's cheek. "You sweet, sweet man," she said. "I am so lucky."*

⸻ ⸻ ⸻

A blinding patch of light burst in from the saloon door. When they could see again, Mitch and Lew found John Turnbell standing beside them.

"Can you believe it?" he asked. "I just get off the phone with the *Record* telling them about Grant and this one calls." He wagged his thumb toward the stage. "Wanted to meet me here. I got the feeling she didn't want to waste the opportunity. The paper would kill me if I didn't go for the story. You have to admit though, it takes guts to squeeze ink out of your fiancé's death."

"Actually, I don't believe she ever did answer Archie's proposal," said Lew. "Not onstage, anyway."

"Hey," said John, "that show you put on yesterday—pretty good. Chuck Nelson told me he's been getting a lot of comments on your performance. This could be your big break."

"Bad timing," said Lew.

"I disagree," replied John. "Not to be callous about it, but a crime like this will only help you stick in people's heads."

"Now doesn't that put us in the same camp as Ann-Dee?"

"Not at all. Anyone can tell in five minutes that your aim is true."

"That's lovely, Mr. Turnbell," said Mitch.

"It was Chuck who found the body, by the way," said John.

"My goodness," said Lew.

"You can bet his blog's getting record hits right now," continued John. He grimaced. "Sorry, I sound like a ghoul, don't I? Newspaper people can be sardonic. It even rubs off on the music critic."

"Say John," said Lew, "You being a journalist and all, you ever cover something like this before? See, I need some help working this thing out. I'm trying to wrap my head around it, find out what I can, but I hardly know where to start. Outside of reading Hercule Poirot stories, I've got no experience with murder investigations. If both you and young Chuck and the police are looking into it, well, maybe I should just call it a day."

"Another set of little gray cells can only help," said John. "In fact, you might think of something the rest of us wouldn't, being acquainted with the victim and knowing the business he was in."

Lew flinched. Despite not being pleased with Archie's behavior, Lew didn't like hearing him referred to as "the victim" instead of by his name.

"My motive for looking into this . . . Maybe I should use a different word. My *reasons* for looking into this, I have to confess . . ." Lew took off his hat and rubbed his brow. "The reason why I'm looking around is mostly because I figure I'm pretty high up on the most-wanted list right now. I'd very much prefer not going to prison, especially for a crime I didn't commit. I know it's probably against your journalistic rules, but I'd truly appreciate it if you'd share any information you find that could exonerate me. I give you my word I won't share it with any other journalist."

John smiled and offered his hand. They shook on it. "I'll do whatever I can to keep an innocent man out of jail. Unfortunately, right now, I have an interview with your ex and I better get over there. I think she's just doing the one song. Later, guys."

Lew watched John stride over to the stage and take a few snaps of Ann-Dee as she finished her performance and thanked the crowd. They moved to a booth next to the stage.

Ann-Dee drew a compact from her purse and checked her face. John pointed in Lew's direction. Ann-Dee saw Lew and Mitch. She waved the bartender over.

She must have whispered something uncomplimentary about Lew and Mitch, for the burly barkeep looked none too happy with them.

He moved like a bullet train to Mitch and Lew. Mitch grabbed a Windsor Seven from a confused nearby patron and cast the contents at the bartender. He then grabbed a longneck and Lew and sped from the saloon.

They hid behind a curtain of sundresses in a nearby merchant's booth. A few moments passed. They seemed much longer.

"Do you think he's gone?" whispered Mitch.

"May as well stay here a mite longer, just to be sure," said Lew.

A bit later: "How about now?"

"A mite longer."

"How . . ."

"Two mites longer Mitch. I'll tell you when."

"This dress would look good on Nancy. Set off her eyes."

"You can come out now," said a voice, most likely the female vendor.

Lew and Mitch peered through the sundresses, then stuck their heads out. Mitch took a swig of his—well, somebody's—beer.

"You can't have glass on the grounds," said the vendor. She nodded to Mitch's illicit longneck. "Or at least take it outside my booth.

FYI, that guy that was chasing you went back inside the bar. I'd make a break for it now if I were you."

"Thankee ma'am," said Mitch. "You've been right kind."

"Now, Mitchell, why'd you have to go and throw that drink?" said Lew. "The man was angry enough as it was."

"Lew, we were in a saloon. I'm dressed as a cowboy. When am I ever going to get the chance to be in a saloon brawl again?"

"Tomorrow night, most likely. You do need a hobby."

A gust of wind blew some dust up in front of the booth. It caused Lew to sneeze. He automatically looked over his shoulder.

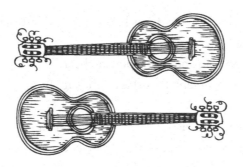

CHAPTER TWELVE

⸙⸙⸙

I t was now a little over a day since their FallsFest performance. Slim had made an early night of it when he'd reached his hotel the night before. He'd ordered in the renowned oven-roasted turkey dinner from Keys Café, put his phone on airplane mode, and gone to bed, sleeping like a man full of tryptophan should sleep.

This morning he'd taken advantage of eating breakfast at Mickey's Diner, an institution listed on the National Register of Historic Places. After sitting for a spell in the majestic Saint Paul's Cathedral and having a contemplate, he finally made it to that splendid Thai restaurant on University.

It was everything he'd dreamed it would be. To work off the calories of the day, he strolled through the splendid gardens and conservatory at Como Zoo. He even took a spin in one of the chariots in the Cafesjian's Carousel there.

Now it was time for music. His cab pulled up to a quartzite Romanesque building in Saint Paul's Lowertown district. He intended to enjoy a few cocktails with his supper so had left the band van in the hotel ramp.

"Know anything about this place?" he asked the driver. "I mean the club in the basement. Heard anything about the food or the best place to sit?"

"Depending on who's playing you might want to use earplugs. It's small. If it's a jazz night, it should be okay. My cousin stops here sometimes after his shift. He likes the sirloin-tip stew."

"Thank you, son." Slim paid his fare and walked down the steps to the club. The band was still setting up. Slim had heard space was limited here. He decided to dine early so he could choose his spot. A waitress arrived at his table. She handed him a menu.

"I hear the sirloin-tip stew's good."

"Best in the Twin Cities, according to the *Record*. Served with a personal French loaf, baked daily."

"Is it a meal?"

"It's a pretty good serving. I think it'll suit you."

"I'll go with that. Who's playing tonight?"

"Dirt Devils. Country/blues band, I think."

"Hmm," said Slim. "Bring me a ginger ale, if you please—Vernors if you have it—a glass of water, and two fingers of scotch in separate glasses. I see you've got a bottle of that Bruichladdich." He nodded to the shelves behind the bar. "I surely would like to try that."

"Be right back."

Slim studied the band. They weren't jazz and the food wasn't Thai, but he was pleased with his circumstances nonetheless. He thought he knew the bass player from somewhere. They must be acquaintances, for the man returned Slim's puzzled gaze.

⫷⫸⫷⫸⫷⫸

The Schroeder Resort was a village of campfires and lanterns.

The stars and moon shimmered on the lake. Lew was relieved to be in this serene place. Even better, he was wrapped in the warmth of the welcoming Schroeder household. They were presently gathered in the resort's combination office/soda fountain. Lew, Gary, and Mitch rested their elbows on the counter and enjoyed some libations. Mr. and Mrs. Schroeder stood behind the counter, arranging supplies but also enjoying their cordial glasses of raspberry schnapps. The room was full of laughter. Mr. Schroeder, Senior poured a dose of the liqueur into Lew's empty glass.

"Oh, you should have seen it," said Mr. Schroeder. "I had a good feeling dropping my line in. I was using leftover sausage from breakfast. Bea makes it herself, you know, so I knew I had an edge."

"Even bait tastes good when Bea makes it," said Lew. They all laughed, even Bea.

"The look on Dad's face"—Gary chuckled—"when that monster took his bait and we finally got the thing out of the water."

"It was four feet long!" said Mr. Schroeder. "Three at least."

"Are you going to have it stuffed, Mr. Schroeder?" asked Mitch. "Put it on the wall?"

"Naw. We threw it back in. You can't keep 'em that size by law." He removed a handkerchief from a back pocket and mopped his brow. "And we Schroeders eat everything we catch or shoot, out of respect. Not that Bea couldn't have cooked it." He winked at his wife.

"I expect I'd have to pickle it," said Bea. "Lucky for us, the boys caught a good supply of whitefish before Mr. Jaws jumped in the boat. We'll be paying our respects to them in about fifteen minutes," said Bea. "Make sure you're washed up."

"None for me, Mrs. S," said Mitch. "My family never touches fish. My granny says it's because her great, great, great grandmother was a selkie. That's a kind of mermaid. Probably just a story—she's told a few over the years—but we never did eat fish. Anyway, I'll be popping off now. I'm meeting that blogger fella."

"Off you go, Finbar," said Mrs. Schroeder. "I'll make you something nice tomorrow then."

Mitch departed.

"Lew," said Mrs. Schroeder, "come into the kitchen and keep me company while I fry up Finbar's cousin." As they walked into the kitchen, there was a knock at its side door beside the refrigerator. Bea opened it and welcomed Ruby with a man dressed like a jazz musician. He had a sleek, short ponytail and the cool demeanor of a feudal warrior.

"Mrs. Schroeder, Lewis," said Ruby, "I'd like to introduce you to Thurgood Buchwald. He handles all the legal work for FallsFest. Gordon thinks he'd be a good resource for you, Lewis, in the next week or so, in case the police consider you a suspect." They all shook hands. Bea pulled out two chairs at the kitchen table and gestured for everyone to sit down.

"Don't mind me now," said Bea, "I'll be taking care of supper. You're welcome to stay, Mrs. Flynn, Mr. Buchwald. The boys had a good day on the lake, so there's plenty for everyone." Bea turned her attention to her cupboards and stove.

"Mr. Sinclair," said the lawyer, "let's start with a few questions."

"Where were you when Archie Grant was killed?" asked Ruby.

"When was he killed?" asked Lew.

"Maybe just give us the rundown on where you were from yesterday afternoon—the last time so far anyone remembers seeing Archie Grant—and early this morning," said Buchwald.

Lew rubbed a finger below his lip and gave the question some thought.

"Well, after the meet and greet, Slim, Gary, Mitchell, and I tossed back a few celebratory beverages at the Artist Hospitality tent at FallsFest. Slim had plans in the Twin Cities and needed to get on the road. He asked if I'd be all right, and of course I said I would be. He must have made a deal with the guys though, because Gary and

Mitchell called me every ten minutes that night to check up on me. I guess they figured a great show and audience doesn't wipe away the effects of breaking up with one's girlfriend. Well, the calls just kept reminding me of my situation, so I eventually turned the ringer off on my phone. Before that though, I caught a couple of the acts. And I went up to the StarWalk. Mr. Morgan was there. He let me have the golf cart he was using so I could drive around. This was about eight o'clock, I guess."

"How long did you drive around?" asked Ruby. "Where'd you go?"

"Oh, I suppose until about ten thirty. The stars were out and it was dark enough to recognize some constellations. We've pretty much been in cities this whole tour. There's a big difference between a city and a pastoral evening sky. It was a treat to be out in the country on such a clear night."

"Did anyone see you?" asked Ruby.

"Might have," replied Lew. "I wasn't paying much attention to people at the time. Didn't know I'd need an alibi. I pretty much drove out to the fence line. Navigated the circumference. I went by a couple of the campgrounds. Someone might've recognized me. I wasn't wearing a hat. As you know, Ms. Flynn, I borrowed Mr. Morgan's for the show. I brought the cart back to your trailer, probably around eleven o'clock. Caught the shuttle back to my motel."

"How long did you know Archie Grant?" asked Thurgood.

"I'd say about three years. The Cowboys and me were playing in a club in Memphis. We didn't have a manager at the time. Archie came up to us during a break. Said he was looking for new clients. He became our manager that night."

"How long have you known Ann-Dee?" asked Ruby. Lew wondered at the protocol here. He looked from Ruby to Mr. Buchwald.

"I don't care who asks the questions as long as I get answers," said Thurgood. "If she misses anything, I'll jump in."

"Well, what's Ann-Dee got to do with it?" asked Lew.

"She's a huge common denominator," said Ruby. "Emphasis on common."

"I met Ann-Dee a little over a year ago in New Orleans. Tipitina's. Slim had his own gig set up there. We were out to give him a good audience. Ann-Dee asked me to dance. We hit it off."

"Did she tour with you?" asked Ruby. "Did she live in New Orleans? Did you live in New Orleans?"

Lew was embarrassed to realize he'd never thought much about how Ann-Dee showed up at their next show, which was in another state. They'd just laughed at the coincidence.

Lew rubbed his eyes. She played him good, and he'd made it so easy.

"Were she and Grant ever an item before Archie proposed? Did they seem to know each other before New Orleans?"

"Archie wasn't with us in New Orleans. That was just the Cowboys. I never noticed Ann-Dee and Archie being overly chummy, to tell you the truth. Now I have a question, if you don't mind. If the victim's head was encased in cement, how do they know for sure it's Archie?"

"His wallet was on him," said Thurgood. "No cash, but his driver's license was still in it. They took his fingerprints. Mr. Grant had a criminal record, so they found a match. Looks like at one time he was some sort of enforcer in Memphis. Hired muscle."

"Archie had a criminal record?" asked Lew. He leaned back in his chair. "Archie had muscle?" He realized what a ridiculously trusting person he was.

"You're a good man, Lew," said Mrs. Schroeder, her back still to the trio. "It's not a character flaw to see the people about you as innocent until proven guilty."

"Let's hope the police feel the same way about Mr. Sinclair," said Thurgood.

"How would you describe your relationship with your mother?" asked Ruby. Lew's eyes widened. He looked to Thurgood. Thurgood shrugged. He looked back to Ruby, concentrated his brow.

"There was a lot of love in that woman, ma'am. Losing her and my pop was plenty painful, I won't deny it. Heck of a lot worse than anything that's happened in the last couple of days, I can tell you."

"The face of the victim being encased—obscured—says to me this was a crime of passion," said Ruby. "Or maybe the murderer didn't want anyone to ever look at this person again. That doesn't look good for you, Lew. I'd be happier if we could find someone who saw you last night on that golf cart."

"Ruby," said Thurgood, "the man I presently use for private detective work is retiring in a couple of months." He slid a business card into her hand. "At that time, if you're interested, please give me a call."

CHAPTER THIRTEEN

⚜ ⚜ ⚜

S lim agreed with the cabbie's cousin. The sirloin-tip stew was
delicious. And the earplugs Slim always carried in his breast
pocket were put to good use.

The band was good, but a little too loud for the space, in Slim's
opinion.

They were now on break. Slim caught the eye of the tall fellow
playing bass and waved him to his table.

"You play a good bass, son," said Slim.

"Thanks. I don't know how well I'm gonna do the rest of the
night though. I did some heavy lifting yesterday and my shoulder's
giving me some problems."

"Might I buy you a beverage? I feel as though we've met somewhere. I'm Slim Pontchartrain. I play keys and fiddle for Lewis Sinclair and the Gentlemen Cowboys."

"Yeah, I recognized you," said the bass player. He took a chair
next to Slim as the waitress arrived. "Root beer please, miss." Slim

motioned he was fine. "Dale Bolger. As a matter of fact, I once knocked over ... I saw you yesterday up at FallsFest. We played right before you, after the gospel choir."

"You don't say," said Slim. "My word. What a small world."

"It is for a fact," said the bassist with a big grin that revealed a sorry set of decaying teeth. He pulled a pack of cigarettes from his breast pocket. "Mind if I smoke?"

"I don't believe it's allowed indoors in Minnesota," said Slim.

"Even bars? I didn't see any kids so I figured it was okay." Dale frowned and put the pack away. He returned his attention to Slim. "I stuck around and gave you guys a listen from backstage. Glad we didn't have to follow you."

"You're a fine musician yourself. I've pretty much decided that bass of yours is what ties this whole band together." Slim gestured toward the stage.

"Thanks." Dale blushed. "We do okay for a bunch of guys who haven't played together for a while. Well, they play together, just not with me. We used to do bars back in Memphis. Started out as a punk band of all things." Dale laughed. "Finally figured out we'd get more gigs if we played country. I still wear the shoes though." He waggled a Doc Marten out from under the table. "Most of the guys moved up here to Minneapolis. Ann-Dee needed a band real quick for this FallsFest gig. So, I got the band back together, so to speak. They asked me to sit in tonight. Feels good."

"Ms. Phillips is fortunate to have you backing her."

"I wish *she* felt that way. Bit of a diva, y'know?"

Slim nodded.

"Don't get me wrong. I love her and all, but ..."

Slim sat back in his chair. Just how many plates was Ann-Dee trying to spin?

"Now, son," said Slim, "I don't think that's wise. Weren't you on-stage yesterday when Archie ..."

"Yeah, I guess I am pretty much a fool when it comes to the heart. I was surprised as anyone when her manager got down on one knee and all."

"It's not a good sign for a relationship when another man proposes to your girl."

"I know that. But she didn't say yes to him, did she? You shoulda heard her last night. Cussing up a storm. See, she and me go way back. Only thing keeping us two from tying the knot is she don't trust my sobriety yet. But I'm holding steady. Got my one-year medallion. On my way to two."

"Good for you, son," said Slim.

"I don't blame her though. She's seen me pretty messed up. Hell, she even knows I spent my rent money on weed once." Dale hung his head. A guileless smirk interrupted his shame. "It's how we met! This was back in Memphis. We were neighbors. I always seen her around. One day I hear this commotion in the hallway so I look out my door. There she is, trying to get her keys in her lock. Looked pretty shook up, so, I ask her if she wants to come over and smoke some weed." Dale hung his head and shook it slowly, but this time he laughed.

"Pretty smooth, Dale. That work for you often?" asked Slim.

"I don't know why I said it. I think I felt bad for spending all my rent money on grass. Like it wouldn't be so bad if I shared it, you know? And anyway, you've seen her—she's gorgeous. I think I just said the first thing that came into my head to tell the truth, and I was a little baked already. But it worked! She walked right in and sat on my couch. Stayed for a week!"

The waitress brought Dale's root beer. "Root beer's on the house for the band," she said and walked away. Dale took a sip of the pop.

"Once I had a couple more tokes, I told her about spending the rent. I can't keep nothing sitting on my conscience, especially when I'm stoned. Well, I don't get stoned no more. I'm Twelve-Stepping it.

You're as sick as your secrets, y'know? These days, I'm telling everything on my mind. Back then though, well, I was blabbing for different reasons. Now here's where you'll be surprised, 'cause everybody thinks she's the devil and all, but Ann-Dee tried to make me feel better that day. Said, 'Don't worry about it, Dale. You won't have to pay the rent this month.' I think she must have gone and paid it for me later, 'cause the landlord never did come looking for it."

"She paid your rent for you?"

"I think she did, yeah. Good thing too. That landlord was a big ol' thug. Scared the living daylights outta me, I tell ya. Old guy, but big. I was spooked going to his office even when I had the money. You can imagine, next time I went to pay up, I was pretty shaky. Well, this tiny old woman was there instead. Talked like she was from another country. Like Hans Gruber in *Die Hard*, y'know? Because of the accent, I missed some of what she said, but I got the drift that her husband was dead and to make the check out to her from now on. She didn't say nothing about the previous month, so Ann-Dee must have paid it, y'know, as a thank-you for taking her in when she was shook up and all. She's got a big heart. People don't know that about her. I never asked her about it in case she changed her mind and wanted her money back. I'm not the kind of guy who's ever flush with cash, y'know? We hung out pretty regular after that. She moved in with me even, despite some bad lifestyle choices I made. I'd drive the Bronco for her, if you know what I mean."

Slim felt relieved that, to the best of his knowledge, none of his friends were likely to require him to "drive the Bronco" for them.

"She's the one got me into rehab," continued Dale. "I figure once I get my teeth fixed, we'll be like a regular couple. I'm saving up for new choppers. Meth makes a mess out of your mouth."

"I wish you luck," said Slim. "I truly do."

"Thanks. I got myself some insurance just in case."

"Insurance, you say."

"Yeah. I got blue paint all over my lucky shirt last night. She was all freaked out about it—on top of being freaked out about the proposal. She went to get me another shirt, and I don't know what came over me. I stole this pin off her vanity." Dale pulled a large, ornate brooch from an inner vest pocket. "I don't know if you ever noticed it on her. She wears it a lot, especially when she performs. She says it's her signature. I figure, even if she did decide to marry that Archie, she'd at least have to see me one more time to get her pin back. Guess I don't trust her as much as I say I do. Now I'll have to confess to her I stole it. She'll probably get angry."

"We do crazy things when we're in love," said Slim.

"That's a fact. I'd do anything for that girl," said Dale. "Listen, could you do me a favor?"

"If I can."

"I want you to hang on to it for me." He rested the brooch on the table, slid it in front of Slim, and grabbed a cocktail napkin. "I'm just thinking this out right now. Got a pen?" Slim removed a pen from his jacket and handed it to Dale. "Thanks. See, I've written songs for her—produced her CD. I never took a dime for it. Not that she offered one. And, heck, I owe her anyway, don't I?" Dale scribbled onto the napkin. "Here's my address in Austin."

"Austin?"

"Her and me moved around. NOLA for a while, then Austin. Ann-Dee's got what ya call an itchy foot. I don't mind; they're fun towns. I probably wouldn't've had the guts to do it on my own. So I've seen a little more of the world now thanks to her." Dale pushed the address over to Slim. "You can mail it to me in about two weeks' time. I should be home by then. I promise I'll return it to Ann-Dee. I'd just like to make it scarce for a little while, 'cause I can be impulsive sometimes—you might say weak-willed, especially if she sweet-talks me. I'd kind of like to not have it at my disposal till I'm back home. I'd be most obliged."

"That would be a felony, Dale, using the US mail to transport stolen property."

"But it's not stolen, I'm just borrowing it. And it ain't worth nothing. Just a dime-store gewgaw. Put a bunch of stamps on it and drop it in a box. No one'll ever know you were involved. Here." He pulled a ten-dollar bill out of his wallet and tucked it under Slim's glass. "For postage." Against his better judgment, Slim took the brooch and napkin. He could be impulsive too sometimes. It seemed so important to this poor young man. Slim removed a business card with his cell phone number on it and handed it to Dale.

"Here. This is my number. Now tell me where you're staying. Let me know that and your cell phone number. We'll check in with each other tomorrow and see if you still feel the same way. If you've changed your mind, I'll bring you the brooch."

"Fine," said Dale. "That'll work." He shook Slim's hand then scribbled the name of his hotel and his cell number on another cocktail napkin. "Now, if you don't mind, I'm gonna head outside for some nicotine before our break's up. I'm sure glad to meet ya."

"Same here, son. I look forward to the rest of your set."

Dale smiled a rotten grin and made his way outside for a quick smoke.

"Welcome to the War Zone," said Chuck. He and Mitch stood at the entrance and gazed at campfires, the smoke alternately delighting their nostrils and cramping their throats. A hint of marijuana slinked through on a breeze. They could just make out the various tents and campers in the dark.

Mitch sipped his beer. "Do you think we should go over there?" He gestured to an area with strings of lights shaped like chili peppers forming a makeshift suspension bridge between an RV and a tree.

Chuck sipped his beer. "I'm not sure."

"How about there?" Mitch pointed his bottle toward a site with daisy pinwheels and a windsock shaped like a peacock where a group of young people huddled around a fire.

"Um, I don't know."

"But you're a veteran," said Mitch. "You were here the other night."

"It was a totally different vibe," said Chuck. "It was all laughing and singing then. It just feels more sinister now."

"Maybe it just seems that way because Archie was murdered," said Mitch.

Chuck looked askance at Mitch. "Yeah, dude. Maybe."

The sound of two men shouting reached their ears.

"It sounds like somebody's ready to start a fight over there," said Chuck. Something made of glass shattered. Something else popped. "Let's wait a little while. If there's more laughing than shouting, we go in. If there's more shouting than laughing, we stay away."

"I endorse this plan," said Mitch. He sat down on the grass and continued drinking his brew. The duo stared off into the darkness. Crickets chirped in the distance. Chuck began humming "Ghost Riders in the Sky." Mitch joined in playing the drum part with his palms on his thighs.

A far-off drunken choir sang the last chorus, followed by much laughter.

"At least they're not shouting anymore," said Chuck.

"Music hath charms," said Mitch. They looked up at the stars and finished their beers. There was more laughter, more singing.

"I think they're done with the shouting," said Mitch.

Chuck remembered Ruby's warning. "Any naked people?"

"Not so far as I can see," said Mitch.

"Then I'd say we're cleared for takeoff," said Chuck. "Let's go that-a-way."

They ambled amid vacant patches of pasture passing for roads, sneaking eyefuls left and right, Chuck's hat cam capturing campers and tents. Some folks lounged on folding chairs and chatted with their campmates—a joke here and there and a gentle chuckle. "Keep on the Sunny Side" rang out on the air like a chorus of silvery fine-tuned bells. It lured them like a siren's song toward a flash of canary satin near a campfire.

"Charla!" said Chuck. "She likes to sing."

"She's got a good voice," said Mitch.

"You should have heard the stories she told me in line at your meet and greet. Crazy stuff."

"She reminds me of my granny," said Mitch. He looked off into the darkness. "I miss her."

"You would not believe all the things she's done," said Chuck. "Moira will definitely get a kick out of her. She'll want her on her *She-Ment* podcast for sure." They walked over to Charla. She sat on a lawn chair, a martini in one hand and a stick with marshmallows on it in the other. "Charla, it's Chuck, the blogger, from the meet and greet?"

Charla shook her head and looked up.

"Oh, Maynard! Sit down doll, you and your friend. I was miles away. Sorry about that. You want a martini? Here, give me them empties." She took their bottles and put them in a bag with other recyclables.

"I do," said Mitch. He extended his hand. "I'm Finbar Mitchell, Miss Charla. I'm in the Gentlemen Cowboys."

"Now yes, you are, aren't you," said Charla. She received Mitch's hand and gave it a gentle squeeze and a jiggle. "I've got some more chairs by the camper." She turned around to scout their exact location.

"I see them, ma'am. No need to get up." He set off to fetch the chairs.

"Pleased to see you again," said Chuck.

"Oh darlin', I hardly know where I am right now. Looks like I don't know where my manners are either." Mitch returned with the opened chairs and he and Chuck sat down. Charla searched a picnic basket at her side and extracted two more martini glasses. She handed them to the boys then fished out the appropriate bottles of liquor. Chuck took silent joy in both the decadence and the *Yogi Bear* quality of Charla's picnic basket. "Here," she said. "You know how to make a martini? No? Hold the glasses. I'll do the pouring." They complied. "I'm glad y'all came by. I don't mind telling you, I was in a pretty sorry state. But now here you two pop up just like guardian angels."

The boys beamed.

"I like being an angel," said Mitch.

"An angel with a martini," said Chuck.

"I about met my maker not ten minutes ago," said Charla. "That's why I'm such a butterfly brain right now. Had to sing 'Sunny Side' to gather my wits."

"Oh, no!" said Chuck. "What happened?"

"You want some marshmellers?" asked Charla. "Here." She handed them a bag of marshmallows. "See any sticks?" She looked around for long twigs to put the marshmallows on. Mitch spied two and retrieved them. He and Chuck stuck the puffs of sugar onto the ends.

"Charla, are you okay?" asked Chuck.

"How'd you come to harm, Miss Charla?" asked Mitch.

"What's your name again, dear?"

"Finbar Mitchell."

"Poke that 'meller a little farther down on the stick, Finbar," she said. "It'll fall into the fire if you don't."

"Charla, what happened?" asked Chuck.

"Well, I almost fell into the fire myself," she said.

"How?" asked Mitch.

"One of them four-wheelers come speeding right on through this campsite. Nearly ran smack-dab into me. I had to jump over the fire not to get hit. Good thing I did too, or I'da broken a hip or something worse. I hope I didn't scorch the satin." She checked her shins for burn marks.

"Where'd they go?" asked Mitch. He stood up like a bird dog looking for the cretins.

"They're long gone, I'm sure," said Charla. She tested her marshmallow for temperature, then plucked it and popped it into her mouth. "And good riddance. That kind just monkeys with a girl's good time. Not a thought for anyone else."

"Did the vehicle touch you?" asked Chuck. "Are you sure you're okay?"

"Oh, just shaken," said Charla. "Not stirred like those martinis." She chuckled a bit.

"There's my girl," said Chuck.

"Oh, it really did shake me up though," said Charla. "It could have been real bad. Watch that 'meller, Finbar. I think it's almost done."

"What about your friend?" asked Chuck. "I'm sorry, I don't remember her name."

"Magda," said Charla. "She's in the RV. Magda don't care for campfires much, y'see, martinis neither. Don't know why she ever took up with me." She laughed. "And don'tcha know, some rascal went and messed with the lock on the RV too. We had to jerry-rig something up with a padlock and a coat hanger. Glad I had 'em on hand. Gonna have to figure out something else for the cooler now though, to keep out the critters."

"I'm glad you're okay," said Mitch.

"Me too, dear," she replied. "So, you're a musician. Goodness, I seem to have stumbled on the two most interesting young fellas in the whole of FallsFest. Lucky me. Well, lucky when I'm not getting run over. 'Course, I didn't get run over, did I, so I guess I'm lucky there too."

"Don't take it for granted," said Mitch. "There's a maniac on the loose. Maybe he's the same one who tried to run you down."

"Oh, I don't think they tried to run me down, hon. I think I was just in the way of their good time. What's this maniac you're talking about?"

"A murderer!"

Charla's eyes widened.

"Charles here found the victim's body!" Charla's big eyes turned to Chuck.

"Oh you boys! Now I want you to stay out of trouble."

"I wasn't doing anything, Charla," said Chuck. "I was just wandering around the StarWalk. Did you know Willie Nelson and Lewis Sinclair have the same thumb-to-forefinger ratio?"

"No, child. I didn't. Now what about this murderer?"

"I found the body at the StarWalk, this morning, about six o'clock."

"You were up at six o'clock?" asked Mitch.

"Still up, actually. There was a party at the saloon. Good time. But the bartender kicked us out. He's kind of a jerk." Mitch nodded his agreement. "One of the partyers invited us back to her motel. The TV was on. They kept making fun of the wrong things, so I left. Not my kind of people, it turns out. Anyway, the sunrise was gorgeous. I caught a shuttle over to FallsFest and walked around while no one was there. Shot some video." Charla smoothed her hair. "It was pretty cool. It's amazing how they get all the litter picked up after the last show and before the morning. I liked walking around. It was a little eerie, but peaceful and quiet."

"Maynard, your marshmeller fell in the fire. Here, try another one."

"The sun was rising behind the StarWalk hill. I walked over there. The only sound was the wind."

Charla and Mitch watched Chuck. They waited for the monster to crawl out of the lagoon and up to their campfire.

"I was just blown away by your set, dude," said Chuck to Mitch. "I was so psyched I went to check out Lewis Sinclair's new concrete. John Turnbell told me your boss got his hands in cement. I passed Willie Nelson's on the way. That's how I know about the thumb-fore-finger thing. I shot it for my blog."

"Maynard, what about the body?"

"Well, Mr. Sinclair's concrete section is the newest so it's the far-thest from the entrance. And just beyond it was this other section, and your manager's face down in it. I didn't realize it was a human body—your manager—at first because it was all wrapped up in sheets and stuff."

Charla gasped. She took a gulp from her martini.

"I went over to him, to pull him out. But the concrete was dry. I couldn't find a pulse, so I called 911 and split to the nearest place with people. That was the trailer with Ruby's office in it. A security guy named Brad was there. I hung out with him until the police showed up."

"Mad stuff," said Mitch. "That would be frightening but exciting."

"I've had enough excitement at the StarWalk for my taste. Time before I was there, two guys were arguing."

"When was that?" asked Charla.

"Yesterday morning. Before the gospel choir. I'd just picked up my press pass and decided to roam around with it. But nothing was going on yet so I went to the StarWalk." Chuck lowered his martini and stared into the distance. "Oh wow . . ."

"What?"

"One of the guys arguing was the dead guy. I forgot all about that. I should tell the police."

"Who was the other guy arguing?"

"The big dude with the muscles. I think he owns the place?"

"That would be Mr. Gordon Morgan," said Mitch. "What were they arguing about?"

"Memphis," said Chuck.

"What?!?" said Charla.

"Some club in Memphis or something. Mr. Morgan called security and I took off."

"Did you have your hat on?" asked Mitch.

"Oh, that hat!" said Charla. She tucked a stray curl behind her left ear.

"Your hat cam. Were you wearing it? Did you record anything from that time?"

"I definitely had it on. It would have been streaming, but I don't know if it was recording. I usually clue Moira in when I want something recorded, but she's been known to do it randomly. She prides herself on her curation skills. I should call her."

"Who's Moira?"

"My lady."

"You have a lady." Charla smiled. "That's nice."

Chuck pulled his cell phone from the inside pocket of his vest. He groaned.

"No bars. John warned me that reception was touch and go around here." He looked around. "I wonder what's blocking the signal. It was fine at my cabin." Chuck pocketed his phone.

"Would it be on your blog?" asked Charla.

"If Moira posted the clip."

"The motel has Wi-Fi," said Mitch.

"Cool," said Chuck. "So does my cabin. You got a minibar? I could use some snacks."

"Just vending machines."

"Good enough. Charla, maybe you should come with us."

"Oh no, doll. I should stay with Magda. And I don't think she'd want to go with you at this time of night."

"Well, stay inside your RV."

Chuck pulled a notepad and pen from an outer vest pocket. He always carried these items since he was an intern and saw John Turnbell use them.

"Here, write down your number." Charla did. Chuck then jotted down his number and handed the sheet to her.

"Don't worry too much about me," said Charla, "I've got a pistol in that picnic basket under them 'mellers and Magda's yarn."

Mitch laughed hard and nearly fell into the fire.

"I'll bet your granny never said that!" said Chuck.

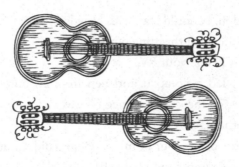

CHAPTER FOURTEEN

L ew Sinclair played a paradiddle with his fingers on his knees as he sat in the backseat of Thurgood Buchwald's Lincoln Navigator. He caught Thurgood's eyes studying him now and again in the rearview mirror. Thelonious Monk wafted from all fourteen speakers of the automobile's THX II certified audio system. Thurgood drew a travel mug to his lips. Lew did likewise with the mug Thurgood had provided him. He took a draft of smooth rich java into his mouth and swirled it around his tongue. The potent coffee and heavy cream both woke him up and soothed him. Why, it was almost a dessert, but better. He'd have to ask Thurgood more about it and tell Slim.

"Now Mr. Sinclair," said Thurgood from the driver's seat, "I suggest you tell the police the truth—not that you wouldn't, but I want to underscore the importance of this advice. It'll save you the stress of remembering what you tell them. They'll ask you the same questions several times over the course of the interview. If you tell them what you honestly think, it'll go better for you. You'll be less nervous, less likely to make mistakes. However, I do want you to pause before you speak and to speak slowly when you do. That'll give me time to intercede if I think it beneficial. If you feel yourself about to blurt anything out, or if you find your speech patterns abnormally accelerated, which frequently happens to perfectly innocent people during police interrogations, I want you to think of Mr. Monk here." He cupped his hand to his ear and listened to the music. "Think of Thelonious Monk turning around as his band plays." Lew closed his eyes and pictured the musician on a stage with his band. "Of course," continued Thurgood, "he didn't turn around while he played the piano, but while the band played, he would stroll about the stage and turn in circles, keeping time with the music. Can you see him?"

Lew nodded. Thurgood must have seen Lew in the rearview mirror, because he went on.

"I want you to think of Thelonious Monk turning in circles three times before you speak. Now, can you do it with your eyes open?"

Lew opened his eyes and reimagined the scene. The notes, the images did make him calmer. He smiled.

"Good," said Thurgood. "Now if I think you're speaking too rapidly, I'll place my forefinger just off center on my lips." He demonstrated.

Lew raised an eyebrow.

"It'll keep you out of trouble. Trust me. If you can talk to the police comfortably, you won't sound rehearsed."

Lew understood rehearsal. He understood practicing until the notes were written on your bones. *That's how the practiced becomes fresh,* he thought.

"Of course, I didn't want you to get confused during the interview, that's why we *did* rehearse, but you want the words to flow out of you naturally as if it's the first time you've said them. It's a performance. You understand?" Lew nodded. "Good, now listen to the music."

Lew and Thurgood arrived at the town park adjacent to a lake.

"Ah, the detectives are here," said Mr. Buchwald, gesturing toward a gazebo on the shore by the entrance to a pier. "I didn't want you to meet them at the law-enforcement center for legal reasons. They agreed to meet us here. There are fortunately some not uncomfortable benches in the gazebo." Mr. Buchwald unlocked the car doors. He waved his finger slowly in the air to the remains of the Monk tune playing. "Remember Mr. Thelonious Monk." He then placed his finger off center on his lips. "Are you ready?"

Lew looked to the detectives in the small, frilly gazebo. He could feel his nerves rising up his throat. He looked at Thurgood Buchwald, whose finger once again lay on his lips. Lew saw Thelonious Monk turning in circles. The music filled him and swirled inside of him, relaxing him. He got out of the car and advanced toward the detectives.

⟪•⟫⟫ ⟪•⟫⟫ ⟪•⟫⟫

"I'm not seeing any clips from yesterday morning," said Chuck. "Here's your noon performance though, at least the 'Ghost Riders' part of it. Don't tell Ruby I recorded it." Chuck swiped his finger along the tablet screen.

"Have you been searching videos all night?" asked Mitch. He sat up in bed and squinted at Chuck, who had just poured some steaming motel-room coffee into his Styrofoam cup at the table by the window. Chuck transferred several ice cubes from an ice bucket to his coffee.

"I gave up an hour after you went to bed. I'm hoping Moira posted more clips since then. She's more of a morning person than I am, so it's possible." Chuck jabbed at the tablet. "Refresh! Refresh!" He gave up and put the tablet down on the table. "Moira's not answering her cell either. She must have night mode on."

"Do you have another phone?" said Mitch. "The kind that plugs into the wall?"

"Don't have one," said Chuck. "Want to watch your clip?"

"Later. I don't know that I want to see myself perform."

"Oh, wait!" Chuck picked up the tablet again. "I missed this. 'More clips Monday at noon.'" Chuck typed a few sentences. "I'm telling her to upload ASAP and to call me. I'll text her too."

"Let's google Archie," said Mitch.

"Sure. Go right ahead."

Chuck began thumbing out a message on his phone while Mitch took over the tablet.

"Would you look at that!" cried Mitch. "Charles, Archie's a criminal!"

"Was, anyway," said Chuck, turning his attention to the tablet screen. "Ooh, assault. Nasty. Racketeering? Really? Looks like a punk, doesn't he?"

"You never said a truer word," said Mitch. "And what sorry aliases. My granny could come up with fifty names better than any of those."

"She did. See, her picture's right after Archie's." Mitch hit Chuck hard on the bicep.

"My granny's a saint!"

"Geez Finbar, chill out." He rubbed his arm. "All this seems to have happened in Tennessee."

"There were other links, weren't there? Go back."

"Okay . . . Archie has a LinkedIn page?" said Chuck. *Click.* "Hmm, he doesn't list racketeering or assault in his skills. Seems like a missed opportunity."

"There's a link to his web page," said Mitch. Chuck clicked on it. Both young men flinched and closed their eyes momentarily.

"OMG," said Chuck. "Females Feeling Feisty. No way. I hate that crap. Don't even get me started on what Moira thinks."

"It's his site!" said Mitch. "That's his face next to every photo!"

"Each one with a cartoon balloon: 'Archie Grant sez.' What a turd."

"The bastard!" said Mitch. "Wait a minute. That's Nancy! What the . . ."

"From-the-office-trailer Nancy?"

"Shut it down. I can't face Gary again if I see any more."

"Look at the wall," said Chuck. He pushed Mitch's head away. "I need to figure something out."

"Shut it down!"

"No really, there's something weird here. I'm not kidding." Mitch grabbed hold of the tablet. Chuck pulled it back. "Hold on! They're not her! Just the head." He enlarged the photo. "And there's a dot pattern on everything in the picture except her head. He Photoshopped her face onto pictures scanned from magazines. What an idiot! That's, like, at least two crimes in one."

"I'm still not looking."

"Wow, Archie was a huge creep show. How'd it take so long for someone to kill him? We've got to show this to the police."

"No!"

"But this could be big."

"It could be a big arrow pointing straight at Nancy and Gary, is what it could be."

"You don't think . . ."

"I don't think anything. But that's bad, that is. Let the police find it out on their own. Nancy and Gary don't deserve the aggro."

"Well, I guess the police can google as well as we can. I don't feel right about it though. We should talk to Gary and Nancy. Get their story."

"That's madness. No way can I look Gary in the eye and tell him I've seen that site. I'd better start drinking heavily. Let's go back to Charla's. Maybe she's serving 'meller-tinis for breakfast."

"Gary doesn't have to know you were with me when I found the site. Dude, your friend could get in trouble. He and Nancy need to get a lawyer."

"All right. You tell him. Just make sure I'm not around, yeah?"

"What was your relationship to Archie Grant?" The detective on the left leveled a steady eye at Lew as they sat across from each other on curved concrete benches inside the gazebo.

I don't know what kind of furniture Mr. Buchwald has in his home, thought Lew, *but I would not under any circumstances describe these seats as "comfortable."* A cold morning breeze blew in from the park's pond, causing Lew to shiver.

He longed for the warmth of Texas.

"He was my manager—my band's manager. Lewis Sinclair and the Gentlemen Cowboys. We met Archie in a club in Memphis three years ago, a place named Kennedy's, if I remember correctly. It had seen better days. Archie was looking to get into the music business. He seemed to know a lot. Had a lot of contacts. We'd never had a manager. Thought we'd see if we liked it. It was a handshake kind of a deal. Both sides said let's try it for a while. That while lasted till Thursday evening."

"That's when you fired him?" asked the detective on the right.

"Yes, sir. You see, Archie hadn't been doing very much for us for a long time—at least half a year—but he still took his percentage. I kept hoping he'd step up to the plate. I know I did make some suggestions in that direction. I don't know if any of the Cowboys had. Anyhow, Archie never did step up."

"Why'd you decide to sack him on Thursday?"

"Well, first of all, he sat on my hat."

⸺

"John," said Chuck into his phone, "it's Chuck. I think I'm onto some-thing with the Archie Grant murder. I need some advice. Give me a call, yeah?"

Chuck hung up. Why was no one answering their cell phones? He'd wait a few minutes for John Turnbell to call back before try-ing Gary. In the meantime, what else could he find on the interwebs about these people?

"What the . . .?" exclaimed Chuck. "That's weird."

John wasn't answering his phone, but maybe he'd check out this link. Chuck pressed "send."

⸺

"You had no idea that Archie Grant and Ann-Dee Phillips were in a relationship?" asked the detective on the left.

"To tell the truth, I don't think they were in a relationship," said Lew. "Not a romantic one. And it's not just my ego saying this, but I don't think Ann-Dee had any idea how Archie felt until he got down on one knee on that stage. I think she wanted free management, and maybe she batted her eyes and cooed a bit to get it, but I highly doubt she'd have been interested in Archie that way."

Quiet enveloped the gazebo. The detectives stared at Lew. Was that pity in their eyes?

I know her better than you, thought Lew.

He looked to Thurgood, who placed a finger to his lips and jumped in.

"My client is obviously a trusting fellow. As it took him so long to fire his worthless manager, I'd like to suggest that he's hardly a man quick to anger. And so, despite the fact that Archie Grant proposed to Mr. Sinclair's former girlfriend in front of several thousand people, it would not be in his nature to kill anyone within twenty-four hours because of it."

"But Mr. Sinclair did exchange words with the victim at the site of the body's discovery," said the detective on the right.

"I didn't just exchange words with him," said Lew. "I punched him in the breadbasket and sent him rolling down a hill."

"Mr. Sinclair," said Mr. Buchwald, "I'm not sure . . ."

"There was a journalist there. He seems like a nice man, but I'm pretty sure he's not gonna keep that tasty tidbit under his hat. I'd like the police to hear it from me if they're gonna hear it from anybody."

"Maybe you're not so slow to anger after all," said the detective on the left.

"Sir, three people within one hour told me how Archie was not only ignoring my career but actively working against my success." Lew skooched forward, his hands on his knees. "My girlfriend dumps me and I find out he knew before I did. He then waddles up the hill trying to shoehorn her into the best piece of publicity—and a damn fine honor to boot—that I'd ever received in my entire career. He was obviously now representing her." Lew sat back on the cold, hard bench. "And he told me just that morning he was on the make for any pretty young woman within eyeshot and he was in a big hurry to do so. Why, I don't think I'd have much respect for myself if I hadn't punched him."

"Maybe you ought to tell us where you were, Friday night and Saturday morning," said Detective Right.

Thurgood Buchwald put his entire hand over his mouth and began to hum "'Round Midnight."

⦁⦁⦁⦁ ⦁⦁⦁⦁ ⦁⦁⦁⦁

Gordon entered his office from its outside entrance. His coffeemaker died that morning and he wasn't in the mood to talk to anyone in the main office just yet. Stealthily, he filled a carafe with water and poured it into the Brewmaster on the table by the door to the next room. He heard voices.

"I know! I know!" Nancy.

"Well, it wasn't smart." Gary?

"I know," said Nancy. "It's just seeing him here, popping up everywhere like a Whac-A-Mole. I . . . I don't know. I had to look at it. I thought I was alone."

"Are you sure she saw what site it was?"

"No. I closed it pretty fast."

"This isn't good," said Gary. "It points right to us."

"She might not do anything about it," said Nancy. "I mean, she thought he was a pig before she knew about the site."

"She's not going to overlook the law."

"She might. It wouldn't look good for FallsFest. She's very loyal. In fact, I don't think she'd sell me out either."

"Well, she's got no allegiance to me," said Gary. "Did you get rid of the recording?"

"I don't remember where I put it."

"What? This is important, Nancy."

"There's been a lot going on since then, if you haven't noticed."

"This isn't like you."

"I've never been in this situation before."

"Please find it and get rid of it."

"I'm never alone long enough to look for it."

"We're alone now. Let's start."

Silence. Gordon crept to his outer door and—not stealthily—opened and closed it. He then returned to Ruby and Nancy's door and opened it.

"You have any coffee in . . ."

He saw Nancy frozen in place, her face ashen. Gary leaned on her desk, his face stern.

"Nancy," said Gordon, "are you ill? Maybe you should go home."

Ruby burst into the trailer, talking on her cell.

"Sorry, Johnny. You know I can't give you that information." She laughed. "Rascal." She shook her head, sat down at her desk, and opened up her laptop. She looked up at Gary, then Gordon, then Nancy. "I gotta go now. Looks like I walked in on a game of statues."

<hr />

Gordon tapped his fingertips on his desk. He was very rarely ever at this desk—or any desk really. It didn't suit him. He was a man who liked to move around. Always had been.

After blasting off from high school, he fell to earth several states south, at his uncle's Memphis music club. Before his uncle sold the place, before that thug Grant beat Gordon up and trashed the bar, it was home and there was always something for an energetic nineteen-year-old to do. True, the place was sticky and stunk like stale beer, but that was just the patina of an appropriately appreciated hot spot.

Every night there was music: a lone balladeer; a jump, jive an' wail band of country-fried hepcats. Sometimes an axman rocked; sometimes he sang the blues.

There were calls to take, deals to make, kegs to tap, and thirst to slake. Uncle Morty put Gordon slapdab in the middle of it all, and Gordon never stopped being thankful for it.

So today, right now, just this very minute, Gordon was pulling at the reins and deeply regretting having to stand in one spot; but Ruby told him he had to. Ruby was the only human on the planet—now that Uncle Morty wasn't around—who could tell him to do anything. He took advice from his lawyer, but Ruby was the only one he ever considered taking orders from.

And today she told him to wait at his desk to meet a potential new hire named Nancy.

FallsFest hadn't brought on a new employee in years. The same crew of friends and fauna gathered every year for the festival. Everyone knew their job well and could take their position in the FallsFest machine for a few weeks each year without missing a beat. A new hire was a big deal. You weren't just hired for the month at FallsFest; you were, hopefully, hired for life. It was important Gordon interview Nancy, but he didn't look forward to it.

It wasn't his strong suit.

At his stage in life, he had little desire to draw people out and discover their potential. He just wanted people to hit the ground running. He tapped, tapped, tapped his fingers on his desk, waiting for the awkward task to be over.

His drum solo was interrupted by Ruby's rolling, crowing laugh. Gordon had never heard anything to match that laugh. It was pure life force moving through the air like a barrel over rapids. It was impossible not to smile when Ruby's laugh was at full throttle. Nancy couldn't have asked for a better introduction. Gordon stopped drumming and picked up a baseball from a stand on his desk. He played a subdued game of one-handed catch.

The door to his office burst open and in came Ruby with Nancy in tow.

"Gordy!" said Ruby. "This is Nancy. Nancy, come along to the front. Stand here." Nancy, being a bright young person, obeyed. "Nancy's just out of school," said Ruby. "She's been to Berklee, McNally Smith, lots of good places. Soaked up the best at the best. I'd like her to be my assistant. I think she'd be a good fit."

Gordon offered his hand. Nancy grasped but did not squeeze it. It was a good handshake for someone who'd be greeting musicians and other people whose livelihoods depended on digital dexterity. Nancy then proffered a genuine gleaming smile to Gordon. It was one of those smiles that drew cameras to it.

Nancy had true likeability—on top of all the other good stuff that goes with being a Hitchcock blonde. She was the crème de la femme. She'd easily charm male management. Gordon tossed the baseball to her. It was a soft throw but it still required quick reflexes to catch. Nancy caught it. She looked up at the Louisville Slugger on the wall.

"That signed?" she asked.

"No," said Gordon. "It's not valuable. Just decoration." It was actually there for a purpose, but he'd leave that to Ruby to explain.

"You play?"

"No, just a fan."

"Who do you root for?"

"Twins and the Brewers."

"Both?"

"Mom's from Minnesota. Dad's from Wisconsin. Now, I have a couple of questions," said Gordon.

"Here we go."

"What music do you like?"

"Ray Charles, Margo Price, Sons of the Pioneers . . ."

Gordon nodded.

"What's the air-speed velocity of an unladen swallow?"

"African or European?"

Gordon smiled and nodded.

"If talent collapses backstage, what do you do?"

"Call a medic on my radio . . ."

My radio, *thought Gordon.* She's already placed herself here.

"Call 911 with my cell . . ." continued Nancy, "assess what's wrong, and see if there's anything without potential harm I can do while I wait for the medic. Call the talent's manager if they're not already there. Call security on my radio to keep crowds from the artist."

"What if you're here in the office and you see someone on the monitor rush talent onstage?"

"First, I call security on my radio. Second, I take that bat down off the wall."

Gordon nodded a third time. Nancy had the job.

"Now, you were driving around in one of the FallsFest golf carts for the majority of Saturday night," said Detective Left.

"Yes, sir," replied Lew.

"How did you gain access to this golf cart?"

"I walked up to the StarWalk to see my handprints," said Lew. He blushed at this admission of ego. "Mr. Gordon Morgan was there smoking a cigarette." Detective Right jotted something down in a notebook. This distracted Lew. He forgot what he was saying.

"You met Gordon Morgan at the StarWalk," prompted Detective Left.

"That's right," said Lew. He brought his focus back to Detective Left. "Mr. Morgan and I talked. It was a nice conversation, couple of laughs. He asked me to take his cigarettes from him, so I did."

"Do you still have them?" asked Detective Right.

"No, sir," replied Lew. "I threw them into the wastebasket in my motel room. They might still be there, but maid service probably disposed of them."

Detective Right scribbled more notes. Lew didn't like when they made notes.

"Is that important?" asked Lew. "I sort of smoked one of those cigarettes."

Thurgood brought a brisk finger to the side of his mouth.

"I didn't get more than one puff from it," added Lew, his gaze darting back and forth between Thurgood, the detectives, and Detective Right's notepad. "I'm not a smoker. I choked right away. And that was that. They weren't poisoned or anything, were they?"

"You don't smoke?" asked Detective Right.

"No," said Lew. "Just the one puff. Made me cough something fierce." Lew felt like coughing right then. "Not the addiction for me." He cleared his throat.

Detective Right's pen hovered over his notepad. "No addictions."

Lew shook his head. Detective Right stared at him. "Except for Hank Williams," joked Lew. "I can't quit Hank." The detective continued his stare. "Don't want to either."

"You met Gordon Morgan by the StarWalk," led Detective Left. Lew looked to Thurgood, who sat very still in his chair.

"Right," said Lew. "I walked up the hill. Mr. Morgan had driven a golf cart to get there. He offered the cart to me, temporarily, not as a permanent gift. It looked fun, so I took possession of the cart—temporarily."

"Where did you go with this cart?"

"I drove around the perimeter of the festival, around the fence line. Went by a couple of the campgrounds."

"Which ones?"

"Um, one of them had three Jay Feathers right in a row by the entrance. That's about the only way I can identify it. I don't remember any signs. And the campground just beyond that one."

"Anybody see you?"

"Plenty of people, I imagine," said Lew. "Don't know if anyone recognized me. I wasn't wearing a hat, but I'm not exactly famous. I'm not one of the headliners at the festival." *Mercy*, thought Lew, *not much of an alibi.* "Folks might remember seeing the golf cart," he offered. "That's something, isn't it?"

The detective wrote down a note. This time that seemed like a good thing.

"I dropped the cart back at the FallsFest offices around eleven."

"You sure about that?"

Lew gave him a brisk nod. "Mm-hmm. I wanted to make sure I could get a shuttle back to the motel. They stop running at eleven thirty."

"You're sure you weren't at the StarWalk after eleven thirty?"

"Very sure. I would have been walking into the motel lobby at that time. That would be on their security cameras."

"Your motel uses an older security camera system." Lew creased his brow. "The cameras were monitored by the night clerk, but he failed to load a new tape, so nothing was recorded."

"You can check with the shuttle driver," said Lew. "I sat kitty-corner behind him. We talked. I was the only rider. He should remember me. I gave him an autograph."

"The motel does have the ability to run a report of key card usage," said Thurgood. "That report would show that Mr. Sinclair indeed entered his room at eleven thirty and didn't reenter it at any time thereafter. That evidence, along with the shuttle driver, shows my client is clearly not involved in this crime." Thurgood eased back in his chair.

"Campers saw a golf cart by the StarWalk later on in the early morning. They saw someone sitting in a golf cart about the same time as we estimate the victim was killed. This witness couldn't tell if it was a man or a woman."

A ghost rider, thought Lew.

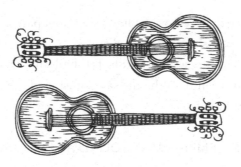

CHAPTER FIFTEEN

━━━━━━━━━━━━━━

S lim opened his eyes to the late-morning sun. It had been nice
having all this quiet time to himself. It was a long tour and
they'd all spent too much time together in that van. He should
check in on Lew, even though he'd promised not to. Maybe after
breakfast. He stretched a bit, bent his knees, then rolled to his side
and looked around his room. He spied the object of his current affection, the coffeemaker. He rose and washed out the carafe, filled it
from the tap, and sent the contents through the coffeemaker's heat-
ing cycle. He poured the results down the sink and refilled the carafe
from a jug of mineral water waiting on the counter. He put a filter in
the basket and spooned in some French chicory grounds from a can
he kept in the valise by his bed.

As the coffee brewed, Slim removed from his bag of tricks a small
china plate. He had bone china at home but didn't dare travel with
it. He then removed from the valise a waxed-paper bag containing
a magnificent chocolate croissant. It found its rightful place upon

the china. Slim then removed a linen-wrapped parcel. From this he produced an exquisite tulip-shaped cup.

He retrieved a newspaper from the hall and brought it to his quaint breakfast setting. What he saw forestalled the rest of his beloved morning ritual.

BODY OF MEMPHIS MAN FOUND AT FESTIVAL

"Mercy," said Slim. He read further. He crossed himself. "Oh, Archie," he said. "Whatever did you do this time?" He sought out his cell phone from last night's suit jacket. Archie dead and not one message? That's when he noticed the minute airplane icon. How long had his phone been in airplane mode? He'd been so happily occupied with his own company and his thoroughly planned excursions, he hadn't looked at any device other than the van's GPS since he'd arrived in the Twin Cities. He released the phone from its hermitage. Myriad notifications popped up on the screen. Slim called his friend.

"Lew, what is this dreadful business?"

"It seems Archie's gone and got himself killed and put the rest of us in a pickle jar."

"Oh, dear. Do the police consider you a suspect?"

"They talked to me just this morning, not half an hour ago. Didn't arrest me though. Unfortunately, I do have the feeling I'm not entirely off the hook."

"What about Ann-Dee?"

"I haven't seen her since yesterday noon. She got Mitchell and me chased outta that saloon on the north side of the festival."

"Have the police questioned her?"

"They didn't mention it."

Slim removed Ann-Dee's brooch and the cocktail napkin with Dale's number from a protected spot of the valise. He looked at the brooch as if it were a compass.

"I'll drive back right after breakfast," said Slim. "Where will I find you?"

"I think I'm gonna ramble around the festival for a bit, then head out to the Schroeders'. Do a little fishing. If I'm not out there, I expect you'll find me in the jailhouse. I'll put my phone on vibrate if I'm out on the lake, so call when you get here."

"See you soon, Lew." Slim hung up. He checked the number on the napkin and dialed. No answer. He'd try again after he ate.

Slim repositioned what was quite likely the prettiest set of English bone china teacups to be found in New Orleans. He moved the cups like chess pieces. One went diagonally just an inch, another went straight ahead two inches, a third hopped forward and to the right like a knight. That cup would be Lewis Sinclair's. These actions might seem fussy to the casual observer, but they made the table more esthetically pleasing and provided increased elbow room for his guests. His waiter appeared at the table.

"I'm expecting two gentlemen shortly. I don't know if they'll be taking tea or coffee, but may as well bring a pot of Earl Grey, enough for three. It won't go to waste. And the cookie assortment, please." The waiter jotted this down. "Hmm . . . four orders of shortbread as well." The waiter nodded and then departed.

Slim looked up to see Lew Sinclair and a sinewy yet angular young man flow in through the café's plate-glass door. New Orleans was experiencing one of its sudden June downpours. Slim's guests took care not to share their dampness with anything or anyone except the entry rug. The angular fellow collapsed an umbrella. He looked for a spot near the entrance to store it. Lew spotted Slim and brought the younger man to Slim's table. Slim rose to greet them.

He extended his hand and Lew took it, smiled, and nodded. The younger man did likewise but with more reserve.

"Well, you almost missed the cloudburst," said Slim. Lew chuckled. He turned his head and checked the rain on the storefront windows.

"It sure is coming down now," said Lew. "I do believe there wasn't a cloud in the sky until the deluge was right upon us."

"The devil's beating his wife," said Slim. "That's what they call it here. You've been baptized New Orleans style. Just you wait, it'll be over in the blink of an eye."

"The manhole covers are floating off the ground!" said the angular one. "There are geysers out there!" Slim laughed.

"Good thing I've got this one with me," said Lew. "He brought an umbrella." Lew patted the lean one on the shoulder. "Slim, this here's Gary Schroeder. He's my new bass player. Hails from up north, like you. Gary, meet Slim Pontchartrain. He plays keys. Caught him at Tipitina's last night. Dynamite."

"Glad you were able to catch me playing with Bernard Thibodeaux. I'm always at my best with him—especially at Tipitina's. Gentleman gave me my first paying gig. When he calls, I show up."

"You sure did show up," said Lew. "I tell you what, I have a great respect for the man myself. He's been around a long time."

"Can't remember a time when he wasn't," said Slim. The waiter brought the tea and baked goods.

"Would you gentlemen care for tea or coffee?" he asked.

Lew looked at the pot of tea, then at Slim.

"There's plenty of Earl Grey if you're inclined," offered Slim.

Gary glanced at the two senior men.

"Earl Grey it is," said Lew. He sat up a little straighter.

"Same here," said Gary, likewise adjusting his posture. The waiter left them to their tea party. Slim poured. Lew and Gary followed Slim's lead with the milk. They watched as he selected a butter cookie and dunked it in his tea.

They repeated his actions. Lew was happily surprised with the result. Gary dunked too long and his cookie crumbled into his cup.

"Timing is all, when it comes to dunking," said Slim. "You'll get the hang of it."

"I'm pretty certain Gary gets the hang of everything he sets his hat for," said Lew. Slim smiled. He unfolded a cloth napkin, dabbed his lip and positioned the linen on his lap.

Gary and Lew followed suit.

"A quick study is a handy fellow to have in a band," said Slim. "So you're a fellow Yankee then. I was born in Iowa myself." Slim offered the plate of shortbread to Gary and Lew. "Try a bar of this shortbread. This tea shop makes them a little sturdier than their butter cookies. They'll hold together better in the tea." They each took a piece.

"I wouldn't have guessed you were from the Midwest," said Gary.

"I imagine I have acquired a tinge of Yat accent," said Slim. "I've been here a good while. It suits me."

"You live here, then?" asked Gary. He looked sideways at Lew.

"It's home base," said Slim, "but I get around. Wherever the muse calls me, I go."

"You mean, if someone asks you to play in Boston, you'll go there?" said Gary.

"I like the way I said it better, but you could interpret it that way." Slim put down his teacup and eyed Gary. He winked. "However, either the money, the company, or the food has to be exceptional to lure me very far away."

"Gary here's been playing in Boston," said Lew. "He studied at Berklee."

"Ah," said Slim. "What brings you to New Orleans?"

Gary looked at Lew.

"Me, basically," said Lew. "I caught him backing a fella at the Paradise there in Boston. The band was having a good night, but Gary was obviously better. I thought I'd see if he'd like to raise my game instead of theirs."

"It was a temporary job, but I would have gone with Lew even if it wasn't," said Gary.

"So, where's home base for you now?" asked Slim.

"Well, I'm from Texas," said Lew. "I keep a place in Austin these days."

"Plenty of good food there," said Slim. "Good music. I could contemplate spending time in Austin."

"I figure on touring a good deal once we're gelled," said Lew. Slim nodded.

"How about you, Fritz?" Slim smiled as he remembered how his father would call Slim's Germanic cousins "Fritz" and "Frieda." "Ready for a warmer climate?"

"Yes, sir," said Gary. He gave a brisk nod.

"The money's not there yet," said Lew. "I hope we make up for it all company-wise."

"I expect we better see how we sound together then," said Slim. He laughed and toasted his new friends. "Once the rain stops, that is. I've got a friend with a courtyard close to here. Not a lot of space but the neighbors are a good audience. I suggest we go pick some."

The door to the restaurant flew open and in blew a sodden, scruffy youth draped in Mardi Gras beads and looking every inch a doused and confused cat. He shook his head, blessing some nearby patrons with raindrops. Their initial anger melted quickly into sweet appreciation at the young man's guileless joie de vivre. The youth immediately zeroed in on Lew, Gary, and Slim. He then noticed the teapot and shortbread on their table and advanced toward them.

"Well, I never expected a tea shop in New Orleans," said the cat with an Irish brogue. Gary looked warily at the drenched figure, probably worried it was going to shake off more rain. "You!" The cat pointed at Slim. "You were at Tipitina's last night. That was some mighty music you played." He pulled a chair up to the table and sat down. The waiter appeared. "I wouldn't mind a drop of tea," said the cat. "And some more of these biscuits—and a beignet, please. Do you have beignets?" The waiter nodded and left for the kitchen. "Do you know of anyone who has need of a drummer?" asked the cat. "I'm a sight better than that fella you played with last night. I'm Finbar Mitchell, by the way. No offense to your drummer.

*I hope he's not a relative. He was lovely. I'm just better. Hey," he looked to
Lew. "You were there last night too. Are you all musicians? Do you need a
drummer?"*

*The waiter arrived with Mitch's order. Mitch poured milk and sugar
into his cuppa. He took a long draft of tea, leaned back, and sighed with
pleasure, tapping his foot to some rhythm Slim wished he was playing to.*

"You got a drum kit at that courtyard?" asked Lew.

"Probably just a set of bongos," said Slim. "Maybe some sticks."

"Let's try 'em out," said Lew. He and Slim nodded and smiled.

⊰⊱⊰⊱⊰⊱

"Mitch!" Chuck rapped on the bathroom door. Mitch opened it. A
toothbrush hung out of his mouth. "Charla just called me. She and
Strudel are sick."

Mitch tossed the toothbrush into the sink. "How bad is she?"

"She doesn't want to go to the hospital. But she's worried about
Strudel."

"Not the wee poodle!"

"She's at the vet's right now. She said she'd stop by the parking
lot on her way back."

"Should she be driving?" asked Mitch.

"She's a tough old peacock. Hard to know if she'd fess up to how
bad off she is."

Mitch threw on some jeans and the red satin cowboy shirt. That
should cheer Charla, thought Chuck.

"Did Moira call you?" asked Mitch.

"Yes. She's going to upload all the footage she's got. She'll call
me when it's there." Chuck picked up Mitch's tablet and put it in a
messenger bag. "Charla said she'd meet us in the parking lot."

"I'll tell Lew where I'm off to," said Mitch. "You grab us some
doughnuts from the lobby, yeah?" He picked up an unused ice-

bucket bag. "Put them in this, so you can keep them clear of my tablet."

"Sure," said Chuck. He popped down to the front desk and beheld the bounty of continental breakfast items available to motel guests.

Lew hung up his jacket and tie, relieved his interview was over and glad that Slim was on his way. There was a knock at the door.

"Lew, it's Mitch. Are you home?"

Lew opened the door.

"Hello Mitchell, are you coming to the Schroeders'?"

"Naw, I'm off with Charles, the web fella, to help out Charla, the lady in satin from the meet and greet. Give my best to Mother Schroeder, would you?"

"Will do, son; but she's not going to like you stepping out with another older woman."

"Ah Lew, stop your teasing. Charla's had a run of trouble. I think she could use an extra friend or two right now."

"You find that out at the meet and greet?"

"Well, Charles and I had a ramble up to the War Zone yesterday."

"The War Zone? Now, Mitchell . . ."

"An ATV had just barely missed running her down. She jumped over the campfire to save herself. I saw the singe marks on her pantsuit. And a fine piece of fabric it was too, twice the shame."

"Well, no good comes from camping in the War Zone. That's what I hear."

"And now it appears someone's poisoned her and her wee poodle."

Lew stroked his chin. This was an odd development.

"Why? A nice old gal like that. Seemed like she'd give you the olive right out of her martini."

"It's a mystery indeed. Charles and I are going to keep an eye on her. Maybe get to the bottom of this business."

"Call me if you need help. I'll have my phone on vibrate. Keep yours on too, y'hear?"

"Right, Lew. Oh! Um . . . I guess I ought to tell you . . ."

Mitch sat down on the end of Lew's bed and looked around the room—anywhere to avoid eye contact. His foot beat a weird tattoo.

"Charles and I found this website. We googled 'Archie Grant.' Oh, it's a terrible site. It belonged to Archie. He put up naked pictures of ladies with Nancy's face on top of 'em. I fear if the police find it, they'll suspect one of the Schroeders for sure. Don't you look at it. You'll not be able to look Gary in the eye if you do."

"*You* can't even look me in the eye. Must be some website."

"Perhaps you could tell that lawyer fella about it. He might know what to do."

"That's an idea worth looking into."

"I best see if Charla's here. I'll check back in with you later, yeah?"

"Yeah."

Mitch sprang off the bed and to the door.

"Now, Mitchell," said Lew. He caught up with the lad. "You be careful. Hard telling what's going on. Keep your wits about you." He clapped the young man on the shoulder.

"Ah, you big sweetie!" Mitch grabbed him in a bear hug. "Tell Mrs. Schroeder I hope to stop by for supper. And try not to catch any fish if you can help it." Lew watched him bound away down the hall.

⛬ ⛬ ⛬

Chuck leaned on the front desk. He was enjoying his chat with the cute clerk behind it. She giggled and blushed. A stack of doughnuts and pastries wrapped in paper plates and napkins formed a garden wall between them.

Mitch rushed into the lobby.

"We've no time for gabbing," said Mitch. "Fetch us some coffee."

"You do it, Finbar," said Chuck. "I'm worn out from pastry acquisition." The clerk giggled.

"Are you Irish?" she asked Mitch.

"Oh sure," said Chuck. He rolled his eyes. "A guy with an accent comes along and it's 'Bye-bye, Mr. New Media.' Harrumph."

"You're married, I can tell. You're just flirting to distract me from the outrageous number of doughnuts you're taking."

Chuck looked at her aghast. Was he losing his touch?

"Now do as the Irish guy says," said the clerk, "and get some coffee to go with that mountain of doughnuts." She pointed at the to-go cups in the corner.

"Next time I'm here I'll have an accent," said Chuck. He made a mental note to watch some voice-coach videos on YouTube.

"I look forward to it," said the clerk. She laughed and retreated to her computer.

Chuck and Mitch poured themselves coffee. Mitch looked at Chuck, then at the clerk, then at Chuck again.

"I'm keeping an eye on you," said Mitch. "You and your beatnik ways."

"She was giving me the hairy eyeball when she saw how many pastries I took," whispered Chuck. "I had no choice but to be charming. Anyway, it's good to keep in practice. Flirting is an important tool in the journalism trade."

Just as they stepped outside with their breakfast items, Charla's RV swung into place below the motel awning. It felt for all the world to Chuck like a getaway car in a heist. Magda stepped out the side door.

"Get in," she said. Chuck and Mitch stepped up and into the RV. Charla looked over her shoulder at them.

"You brought us breakfast! How sweet. Just plop everything down on the table there and buckle your seat belts." The boys obeyed. Once they were safely ensconced, Charla put the hammer down and tore out of the motel lot. "Sorry to wake you boys, but Magda insisted, and she never insists on anything, so . . ."

"Where are we off to, Miss Charla?" Chuck and Charla made eye contact via the rearview mirror.

"Back to the vet's, to check on Strudel."

Magda twisted around to look at Mitch. "You are musician?"

Mitch nodded. "Yes miss . . . missus . . . ma'am. I'm a drummer. I play the pipes too."

"My husband was musician. Not professional. For joy."

"That's a lovely way to put it . . . ma'am."

"Your manners are good. Like mine when I come here from Germany. Everyone in America so easy with first names. No 'Mr.' or 'Mrs.' to be found. I like you. You may call me Mrs. Herman."

"You're German?" asked Chuck.

"I am Polish," replied Magda. She sat up straight. "But I live for many years in Germany. I come here from there."

"What instrument did your husband play?" asked Chuck.

Charla took a corner. Chuck grabbed the coffee as they lurched.

"Harmonica, guitar, concertina. Much *muzyka* in him. Good man."

Chuck noticed Charla's eyebrows spring up.

"Ha!" said Magda. "I surprise you all. No one thought of my husband in such ways. But I know. I know." Magda's gaze fell upon the doughnuts. "Did you bring us cake?" Chuck thought he saw a hint of a winsome smile in Magda's placid expression. "Oh, I also know how he got his money. I'm not naïve. He 'leaned' on people, but me he did not lean on." She looked back up at Chuck, then Mitch. "Me he lifted up. You see, where I come from there were lots of criminals. You couldn't be picky or choosy about who you kept company with—or you'd never eat!" Magda plucked a doughnut hole from the top of the baked-goods offering. "My husband got things done." She pulled the doughnut hole into two pieces. "He got me out of Germany." Mitch's eyes grew wide. "Oh, he stole such good things!" She popped a piece of doughnut into her mouth and chewed. "Much better than what other people stole." Magda laughed. "And he gave them to me!" Chuck laughed too.

"You understand, little clown."

"Yeah, I get it," said Chuck. "For you, he played music."

"Yes." Magda smiled. "*Muzyka*." She ate the rest of her doughnut.

⫷⫸ ⫷⫸ ⫷⫸

Magda dabbed Frau Holthaus's brow with a damp cloth. The frail woman did poorly in hot weather, so Magda made potato soup the day before. It heated up the kitchen, but could be served cold for days. It was one of her hostess's favorites.

Gertrude entered the bedroom. Magda wished Gertrude was less serious and talked more about unimportant things. The child was quiet, like Magda. It was Magda's mission to nudge Gertrude along toward aimless speech. Magda had had to teach herself this art. Days were long for Frau Holthaus without conversation. It didn't matter what was said, just the exchange of friendly noises comforted the woman. In time, it comforted Magda as well. It bonded them and erased—at least for the moment—the suffering of the past. There was plenty of time for quiet at night.

Gertrude was welcome also because now Frau Holthaus could be moved to and from her bed to a bath chair. They used a sheet to transfer her. They practiced for a good two weeks with sacks of flour and potatoes before moving their benefactor.

Frau Holthaus became even chattier once she could explore and rediscover the comfort and familiarity of her home. She delighted in sitting before a fire or patting the solid kitchen table. On good days she helped peel potatoes and similar homely tasks. The rewards of movement, of being busy and being useful, filled and soothed her.

"Babciu, do you want to be in your chair today?" Despite her weak condition, she did. This was good. She ate more when she was sitting up in her chair. Gertrude and Magda performed the gentle yet strenuous task of moving Frau Holthaus to the bath chair. Gertrude trotted into the kitchen. Magda followed pushing Frau Holthaus. "Run get the soup from the back, Gertrude." Gertrude departed to retrieve the metal canister from the stream behind the cottage.

"Such a relief that the girl is good," said Frau Holthaus, "like you. Not all the girls who have lived here were so." She reached for Magda's hand. She smiled. Magda nodded.

They were still training the new boy in the sheet-transfer process. He was mainly kept busy with outside tasks until they had a better grasp of what he was capable of. For now, he slept in an outbuilding. They'd made it homey for him. It would suffice for the summer. It was surely better than sleeping in the grove. He ate meals in the kitchen with the women. He seemed consistently gentle. They kept rolling pins in easily accessed but hidden places. Frau Holthaus had a surprising number of rolling pins. She never explained why. Magda assumed she'd inherited them from her mother and aunts. At one time, she'd had many of them as well.

Gertrude appeared in the doorway.

"The soldier is here," she announced.

She moved inside the room. The American's large frame now filled the doorway. He held a concertina in one arm. In the crook of the other slept a small calico cat. Magda ran to him and transferred the cat to her own arms, cooing to it and chucking it tenderly beneath its chin.

In lieu of speech, the soldier performed a flourish of chords on the squeezebox. A grand smile filled his face as fully as his body filled the door.

Frau Holthaus clasped her hands together and beamed. The soldier reached outside behind the doorway and produced a bag of sugar.

"I brought sugar too," he said in English. "For kuchen?"

"Kuchen," said Magda. She nodded and beamed as well.

⋘◈⋙ ⋘◈⋙ ⋘◈⋙

Charla pulled the RV into the veterinarian's parking lot at a speed that caused Chuck to slide half off his seat. He saved his coffee from capsizing.

"I'm just going to check back in on Strudel," said Charla. "You folks go ahead with your breakfast. Thanks boys, for bringing it." Charla leaped out her door and sped into the clinic. Magda left her seat and moved to the other side of the table.

"Remove your seat belts. Charla may be gone for some time. It's safe while we are parked." She chuckled softly to herself. "Now, more cake!"

Chuck began to separate out the various pastries and rolls. Mitch uncapped the coffees.

"So boys," said Magda, "if Charla brings back the pup, you are not to be surprised it's not poodle."

"What?" said Chuck.

"It is bichon frise. Don't tell her."

"Doesn't rhyme nearly as well, does it?" said Mitch.

"Exactly," said Magda. "Rhyming gives her joy, so call it a poodle."

"Yes, Mrs. Herman."

"This woman," said Magda, "who sang before you at fair. The blonde one who the dead man proposed to. Do you know her?"

"I do," said Mitch. "But I'd be better off if I didn't."

Did Magda just smile? wondered Chuck. Something had changed in her eyes.

"Ah, so she is troublesome. Is she causing problems in your hotel?"

"I don't know where she's staying," said Mitch.

"Did manager book her room?"

"I suppose he did. He booked ours."

Magda lowered her eyes. Chuck imagined gears turning in her head like in a cartoon. She looked up again.

"Can you drive this?" Magda gestured to the steering wheel.

"What do you have in mind?" asked Mitch.

"I need to go to blonde woman's hotel. I want to see her room. She has something that is mine."

"I don't know . . ." said Mitch.

"I'll do it," said Chuck. Magda looked at him. Now that was definitely a smile.

"Good boy. You, Finbar, you go to Charla. Help her with puppy. Do not tell her what we are up to. She would just worry. We'll be right back. No harm will come."

"Give us your room key," said Chuck. Peer pressure was another good journalist's tool.

Mitch paused and frowned, but dug the key card out of his back pocket and handed it over.

"Thanks," said Chuck.

Mitch stuffed the remainder of his bear claw into his mouth and grabbed a coffee. He shook his head as he left the RV.

Chuck gingerly moved into the driver's seat and took the wheel. He looked at it with a tinge of dismay. It had been a while.

"Ring if you need me," Mitch mumbled, waving.

The RV pulled away, slowly at first, then lurching into warp speed, narrowly missing a fire hydrant, and then beating a stuttering yet hasty retreat to the motel.

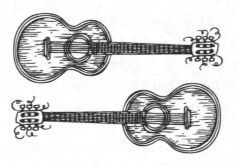

CHAPTER SIXTEEN

itch's news about Archie's website lit up a couple of synapses in Lew's investigative brain. Now, he wasn't just looking to save his own skin, but possibly Gary's or Nancy's too. He stuffed into a pocket a pair of white cotton gloves he wore when dusting his guitar, grabbed a doughnut from the lobby, and hopped the shuttle to FallsFest. There he picked up a doughnut-esque Norwegian taco and sat himself down at the summit, gazing out at the festival. It was humid today, so Lew patted his forehead with an extra napkin while he gathered his thoughts.

The detectives had asked him questions about the golf cart. *Was that golf cart still around?* he wondered. Maybe they were curious about a different golf cart than the one Lew had driven. He remembered the ruts he spied at the StarWalk. He oughtta check the tires of every cart he could find for mud and grass, maybe concrete. He'd check their floorboards and accelerators as well. The driver, or whoever, might have tracked evidence back into their ride when they were done with their work. Lew shuddered, then regained his composure. The festival golf carts were likely scattered all over the festival, but there might be one or two parked by the FallsFest office trailer.

He'd start with those first.

And whom should he be looking at as a suspect? The website would suggest Gary or Nancy. The idea of one of the band being a murderer was almost too much for Lew to bear. It was easier for him to look at Nancy. He liked Nancy, but he didn't know her like he knew Gary. He didn't love her yet. Lew might find out more if he went fishing with Gary and his dad, ask a few questions. He'd have to be subtle though—could he be that subtle?

Maybe he could spend some time with Bea in the kitchen. But she'd be onto his motives far before the menfolk caught on, so maybe not. Why not talk to Nancy herself? Go down to the FallsFest office and act like he was interested in learning how the festival worked, then shepherd the conversation around to something more motive focused.

Who else could he suspect? Gordon? Gordon intimidated him. Questioning would be harder. But why even suspect the man? He'd been nothing but generous to Lew. Well, maybe that was a ruse. Maybe Gordon meant to endear himself to Lew and then peg the murder on him. Maybe that's why he offered the festival lawyer to "help" Lew. It could be a way for Gordon to control the situation, keep the heat on Lew instead of himself.

Lew felt foolish for even thinking such a thing. Why, he'd worn the man's hat! Lew didn't like the way his mind had been working since the murder—since the day the Cowboys set off for the festival even! He didn't like the way that Norwegian taco was sitting in his stomach either.

Time to get moving around. Time to head down to the FallsFest office trailer.

There were two golf carts parked outside the FallsFest offices, one at each end of the trailer. He chose to check out the one near Gordon's door first. He squatted down and got a look at the tires. Yep, there was mud and grass, maybe even some cement crumbles, but it could be clay too. Then again maybe all the cart tires looked like this. He looked for footprints, hair, scraps of cloth. Nothing. Maybe the other cart—

The door to the trailer swung open and Nancy flew down the steps, followed by Brad. She carried a bat.

"Okay, okay, Ruby! We're on our way," she yelled, her fingers pressing a button on the walkie-talkie as she rushed away from Lew and the cart. "We'll be with you in one minute."

Lew realized this meant both Nancy and Ruby were away from the trailer. Now was his chance to talk with Gordon alone—look at his shoes—or, if no one was there, maybe snoop around the offices. He walked up the steps and knocked on the door. No answer. He stepped inside.

"Hello?" No answer. "Gordon?" Still no answer. He knocked on Gordon's door. "Hello?" He opened the door and looked around. Empty. He crept around to Nancy's desk. Her laptop. Start there. As he reached to open it, his sleeve caught some pencils in a caddy and spilled the whole collection across the desk. Lew moved to upright the caddy. He froze, his fingertips a mere quarter inch from it. Fingerprints! He didn't need to give the police any extra cause to suspect him. *Put your sleuth hat on Lew! This isn't a Tuesday crossword puzzle. This has real consequences.* He remembered the white gloves in his pocket and donned them, then tidied the pencil spill and opened Nancy's laptop. First, he checked her browser history. Nothing. He clicked on the hard-drive icon. He sorted the window by date. The most recent file by far was "Talent Info." It appeared to be a list of the performers at the festival, how to contact them, and their tax information. There were two tax columns. Some performers had vendor ID data, some Social Security numbers. Lew scrolled through the file to see if anything jumped out at him.

A rousing ringtone of "The Irish Rover" sprang from Lew's phone and he jumped out of his skin instead. He slapped the laptop shut. Once he returned to his skin, he realized it was Mitch calling. He answered his phone while reopening the laptop, quitting the program, and closing it once again.

"Mitchell, are you all right?"

"Yes, Lew," said Mitch. "I just wanted to fill you in on some matters. I'm safe and sound here at the veterinary clinic with Charla. Her poodle *was* poisoned."

"What?"

"We think it'll be okay. What I wanted to tell you is that Charles went off with Magda—that's the other lady from Memphis, the Polish one?—and they're going to try to get into Ann-Dee's motel room to look for that brooch Ann-Dee wears. Magda says it's hers."

"What on earth?" said Lew. "That lady's from Memphis, you say? But Ann-Dee's from New Orleans. I wonder when—"

"The doctor's coming out now," said Mitch. "We'll talk later, yeah?"

"We will. Thanks for clueing me in. Keep me up to date when you can."

They rang off.

Lew began looking through the drawers in Nancy's desk. When he got to the lower left one, he discovered—beneath an impressive number of envelopes, erasers, and pens—a Zoom Handy Recorder. Lew had one like it. So did Gary. It had a pretty decent microphone setup. Lew used his to record pieces of new songs, or rehearsals, or a set when they were on the road.

It had better sound than his phone.

He played the first track. It was a decent groove. He played another. Now that was more than decent. Lew made a mental note to let Gary take a solo now and again. The third and last track was a conversation. Gary first—his voice somewhat heated. Archie next, oozing out something vague or evasive. Then, some kind of low screech. A chair moving heavily but quickly across the floor? Followed by a loud clatter, like something rigid and metal colliding with the floor.

"All right, all right," said Archie. *"I can do this, just settle down. There's a lady present."*
"Like you have any respect for women!" said Gary.

Gary sounded mad. Lew was thankful Gary'd never been mad at him. There was a scuffling noise. Lew couldn't quite make out what it was, but it didn't sound good for Archie.

"Okay, okay," said Archie. *"Just stand farther away and I'll say it."* A pause. Archie took a deep breath. He recited the date, some day in March of this year. *"My name is Archie Grant. I took unauthorized photographs of Nancy Hirsch when she and Gary Schroeder were at a private beach near Galveston, Texas."* There was a pause. *"Oh, yeah, I also used other photos of Ms. Hirsch in combination with pictures I found in magazines and screen grabs to create false—what's the word?—right, composites. I made composites. I have since taken the website down and will not repost any of the photos or composites . . . oh, and I make this recording of my own volition . . . so help me God."*

The track ended there.
That dirty skunk Archie, thought Lew. *He must have put the site— and Nancy's photos—back up when he thought Nancy and Gary were convinced he'd done the right thing.* Lew thought about the date. March.

Just a bit after the band took a tour break. Gary and Nancy went to Galveston during that break. Nancy would have headed back north not long afterward to start working for the festival.

Lew rewound the track and recorded it on his phone. He glanced up and through a window saw Gordon and Thurgood moving toward the trailer, perhaps thirty feet away. He carefully but briskly stored the recorder back in the drawer. He looked up again. Gordon and Thurgood were much closer. Their direction suggested they were headed for the trailer door leading into where Lew now stood, so he made a quick relocation to Gordon's office. Because the air was humid, the door didn't close all the way. He positioned himself so that he could peek through the crack but was far enough back so that he (hopefully) couldn't be seen.

Gordon and Thurgood entered the trailer.

"You know she's right behind us," said Thurgood.

"She's going to grill me about the murder for the ten thousandth time," said Gordon, "Quick, let's see if we can get a few moves in on our game. Maybe it'll distract her." They sat down at a chessboard that was perched on a lamp table between two guest chairs.

Ruby entered the trailer.

"Where have you been?" she said to Gordon.

"Now, help me remember," said Gordon. "Do you work for me? Or do I work for you?"

"You're the boss, Gordy," said Ruby.

"Sometimes I forget. I don't know why."

"Where have you been?"

"How is it," replied Gordon, "that I'm sitting in the office, deep into a game of chess with our company attorney, and *you* enter asking *me* where I've been?"

"I've been calling you on the walkie-talkie every ten minutes and you didn't answer." Ruby's back was to Lew. She was in superhero pose, her hands balled into fists perched on her hips. "Some nut job jumped onstage and started dancing with Lucy Hucknall. She was a good sport about it, but it took security until the end of the song to waltz him back to terra firma."

Gordon sat up. He was partially hidden from Lew by Ruby.

"Is Lucy okay?"

"She's a pro. She dedicated the next song to him. Said he was her fiancé. Crowd ate it up. I guess they forgot the last fiancé onstage wound up dead. Speaking of which, you." She addressed Thurgood. "What's going on with Archie Grant's murder investigation? What do the cops have to say?"

"Can't tell you. Attorney-client privilege," said Thurgood.

"You're also the FallsFest lawyer," said Ruby. "Tell me on that level."

"Can't."

"Just how am I supposed to nose out information if you won't fill me in on the down-low?"

"Oh, that's right," said Thurgood. "You're my new private detective."

Gordon, still obscured from Lew's sight by Super Ruby, said, "She could be helpful, Thurgood." He crossed his legs, which brought one of his Doc Marten-clad feet into Lew's view.

Thurgood, who was fully in Lew's sightline, unbound his glossy black hair, smoothed it and refastened it into a short ponytail.

"The interview with Lewis Sinclair went all right, I suppose. I called the detectives afterward to see what I could find out. They've lost contact with the witness who claimed they saw someone at the StarWalk around the estimated time of Grant's death. Until they can reconnect with that witness to organize a lineup, all they have to go on is that the person was tall and most likely male. That's good for Mr. Sinclair. He's by no means short, but I wouldn't classify him as tall.

"They're still waiting for a toxicology report, but expect it soon. They're especially looking for a sedative of some kind. Grant had no head injuries, so they're anticipating he was sedated somewhere else where it was convenient to do so, then moved to the StarWalk where he was suffocated in the cement. That 'sedated elsewhere' is likely why they're so curious about golf carts. Even a tall man would need some kind of help getting an unconscious body up the StarWalk hill. Or at least something less conspicuous than a fireman's lift."

"The witness only saw one person?" asked Ruby.

Thurgood raised his eyebrows. "The witness they haven't reconnected with said that, yes."

Ruby moved out of sight, exposing Gordon. Gordon put his fingertips to the top of his bishop.

"Don't do that, Gordy. He'll have your queen in two moves."

Gordon released the piece.

"Speaking of golf carts," said Ruby. "When we escorted Lucy Hucknall's 'fiancé' back to the War Zone—of course he's camping at the War Zone—we passed by one of our carts by Big Pearly Lake. I was gonna drive it back here but the keys were missing. Lucky I noticed it. If I'd climbed in I would have got FallsFest blue all over my favorite pair of flip-flops. Paint all over the floorboards." Ruby's fashionably sandaled foot entered Lew's view. She shook it.

"Only you would call those flip-flops," said Gordon.

"Some other poor slob wasn't so lucky," said Ruby. "Big old footprint right in the middle of the paint."

Thurgood shaped a tighter curl to his short ponytail.

"FallsFest blue. Is that the paint they found at the murder scene?" he asked.

"Yes. A perfect match for our logo," said Ruby. "Wasted on golf carts and concrete."

"Hmm, and it has a footprint in it," said Thurgood, still curling his ponytail. Gordon eyed him intently.

"The golf cart was at the murder scene?" asked Ruby. "Why didn't I think of that?"

"You're still learning," said Thurgood. "Psychology is your forte at the moment." Thurgood removed his cell from its holster. "I guess I should call the detectives."

"Tell 'em our Cinderella has at least size twelve tootsies."

Lew decided it would be best to leave the trailer in case the detectives swung by on their way to the lake. He paddy-pawed out the door to the outside world and had gotten a ways away when his phone vibrated in his pocket.

"Slim! Are you at the Schroeders' already?"

"I'm at a rest stop about forty minutes outside Big Pearly Falls."

"I'm glad to hear it."

"I've got some extra information I forgot to share earlier," said Slim. He paused, cleared his throat. "Y'see, well, I bumped into Ann-Dee's bass player last night. He backed her for her performance, the one before us."

"Yes."

"Well . . . the boy said he was in love with Ann-Dee. Said he hoped someday to have more than a professional relationship with her."

"I see."

"And he sto—" Slim stopped, cleared his throat again. "He borrowed that brooch she wears when she performs. Some insurance that he'd see her again, he said."

"Brooch!" said Lew. "Why's everybody so danged concerned with that brooch?"

"Hmm?"

"Mitch called me just a bit ago saying that the blogger fella and the little Polish woman with Charla . . . Maybe you didn't meet her. Anyway, they're looking for the brooch in Ann-Dee's motel room."

"Well, I'll be," said Slim. He felt the kerchief pocket of his vest.

"I'm gonna run a quick errand," said Lew. "Then I'll meet up with you at the Schroeders'. Tell you everything I know then."

"Sounds good," said Slim.

Lew was puzzling over this brooch business when—

"Lewie!"

Lew pocketed his phone and turned around. "Ms. Flynn."

"You busy?"

Lew's brain was busy. He wanted a break from FallsFest. Some quiet time on the lake with two somber Schroeders would help him process all this information.

"I'm headed for the shuttle," he said. "I'm fixing to go fishing with Gary and his pop. I'd like to buy a gift for Bea first though. Does the shuttle go downtown?"

"I'll give you a ride," said Ruby. "Gordon's sent me on a mission to get more FallsFest blue paint. Said he wants to show it to the detectives. I think he wants me out of the way when the detectives show up. Thinks I'm a loose cannon." She laughed. "Maybe I am." She walked over to the golf cart on the other end of the trailer. "Good. We've got a clean one. Climb in."

Off they sped to downtown Big Pearly. Ruby had a rather heavy right foot so they took off with a lurch. Lew looked back, not to see Lot's wife, but Gordon on the steps of the trailer talking animatedly into his phone.

⸎⸎⸎

"Here's your stop," said Ruby. She paused the golf cart momentarily in front of the Grocery Basket supermarket, next door to Hoffman Hardware. "I'm going to park behind Hoffman's. Meet me inside if you finish your shopping before I do. I'll be in the paint section or at checkout." She zipped away around the corner.

Lew noticed the chrysanthemum display in front of the grocery store. Buying a hostess gift for Bea was a challenge. The Schroeder larder was the most completely stocked kitchen resource in the tristate area. A loaf of marble rye was simply not necessary, and perhaps insulting, in a household with a baker as talented and prolific as Bea. And the Schroeder palate for spirits was particular. Lew had yet to figure it out. They weren't teetotalers, but the stern looks that greeted a bottle of Pinot Noir Lew once brought were curious to behold. Perhaps it was a Germanic thing. Come to think of it, he could only remember seeing Liebfraumilch and schnapps decanted at their table. Best to skip the bakery and alcohol sections.

The chrysanthemums were a perfect choice. Bea would appreciate the practicality of them. She could enjoy their beauty upon presentation and later plant them at the resort, thus improving the camping experience of her guests. Lew almost regretted being allergic to mums, but as he was often not home to enjoy his yard, it was not a regret worth having. He bent down and chose two lovely specimens. Bea would surely find them jolly and rewarding. Their pollen took little time finding Lew's olfactory organs however, and he released a mighty series of sneezes. He shook his head to recover. He wondered which pocket his handkerchief was in and whether he'd make it to the checkout before it was crucial.

"Silly," a soft voice behind him cooed. "You know you're allergic to mums."

Lew turned toward the familiar voice. There stood Ann-Dee. She tucked a tissue into one of his hands. Her eyes were misty. He remembered why he'd fallen so blindly for her. He glanced down at her bag of purchases. A rotisserie chicken, Asian barbecue sauce, some kind of cheese he'd never known the name of. That was *their* picnic menu. Lew's heart ached. He hoped his allergies covered for the water that was building in his eyes. Oh, if only they were going on a picnic together and this whole sordid Archie business had never taken place. Then he glanced down again and saw the bottle of antihistamine pressed against the thin membrane of the bag. Antihistamines could be a sedative. This brand anyway. Ann-Dee sometimes took one to help her sleep when it was late and she was still up after a performance. Could she? He'd never seen her in a size-twelve boot. Still . . . He looked up into Ann-Dee's eyes. Those beautiful, beautiful eyes.

"Sorry about that scene in the saloon," she said. "I didn't know the barkeep was going to react that way."

She reached up to touch his cheek but stopped. Her hand fell to her side, but Lew felt her fingertips brush ever so gently against his face just the same. Ann-Dee's gaze dropped as well. She rushed off to the checkout, but Lew had enough chance to see that the mums had affected Ann-Dee's eyes as much as they had his.

<hr />

They were enjoying one of their Sunday mornings. Hanging around at Lew's house—the house he'd inherited when his parents died—drinking coffee, not saying much, reading the newspaper on the big cozy couch in the sun.

This Sunday morning was different for Lew because it was the anniversary of the day his parents died. On this day, he performed three simple rituals to celebrate his folks.

The first was a meal of chili beans and fried potatoes. It was the first meal Lew's mom had ever made for his dad, and so it was his dad's favorite—which was good because it was cheap and they ate it often.

Lew loved the sparkle in his parents' eyes when they told him this story, which they did almost every time the meal was served.

Hence, he made chili beans and fried potatoes today for their Sunday-morning brunch. He didn't explain why. Ann-Dee ate her plateful with relish and it pleased Lew and warmed his heart.

After the last spud was stabbed, Lew brought out the second ritual, a silver plate with two small rectangles of white cake with fluffy white frosting coated in crushed peanuts. Lew's parents had eloped as soon as they'd graduated high school. They were, of course, poor, and two pieces of this dessert picked up at a bakery near the courthouse had served as their wedding cake. This was another tale they told Lew with sparkling and sometimes dewy eyes.

Ann-Dee watched Lew present the cakes. She ate every morsel, licking her index finger and dabbing up each remaining crumb. The kitchen was warm from the sun. Ann-Dee looked into Lew's eyes. She took his hand and smiled, brought his fingers to her cheek, then closed her eyes.

After the meal, they went out to the couch on the porch. Lew drew up a guitar that leaned against the sofa's arm. He began strumming the tune of the third ritual. An old instrumental his parents taught him when he was a child. They called it "The Wind and Rain." His pop would play the guitar and his mom the autoharp. Ann-Dee surprised him by singing words to it. He didn't know it had words. And she sang, "Oh, the dreadful wind and rain." The wind blew in from the woods and moved fair strands of hair from her shoulders. The words were grim, but the melody lovely. Lew choked back tears and lay back against the couch. Ann-Dee rested her head on his chest. The restless wind blew through the trees.

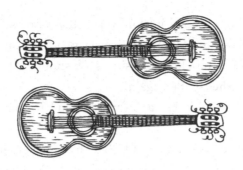

CHAPTER SEVENTEEN

"**H**ey there, cowboy!" said Ruby.

Lew looked away from the mums to see Ruby marching toward him out of the hardware store with a can of paint.

"You're not thinking of getting back together with the blonde bomber, are you?"

"Hmm? Oh. No. Just thinking of buying Mrs. Schroeder some mums. Do you like mums? I reckon I owe you a gift or two."

"The pleasure of your company's enough." Ruby laughed. "Besides, I'm paying you to be here. Gifts aren't necessary in a business transaction." She looked at Lew's bare crown. "You need a hat. If you're going fishing you'll burn without one."

"I got one yesterday, but it was a rash decision. I was all addled on account of Archie. Just didn't seem like something I wanted to wear today."

"They'll have a good lid for you in the hardware store," said Ruby. "Come with me. Old Hoffy'll give you a discount if he sees me with you. We give him lots of business. Or should I say we give him the business!" She laughed again.

"May I?" Lew took the can of paint from her. They entered the hardware store.

"Fishing's at the back," said Ruby. They made their way. "Now, Lewie, I've been googling and noodling and asking around. Trying to make sense of this Archie murder."

Lew nodded.

"I was talking to the acts and their management earlier," she continued. "Just casual. They're used to me. But I've been trying to get a sense of who knows who. Know what I mean?"

"I guess."

"Trouble is, I'm not finding anyone with as much motive as you or one of the Cowboys."

"I wouldn't look at any of the Cowboys, ma'am."

"So where were your boys that night?"

"Slim was in the Twin Cities; Mitchell was with that blogger fella; and Gary was with the Schroeders all night."

"Gary," said Ruby. She rubbed her chin. "He's a tall drink of water."

"Now, Ms. Flynn—"

"And those Schroeders are a close-knit bunch. Good people, but very close-knit."

Lew stopped cold and set the paint on the floor.

"You're a trusting man," said Ruby. "I'm not. I'm a woman with a keen intuition. You don't work around people in the music business as long as I have without developing a keen intuition. That and my father was a forensic psychologist. We had a lot of interesting Sunday dinners. Now, pick that paint can back up."

Lew picked up the paint.

"No Cowboy or Schroeder had anything to do with Archie's death," said Lew.

"So help me out. Who did?" Ruby's keen eyes bore into Lew's. "How about Blondie? Any more info on her whereabouts that night?"

Lew swallowed. "I have no idea where Ann-Dee's been. Just now was the first time since the saloon that I've seen her."

"The saloon?"

"Yesterday. Mitchell and I were in the saloon there on the festival grounds. Ann-Dee performed a song."

"Tammy Wynette?"

Lew grimaced.

"Then John Turnbell interviewed her," continued Lew. "Mitchell and I took our leave about then. How about your Gordon Morgan? Not that I suspect the man. Just that if you're going to suspect Gary and the Schroeders, seems like fair play."

"When I was googling, I found out that Archie has a record in Memphis. A criminal record, not a music one. Now, Gordon's *from* here but he did spend some years in Memphis at his uncle's club, Kennedy's I think the name was."

"Kennedy's! That's where we met Archie!"

"When was this?"

"Around three years ago."

"That was after," said Ruby.

"After?"

"After some mob guys trashed the club and beat Gordon up. His uncle sold the place and Gordon moved back here."

"Was Archie involved in that?" asked Lew.

"I don't remember him mentioning anyone by name. He didn't say anything when we made your deal with Grant." Ruby looked long and hard at Lew. "I can tell you this for sure: Gordon would never do anything to jeopardize FallsFest. Not the festival, its employees, or the acts. Never."

"I believe you," said Lew. They stood at the back of the store and studied a display of hats. "And how about me?" He looked sideways at Ruby.

"Well, you're not in the clear." She laughed. "But like I said, I have intuition. It says you didn't do it."

Lew reached for a standard-issue fishing hat.

"Nope," said Ruby. She reached over his arm and selected a woven ranch style and positioned it on Lew, giving it a slight tilt forward toward his left eye. "Now that's a proper hat for a country-western star out fishing. It's not a performing hat, but it'll do on a boat. She stepped back and studied him. "Let's get you checked out. Then I'll drive you over to the Schroeders'."

"I still need to get the mums for Bea," said Lew.

"Fine," said Ruby. "I'll get the cart after we pay and swing around front. That Bea will love those mums."

"She's good people," said Lew. "All the Schroeders are."

"Mm-hmm," said Ruby. "Close-knit."

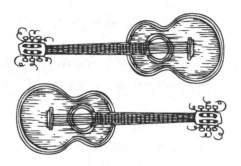

CHAPTER EIGHTEEN

uby dropped Lew off beside the Schroeder propane tank. He
fetched the mums from the back of the golf cart and tipped
his new ranch hat good-bye to the jewel-haired dynamo as
she sped down the hill toward the FallsFest grounds. As the sound
of the cart faded away, his ears were met with a very non-Schroeder
sound: the wail of a woman in distress.

"My boy! My boy! Someone fetch the gun. We've got to get him
back!"

Lew ran through the resort office and into the kitchen. It was
but an echo of the cozy room from two nights ago. The coffeepot sat
cold on the stove. A potholder languished on the floor. No baking
bread or aromatic anything. No cooking projects at all, just a spat-
tered mess of flour and a discarded apron puddled up next to the
violets on the counter. Bea Schroeder sat at the table, her elbows on
the oilcloth, a dish towel held to her face.

She wailed in horrible sorrow.

Mr. Schroeder's head was next to hers, his arm around her shoulders.

"He'll be back, Beatrice. It's all a mistake. Nancy's got a lawyer on his way to the jail now. You've got to be strong. Gary needs you to be strong."

Nancy braced herself against the sink. The smashing blonde was now shaken and pale. She turned her wan face up to Lew when he entered.

"Lew," she murmured, "the sheriff's taken Gary to the police station."

Mrs. Schroeder lowered her towel to look at Lew.

"They've taken my son! My beautiful son! Gary's no murderer!" She collapsed in tears, her face again submerged in the dishtowel.

Lew's face blanched. It was bad enough when he was fretting about his own hide, but worrying about Gary's future was ten times worse. He stepped over to Nancy.

"When did all this happen?" he asked.

"Not five minutes ago. You must have passed the car on the way here. No, they'd have taken the south road." Nancy's eyes were red from crying, but there was also anger in them. "Let's step outside."

They walked down to where the family's johnboat was moored at the dock. "It's that hideous Archie's fault. If he weren't dead, I'd strangle him myself."

"I wouldn't blame you. You've got plenty of reason and that's a fact." Nancy's eyes now held questions. "That blogger fellow found out about Archie's website," said Lew. "I'm mighty sorry. No one believes the pictures are real, but I know they must bother you."

"Did you . . .?"

"Gosh no!" Lew took off his hat.

"If I weren't so angry," said Nancy, "I just might let the fear in . . ."

"Even with the website, though, I don't see why they'd arrest Gary. Just doesn't seem like enough motive to me. Why, it's cut-and-dried illegal, what Archie did. Seems like it'd be a whole lot easier to file charges against a man than to take his life."

"Law takes time. Besides, there were some other photos too. Real ones Archie took with an extremely long lens when Gary and I were on vacation back in February. It was an isolated beach. I don't even know how he knew we were there. I don't know what's creepier, that he found us or that he took the photos."

Lew patted Nancy's shoulder.

"We saw someone with a giant camera lens when we were on the beach. We eventually figured out it was Archie because he started bragging about his new whizbang camera and lenses. We confront-ed him and he blabbed about the website." Nancy reached a knuckle up to her eye and rid herself of some tears. "Around spring sometime we got Archie to admit it all into a recorder," continued Nancy. "We got him to take the website down and kept the recording for insur-ance. I'd check from time to time. He put the site back up just before you guys drove here for the festival." She looked out onto the lake. Some people were gathering on the other side of it. "I have to find that recording and get rid of it. It might not look good for Gary if the police find it."

Lew's hand twitched. He was about to tell her it was in the lower left drawer of her desk, but should he?

"And I never should have confirmed that Social Security num-ber to Turnbell. But I had to get people to look at someone besides Gary. It seemed like a gift when he called. If they trace that back to me . . ." Nancy peeked sideways up at Lew. "I never told you about this, okay?" She nudged the johnboat with the toe of one of her Ree-boks. She looked out across the water. "Someone says they saw Gary at the StarWalk the night of the murder."

"What?"

"They won't tell us who it is, of course."

Nancy started to cry. Guess the fear got in.

Lew put his arm around her shoulders and let her weep against his chest.

⸭⸭⸭

Chuck had driven his grandparents' RV several years ago, but he still found Charla's vehicle a little unwieldy. He soldiered through after his staccato start, however, by driving slowly.

"Magda," said Chuck, "do you miss your home country?"

"No," said Magda. She thought for a few moments. "I miss mother—what I remember of her. She is dead a long time. Still, I suppose I can miss her anyway, yes?"

"Yes," said Chuck.

"I am gone so long from my old country, long enough to speak like an American. You must forgive me. It was sad and poor where I come from. Everyone miserable. My husband shows up and there is *muzyka* and dancing and good things to eat. I said to him I had nothing to give him in return. He says my *language* is my gift. Again and again he says he loves my speaking. It is my *muzyka* for him. Well, once such a handsome man tells me that, I am never going to throw away this accent! And now it reminds me of him, so I still have it. He is still beside me when I speak."

"That's beautiful. I hope Moira and I still have that decades from now."

"My husband gave me *broszka*—uh, uh, brooch—on our wedding day. Instead of bride's gown, instead of ring, I had brooch. We got married very quickly, you see, so he could bring me back to America with him. He was a soldier at the training camp, Hohenfels. Before the soldiers, the Yanks"—she smiled—"moved into Hohenfels, it was displacement camp. This is where my mother and I live when I was small." She looked at her hands. "My mother died there, from typhoid. Many others died with her. All Poles." Magda's hands curled into tiny fists. "They take me and put me on close-by farm with frail woman. She was kind. I stayed. Until camp becomes Hohenfels and my husband shows up to train there." Her hands opened. "He was resourceful." She smiled and brought her gaze to Chuck. "He bought me a brooch so I could have something pretty on my wedding day. He said this brooch was better than a ring. Fancier. I think it was all that could be found after the war, no matter how resourceful. But it is all I could want. This is what we are going to look for in blonde woman's room."

"We'll find that brooch," said Chuck. "We'll keep searching until we find it."

"Dear little clown," said Magda.

"Any news on the wee poodle?" asked Mitch as he approached Charla in the veterinarian's waiting room.

Charla, wringing her hands, looked up at him from her chair.

"Oh, I'm glad you're here, Finbar. I'm so worried about Strudel. Poor little thing got so dang sick. I just don't understand it. Them wieners shoulda been fine. See, I had a fire going to make coffee. Had the wieners out for Strudel's breakfast. Must have let 'em set out too long, I guess. But it really wasn't that long at all." She stared ahead, gestured each stage with her hand. "I took 'em out of the cooler, but the fire went out, so I walked over to the woods to get some kindling. That only took ten or fifteen minutes. I didn't think hot dogs would go bad that fast. They're precooked and all. Oh, wait. I left the cooler outside. I know you're not supposed to what with bears and all, but there's so many folks around. I might have left the top off. Now did I? But anyway, there was enough ice in there to keep 'em until next Easter. But maybe something crawled in there. Oh dear, oh dear . . ."

"I don't half wonder if Strudel wasn't flat-out poisoned," said Mitch. "Someone might be up to some mischief."

Charla's eyes widened.

"Now, son, why would anyone want to trouble old Charla?"

"I don't know, miss, but you said someone fiddled with your locks, and now this poison. Did Magda eat any of the sausages? Did you?"

"Magda didn't eat a bit last night. Good thing, as it turns out. It was all the excitement I expect, the festival and all. I just had a bite of one of them dogs myself. And a martini. Martini's probably why I ain't had many problems. Alcohol killed all the germs."

"We should take the leftover hot dogs to be tested for poison."

"Whoever does a test like that? The police ain't gonna just 'cause one dog gets sick."

"I think we should all bunk in together at Chuck's cabin until we find out what's going on. There's safety in numbers."

"Now, I don't want to be a bother. I like having my own place, with wheels on it and all."

"For Magda's safety then," said Mitch. "And the poodle's."

Charla nodded. "I'm glad Magda didn't eat any. She's been kinda owly lately. Except for talking to you two she's been sadder than usual."

"How is she usually?"

"Well, old Magda, she does okay. She's set for money it seems. She's got rental properties back in Memphis. Her old man bought 'em. Her husband, that is. I tried to ask her once how he got enough money to buy all them apartment buildings. Didn't seem like the type to inherit money, you know? But whenever I'd ask, that's when old Magda'd forget how to speak English. Ha! What a character."

Charla pulled a canary-yellow handkerchief with scarlet tatting from her sleeve and gave a small cough into it.

"She says he already had the property when they met. But that don't make no sense, because they met when he was in the army, over in whatever country it is she comes from—Poland or Germany or something. She don't talk about that either." She kneaded the handkerchief between her fingers. "Aw, it's none of my business. She's good company. And she runs her properties legit and she's kind enough to about everybody I ever see her meet, so . . ." She traced the handkerchief's lacy edge with a matching red nail. "I gather Magda's seen some pretty hard times. Some pretty shady characters. I suppose even an old dodgeball like her husband seemed like Prince Charming after what she was used to."

"Well," said Mitch, "you don't ever know all a person's been through, do you?"

"That's a fact," said Charla.

⸺⸺⸺

Derrik clomped through the dusty gray streets of the village. Even for a big man like himself, these military boots were heavy. There'd be no tap dancing in these army-issued brogans. He was the only soul in sight, the only sound to be heard. Thud, thud, thud. *No children playing, no dogs barking. No birds. (Not like at Magda's farm with the clucking of the chickens, and Magda's singing and humming.) His comrades found the empty, rubble-strewn byways of the town demoralizing. Derrik joked he had no morals to start with so he was unbothered by the pockmarked houses, crumbling cornerstones, and cracked or missing windows. To him they were treasure troves. If people were dead, there was nothing to be done about it now. May as well carry on and survive as well as one could. And if the dead people's possessions weren't in the hands of their heirs, then they may as well be in the hands of Derrik. That's how he saw it. He studied a block of storefronts, gaps and half structures where whole buildings used to be.*

"Looks like that punk Stossell's mouth of broken teeth after I socked him in the jaw last week." The soldier chuckled. *"Fool picked the wrong*

guy to accuse of stealing his poker winnings." Not that Derrik was above stealing, but he wouldn't do it in his own barracks. And he wouldn't steal from a soldier he was stationed with. Derrik was rarely scolded by his conscience, but he did have some form of moral code to guide him, even if it was hidden from most everyone else.

He paused in the middle of the road. There was a possible disruption to the eerie, still morning. He made himself quiet. He was a man who liked noise, but he could command discipline and quietude if need be. He commanded it now and accustomed his ears to the absence of his footfalls.

The odor came to him before the sound returned. A rotting smell. Could be an abandoned butcher shop. Could be something else, something his fellow soldiers took a while to stomach. It was just a hint. He'd discovered it just in time. It appeared no one else had stumbled across it as a source of spoils. Spoils. Kind of a joke there. Few would laugh besides him. He inhaled slowly. Yes, that was the smell. Just a hint of it.

And then the sound. A cat. Behind a window in one of the unbroken buildings. A meow. Just a tiny one. Derrik strode to the window. The cat called to him. It put a dainty paw up to the pane. He touched the spot with his index finger. Mew.

Well now, here was a second reason to open a locked door (for the smell was a little stronger by this window). He hadn't seen a cat at Magda's farm. He called it Magda's farm. He'd visited several times since he'd brought the boy to them, but he could never remember the old woman's name. He just called her "Frau" which seemed to work okay. Every farm needs a cat. He'd bring Magda this one. Its gentleness. They'd get along fine. A calico, it would be visually interesting for them. Its face cut right in half between black and orange with a spattering of gray and a patch of white. A fine cat to sit next to the ladies in their farmhouse at night.

Derrik jiggled the knob and leaned an ox-like shoulder against the door. It gave way easily. The cat rushed out. Derrik stepped inside.

Lying near the cold hearth was an old man in full Sunday dress. He perhaps had known he was at death's door and had readied himself for his *funeral. Derrik checked behind the open door to make sure no intruder hid there. This could have been a robbery, an attack. He returned to the prone body and checked for a pulse. None. He inspected the body for bruises, cuts, marks of any kind. None. No jaundice. A natural death—a blessing in this place and time.*

Derrik cast an eye about the room. An odd collection of items. Homey things like vases and lamps—too many for one room—heavy tools, a treadle sewing machine, a guitar, a concertina. He'd seen such a collection before, in his father's pawn shop. He rolled the poor fellow over and lifted him to the nearby sofa. It might ruin the sofa, but it didn't seem right to leave the old guy on the floor. He adjusted the man's collar and tie and smoothed his hair, which had ruffled when he fell. Derrik cast another eye around the room. He was shrewd in his appraisal.

Where was the jewelry? Every pawn shop had jewelry. He spied a doorway at the back of the room and passed through it. A desk occupied the farthest part of the new room. Derrik checked behind the door, then advanced to the desk. This was the room where the valuables lived, he was sure of it. He felt like a pirate searching for buried gold.

He tried all the drawers but each one was locked. He went back to the man on the sofa. He gently searched every pocket, to no avail, so returned to the other room.

The treasure hunter hunched over the desk and rifled through the papers and mementos piled higgledy-piggledy across it. In time, the offending clutter was parted and the treasure revealed. A key. It nestled with some string beneath a blanket of paid redemption tickets, a clever place to hide. The key fit the keyhole in the top center drawer and that unlocked all the others. In the left-side second drawer from the bottom he found his prize. A brooch lay in a bed of ivory satin. He removed the brooch and satin together and gently placed them on top of the desk. He lifted the brooch up to catch the light shining into the room through a window to his right. Several large stones of various colors but matching cut sat above gleaming gold filigree. Two of the stones were the light blue of Magda's eyes.

Derrik smiled. He held the brooch with tenderness and even a little rever-
ence. If he'd been a man who could cry, he would have. The jewels spar-
kled. Derrik's eyes sparkled too.

So pleased was he with the glittering, glowing treasure and the joy it
would bring that he was oblivious to the small cat as it jumped up on the
desk and rubbed its wee head against his side.

⫸⫷⫸ ⫷⫸⫷ ⫸⫷⫸

Slim dabbed the last crumb of a vending-machine granola bar from
his lip. He pulled out his phone and called Dale's number. He felt the
anxiety in the pit of his stomach as the phone rang and rang. He felt
even worse when Dale's voice mail kicked in.

Hi there. Leave a message for Dale. You won't regret it.

Kind of sweet, actually.

"Dale, this is Slim Pontchartrain. I surely would like to touch
base with you today. Give me a call, son. Good-bye." He pocketed
the phone and leaned back. He surveyed the grounds of the rest stop
and tapped out the melody to "Ghost Riders in the Sky" with his
right hand. He played it two more times, then dialed once again.

⫸⫷⫸ ⫷⫸⫷ ⫸⫷⫸

"Hi doll face! I'm back." Chuck leaned over the motel desk and batted his eyelashes. Magda stood small and mute behind him.

"You run out of doughnuts?" asked the clerk.

"I need information," said Chuck. "I need to know if someone's
staying at your motel."

"We don't give out that information."

"Is it against the law?"

"I don't know. But I'm pretty sure we just don't do that. I wouldn't
want some rando blogger knowing if I was staying someplace."

Chuck folded his arms and thought fast. "How about this? Can you tell me how many rooms Archie Grant booked this weekend?" The clerk's eyes widened.

"That's the dead guy."

Aha, thought Chuck. *I've got an in.*

"Yes, it is. I need to talk to someone who could shed some light on his murder." Her eyes grew larger still. She consulted her computer. *Tap, tap, tap. Click. Click.*

"Six."

"Six. Let's see." Chuck looked at Magda and started counting on his fingers. "There's Lew, Mitch, Archie—of course—Slim, Gary— would Gary stay here or at the Schroeders'?"

"You are at only five. Have you run out of Cowboys?"

"Yep. That leaves one room left for the blonde."

"Call her room, miss," said Magda. "We must talk to her."

"This doesn't feel right," said the clerk.

"We happen to know she's a very unstable person," said Chuck. "As you can imagine, she's very distraught over the murder of her fiancé—especially after such a public proposal. Why, she could be lying—right now—on the floor of her room, life ebbing away."

"Your call could save life," said Magda. "Such simple thing to do."

"Oh all right," said the clerk. She consulted the computer screen. "Oh, uh . . ." She clicked a few times. "Oops. Wrong." *Click, click.* "Okay." She dialed Ann-Dee's room.

Chuck tried to remain calm. He'd flirted to get information before, but he'd never lied, and the stakes had never been this high.

"I don't know what I'll say if she answers," said the clerk. She waited a tidy amount of time. She drummed her fingers on the desk. She waited some more. "No answer." She looked worried.

"Perhaps you should—" started Chuck before Magda kicked his shin.

"I'll leave a message for her to call the front desk," said the clerk. She did so.

"Thank you, miss," said Magda. "Might be wise to check woman's room if she does not respond in timely manner."

"I don't know why you two are so worried," the clerk said.

"I have sixth sense," said Magda tapping her temple. "I see trouble for her." The clerk's eyes grew wide again, as did Chuck's. He absorbed her technique. "And for you, young one, I see you standing on shores of roiling sea. Much excitement." The clerk's eyebrows rose. "Thank you again. We will stop bothering you." Magda grabbed Chuck's hand and pulled him out the lobby doors. Chuck grabbed a bear claw on the way out. "Come, little clown," said Magda. "We must move RV to back of building. You have key to get into building, yes?"

"I've got Mitch's key card right here." He pulled it from a pocket. "What are we going to do?"

"We go to Blondie's room. Number 237. I peeked over girl's shoulder. It is likely maids are cleaning rooms. We'll see what we can do."

Chuck swallowed a morsel of cruller. He certainly liked these senior ladies from Memphis. There were a lot of tricks he could learn from them on his way to media glory.

On the second floor, they found room 237. They looked around for the maid's cart. Chuck spied it far down the hall, past a door with yellow caution tape across it.

"That must be Archie Grant's room," said Chuck. "The one with the yellow tape."

"He does not book connecting room to future fiancée. Interesting."

"Well, if he booked them at separate times, it might not have been an option."

"Perhaps relationship is not so strong as he pretends" said Magda. Her eyes narrowed. One eyebrow rose. "Go charm maid like you did clerk. I need distraction."

Chuck worked on conjuring up some swagger. He cocked his head and rubbed his soul patch for luck.

"I think I'm ready," he said.

"Go ahead," said Magda. "I will follow." They strolled to the maid's cart. Chuck stopped on the far side of the door next to the cart. The maid came out of the room and paused when she saw Chuck. Magda stayed behind on the maid's blind side.

"Sorry to startle you, miss," Chuck began, in as close an imitation of Finbar Mitchell as he could muster. "I'm needing an extra serviette, I mean, towel, for my room. Might I bother you for one, then?" He smiled ever so sweetly at her, and never broke eye contact.

"Of course." The maid reached into the clean towel section of the cart. "Are you from Ireland?" she asked.

"Oh, aye," he responded. He tried to hide a wince. Did he sound Scottish just then? "Originally. I've been in the States for some time now, yeah."

"How do you like it here?"

"Oh, brilliant. It's brilliant. Especially the people. So kind. You're all so kind." He was verging on 'faith and begorrah' but it helped pull him away from his inclination to sound Scottish. Oh, why had he watched *Brigadoon* last week? "I miss home sometimes though. Little things, like lamb stew. And potatoes."

"You can't find potatoes here?" asked the maid.

"Oh, not like me Mam's. Me Mam made right grand potatoes, she did. Oh, how I miss me Mam as well. As well as her potatoes."

"How did she make them?"

Chuck noticed Magda swiftly and silently remove the master key card from the maid's smock pocket. He had only ever seen someone on TV, like Newkirk on *Hogan's Heroes*, do such a thing. He hadn't thought it was actually physically possible.

"With love," said Chuck. "No one else can do that like your mam."

"That's sweet." The maid began to turn back to her cart. Her hand moved toward her pocket.

"Oh, and the beer!" he shouted, bringing her attention back to him. "Oh, how I'd love a pint of Harp right now."

"Little early, isn't it?"

"Guinness then." The maid looked confused, perhaps alarmed. Chuck laughed. "I'm pullin' the mickey on ya." She smiled. "Maybe later though, yeah? Might I interest you in a pint round the old local later tonight?"

"Oh, um . . ." The maid blushed. Chuck noticed her ring finger.

"Ach! I'm sorry. I didn't notice your wedding band. I was that swept away by your beauty. I didn't realize. It's just your eyes, miss. I mean missus. They're fair magic, they are." The maid looked down.

"That's all right. No harm done."

Chuck was near fainting. Magda crept up behind the maid and placed the key card back into her pocket. He revived.

"I'm that sure that I'm sorry, so I am," said Chuck. "He's a lucky man, your mister, and that's a fact. I'll tarry you no longer. Fare thee well miss . . . missus." Chuck smiled, bowed, and stepped away to let the maid pass. He strolled with his towel to Ann-Dee's room, blotting the sweat from his brow. Magda was already inside conducting a search. He moved the swing bar lock out of the way and closed the door completely.

"Will this performance be on your website?" asked Magda.

"Just the part where you stole the key." Magda's eyes widened. "Just kidding. I turned the camera off before I talked with the desk clerk." Magda did not look at ease. "You can trust me. Watch." Chuck took his hat off and wrapped it in the towel. He placed it on the unmade bed. The maid hadn't been in to tidy or make the bed as the Do Not Disturb sign still hung on the doorknob. It was gutsy of Magda to enter the room. Ann-Dee could have been inside. Magda and Chuck stood quietly and took the space in.

Multiple hairpieces lay on the desk. They looked for all the world to Chuck like blonde creatures Ann-Dee had caught in a series of snares. Cowboy/cowgirl hats sat on the bed, the desk, the desk chair, and akimbo off the TV. *Ann-Dee wears many hats,* thought Chuck. He smiled at his pun. He noted that her suitcases were completely un-packed, their contents strewn around the room. *It's like Ann-Dee was searching for something too.*

"What does this brooch look like again?" asked Chuck.

"About this big," said Magda. She indicated the size with her fin-gers and thumbs. "Different colored jewels in it. Gold filigree."

"And if I find other jewelry?"

"Not important. I seek only brooch." Magda pulled open draw-ers and peered inside. Chuck moved to the bathroom.

"Hmm. Bags." He reached for two plastic shopping bags on the counter and began to open one when there was a knock on the main door. Chuck spun around to look at Magda.

"Hello? Miss Phillips? It's the front desk clerk. Are you in?" Magda dropped and rolled under the bed. There was just enough mattress overhang for her to tuck in next to the platform and pull down some bedspread for cover. (She was indeed a petite woman.) Chuck flattened himself behind the bathroom door. "Miss Phillips, are you there?" The clerk knocked again. There followed the click of the door unlocking and opening. Chuck peered through the crack between the bathroom door and its frame. He could see the bed. He could not see Magda.

The towel! The hat cam's rolled up in it. Please, please, please, don't pick up the towel.

The clerk entered Chuck's sightline. She looked down at the towel and frowned. She started to reach for it. Chuck's stomach flipped over three times. He stifled a small whimper and worked on slowing his breathing. The small whimper was enough to draw the clerk from the bed to the bathroom.

She paused several moments, then pulled back the shower curtain. Chuck held his breath.

"What the—" said the clerk. "I'm done here." She exited the rooms in haste.

Chuck stayed in his hiding place.

"Safe now, little clown."

Chuck exhaled and stepped out from behind the door. He managed a weak smile for Magda, then poked his head into the shower. "Hmm. Weird."

Magda extended a hand and patted Chuck on the shoulder. "There is no brooch here. Time to go." Chuck turned toward Magda. He realized he was still clutching the bags to his chest.

"It might be in one of these," he said. Magda's face lit up. Chuck un-crinkled the first bag and looked inside. He pulled out a long auburn wig and tortoiseshell spectacles. He shook the wig and turned the bag upside down. Empty. He opened the second one. "Yikes!" He dropped it. A number of syringes spilled out. "Is she diabetic?"

Magda shrugged.

"That's all that's in there. Sorry." Her shoulders slumped. "I suppose she's wearing it. Did you check her luggage?"

"Yes. Is not here. Let's go. Thanks for taking old lady on adventure." Chuck jerked his head toward the bathroom counter.

"She likes cola," he said. Three mostly empty two-liter bottles of a local brand of cola sat along the sink ledge.

"Bad for teeth. She must use white strips," said Magda.

"And she seems like kind of a slob?" said Chuck. "But she washed a baseball bat in the shower. I mean, what's that about? Unless maybe she was trying to kill a bat. Huh, a bat with a bat. Smells like chlorine. Maybe she got it."

Magda pushed past him and stared at the bat leaning against the bathtub rim. She stood still and silent as the grave for what seemed like an hour, then she began to shake. Chuck wrapped his arms around her. She felt cold. He feared she was going into shock. He held her until she warmed again.

Chuck said, "Let's get out of here."

Huddled together, they left Ann-Dee's rooms. Just as the door was about to close, Chuck sprinted back in to retrieve the hat cam.

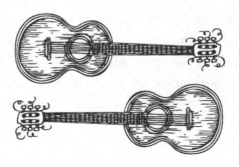

CHAPTER NINETEEN

Detectives Left and Right stood at the crest of the festival next to the Norwegian taco stand. They were not dressed as detectives at the moment, although they were on duty. They decided to spend a small amount of time getting a feel for the place where this murder happened.

Detective Left looked down at the deep-fried flatbread and meat in his hand. He had a bad feeling in his gut, and it wasn't just the snack's fault (although it wasn't entirely innocent; Detective Left had problems digesting fatty foods since the removal of his gallbladder). Truth be told, he just wasn't feeling right about the Schroeder arrest. It wasn't that the guy was a local. Detective Left wasn't from Big Pearly Falls either and the law was the law no matter how long your family lived somewhere. It was just that the arrest didn't have that good clicking-into-place feel to it. Schroeder certainly seemed to detest the victim. Confronted with Grant's website, he spoke freely about the victim and his dealings with him. His undisguised disgust fit the signature, but he appeared genuinely confused by the eyewitness placing him at the crime scene. He claimed it was absolutely impossible for anyone to have seen him there because he hadn't left his parents' resort—indeed, hadn't left the sight of either his parents or his girlfriend—since his band played their set at the festival. Detective Left's instinct told him Schroeder was telling the truth.

Thus, Left and Right decided to question the witness a second time, but they weren't having any luck contacting her. She hadn't returned their calls. They'd stopped at the RV site she'd given as a temporary address but no one was home. They requested a squad check in on the location periodically.

Presently, they decided to see if they could find her at the festival. She'd expressed an enthusiasm for Chet Brinkley, who was just about to take the stage. They'd check the crowd. If nothing else, they'd get some background color of the festival. What was the sociology of this event?

If they didn't see the witness during Brinkley's set, they'd check the meet and greet after the show. Detective Left hoped to see her here first so he could observe her with her guard down. He scanned the crowd for the redhead with glasses and dingy teeth.

"Y'know what I don't like?" asked Detective Right. "Where's the fiancée? We've got a guy in jail and we haven't even talked with her yet."

"She didn't answer his proposal—not that we know of—so technically we shouldn't call her the fiancée."

"She was seen with him afterward, so . . ."

"He's her manager. She might have to stay with him for other reasons. You just shouldn't get used to calling her the fiancée because it's not a proven fact."

"You're right. I just wish we could talk with her."

"Hotel clerk said she'd call us when she returned to her room."

"And what's up with that?" said Detective Right. "Why's the hotel clerk checking the fiancée's—Ann-Dee Phillips's—room every hour?" Detective Right took a few bites of taco and chewed thoroughly. He pondered the feel of the food in his mouth, savored the flavor and swallowed. "I think they should put powdered sugar on this," he said. "It's basically a doughnut with meat." Detective Left took a bite.

"It is pretty good," he said. Detective Left's phone rang. "Yeah, what did you find?" He listened. "So just that? No poison?"

Detective Right cocked his head. He watched Left listen.

"Mm-hmm," murmured Detective Left. "Is that a lot? . . . I see." He nodded. "No injections? So how would . . .? Okay. Thanks."

"Was that the medical examiner?"

Left nodded.

"What did she say?"

"Toxicology results came back. Grant had a very high level of antihistamine in him."

"Did he have allergies?"

"She said this was more than someone with allergies would be taking. More than if they were taking a daily pill, forgot, and took another."

"Maybe he was having an anaphylactic reaction to something and—"

"No record he'd been to the emergency room and no signs of injection on the corpse. ME said it's likely the drug was administered over several hours and the effect was cumulative."

"Why not all at once?"

"Have you ever tasted one of those pills? I chewed one once."

Detective Right raised his eyebrows.

"It's not relevant why. I chewed it so it would take effect faster. I found it quite bitter. Made my tongue numb."

"Well, if he'd been drinking he might not notice."

"True. Especially if he was drinking or eating something bitter. Beer or ale, for instance."

"Gin and tonic."

"Champagne."

Detective Right nodded. The detectives were thirsty from the heat and their tacos. They had miles to go before they could rest.

"I need a beverage," said Detective Right. "Let's get some pop or something before Chet Brinkley."

"There's a lemonade stand," said Detective Left pointing ahead.

"Lemonade. That's bitter."

They headed for the stand.

"Drugged," said Detective Left. "Seems like something a woman would do."

"You get that from Agatha Christie. Plenty of men dope women."

"Do men dope men though?"

"Why not, if it makes killing them or robbing them easier?"

"My gut says it's a woman."

"Your gut's full of fair food."

They both laughed.

Detective Right's cell phone rang. He answered it.

"We're a ten-minute walk from there. Thanks." He put away his phone. "A golf cart that was likely at the StarWalk the night of the murder is at the edge of Big Pearly Lake. It has blue paint on the floorboards that matches paint at the crime scene and there's a footprint in it."

"Let's get over there then. I don't see our witness. We can check the meet and greet after we wrap it up with the golf cart.

"Might take a little longer. A body showed up in the same lake. We should treat it as part of our investigation. Just a gut feeling."

Chuck unlocked the door to his cabin and ushered his guests in.

"Nice," said Mitch.

"John Turnbell booked it," said Chuck. "How come the Cowboys aren't staying here? I mean, if Gary's parents own it and all."

"I don't know. Archie made the arrangements," said Mitch. "It worked out okay. The motel's close to the FallsFest grounds. None of us are morning people, so that helps."

"But y'all went on at noon," said Charla.

"Noon's early enough to be morning in my book," said Chuck.

"But this here place is just ten minutes away," said Charla. "Even closer if you took one of them golf carts past the lake and down the hill. Heck, I can see the stage out this window."

"The motel's closer, I believe, at least to the backstage trailers," said Mitch. "And there's a shuttle. Now what have you got for nibbles, Charles? I'm famished."

"Remember? My cupboard is bare. But the resort's got a soda fountain and convenience store," said Chuck. "I could pop over and bring something back." He'd eaten nothing but fried dough today. He yearned for protein and fruit.

"Maybe Mother Schroeder's got something cooking," said Mitch.

"We don't want to be any bother," said Charla. "We have our own food."

"No bother," said Chuck. "We all have to eat. And there will be no touching any food that's been in your possession."

"There's something on your balcony," said Mitch. He walked to the glass door, unlocked it, and slid it open. Chuck walked over to him and removed a card taped to the glass.

"Chuck," he read aloud, "I'm meeting Ann-Dee Phillips for an interview at a picnic area in Big Pearly Falls State Park. There's something fishy with her Social Security number. Should be back by two. Let's check in with each other if you're around. Can you access your hat cam video? Later, John T."

Chuck thought a few moments. "He already told me this in a text. Why the note?"

"Maybe 'cause you young people think morning is noon," said Charla. "Figured you'd sleep right through your phone going off. Now I'm feeling bad I called y'all up so early."

"I'm glad you did," said Chuck. "Who knows what danger you'd be in if you went back to the War Zone?"

"Curious," said Magda. "He is talking to this Ann-Dee."

"For the second time," said Mitch. "He interviewed her yesterday at that FallsFest saloon."

"She gave an interview just hours after that poor dead man who proposed to her was found?" exclaimed Charla.

"I believe she likes publicity," said Mitch.

"I found something weird on the internet this morning," said Chuck. "Turns out there's another Ann-Dee Phillips. I thought it was weird because what are the odds that there's another person with that name spelled exactly the same way? I mean, 'Ann-Dee' with a hyphen?" He looked around the room for agreement. Mitch shrugged. "It was just a photo from the Tennessee State Fair. They were polling people about their favorite fair food or something—anyway, they'd tagged this Ann-Dee Phillips. I just looked at her world-weary face and thought, 'Now there's a person no one would report missing.' I sent the link to John."

Everyone paused to digest this.

"Maybe I should have sent that link to the police," said Chuck. "I wonder if they've questioned Ann-Dee yet."

"This woman is bad," said Magda. "Call your friend now."

Chuck found his cell and called John Turnbell's number. "I've been calling and leaving him messages for an hour but he doesn't call back." He waited. "Voice mail."

"What does it mean?" asked Mitch.

"Could just mean he's got his phone muted during the interview," said Chuck. But the baked goods in his stomach weren't sitting well.

"Maybe he's leaving evidence for the police," said Charla. "The note, I mean. Maybe that's why he mentions the Social Security number and your hat-cam video. I've seen a lot of *Matlock*s in my day. Sounds to me like he thinks he's onto something and he's leaving a trail in case he goes missing. We may end up turning my cooler over to the police after all."

⸱⸱⸱

Lew watched Slim and Nancy fuss with their phones. Normally, the aromas of Mrs. Schroeder's cooking would have them all in a swoon of delight, but the events of the day must have taken their toll on the master chef. With her boy at the police station, Bea Schroeder just moped around the kitchen, nudging things and then nudging them back to where they'd been. Without Bea's magic, they all sat glum at the table, which was empty except for Slim's phone lying flat and exposed.

Slim checked his voice mail, his texts, but to no avail. He then dialed a number.

"Who you trying to reach?" asked Lew.

"That bass player in Ann-Dee's band I told you about." Slim tapped the phone and hung up. Then he tapped his fingertips on the table. "I'm a little uneasy about him. Seems anybody who gets involved with that woman comes to mischief. We agreed to check in with each other today and I can't get hold of him."

Normally Lew would have come up with some logical excuse for the situation, such as *the fellow's a musician and was still asleep after a late gig.* This weekend, however, had convinced him to keep his Pollyannaish reflexes in check. If anything was amiss, it could likely mean foul play.

He needed to use his puzzle-solving mind. How did this piece fit with the others? He conjured up an image of the bass player as well as he could from his memory of their performance. Was that him with that rowdy group up by the StarWalk yesterday?

"I rang him several times this morning," said Slim. "Called his hotel too. Got them to check his room. Didn't find him. I felt my place was here, so I drove back. I still would like to hear from the boy though." Slim and Lew stared at the phone. Slim dialed one more time.

⫷⫸ ⫷⫸ ⫷⫸

Ann-Dee ignored the incoming call.

"Do you want to answer that?" asked John Turnbell.

"It's not important," said Ann-Dee. "I should just turn it off." She did. She also placed a linen napkin over the picnic basket as some clouds had formed overhead and a sprinkle or two was baptizing the victuals.

"If you don't mind," said John, "I think I should check my messages myself. Someone's been calling every five minutes. It might be an emergency." John interacted with his phone and put it to his ear. The volume of the voice mail was loud enough for Ann-Dee to hear it.

"John, this is Chuck. I might need to bunk in with you tonight. Sorry to spring it on you, but the two elderly ladies from the meet and greet need a safe place to stay. Remember I told you about them? They're with me now at the Schroeder resort. Anyway, they're in my cabin now, so I might have to bunk in with you later. Hope that's okay. Give me a call."

"Sorry about that," said John. He put his phone in a pocket. He looked at the picnic basket. "You didn't have to feed me. If anything, I should be treating you. I'm the reporter."

"Oh, it's the least I could do with you taking the time to interview me again." She removed a container of barbecue sauce from underneath the linen. *Maybe if I stir it . . .*

"Have some more barbecue sauce, John. I was so happy when I found it at the Grocery Basket."

"It's kind of bitter," said John.

"That's because of the special Thai fruit they put in it," said Ann-Dee. "If you have some more, it won't taste bitter. Once you get used to it, you'll be a fan, I'm sure."

"Well . . ."

I do wish you'd take to the Thai fruit, John. It sure is special.

"I guess if you don't like it, you don't," said Ann-Dee. "I don't want to pressure you. Everybody's got their own tastes." She reached for the lid. "My feelings won't be hurt."

"Okay," said John. "It's always good to push beyond one's boundaries."

Ann-Dee smiled, inside and out. She put a slice of chicken and a glob of barbecue sauce onto a crust of French bread and handed it to John.

Indulge, darlin'.

"Maybe if you like this barbecue enough, I'll get a Sunday feature! And all on account of that silly number." She refilled his go-cup. "Don't you just love this champagne? Almond. My favorite."

John took a bite. "Y'know? This is growing on me."

"Didn't I tell you? Anyway . . ." She put down the bottle. "I was named after my dad's sister. Such a good woman. Took care of us after the accident. Taught us to make sacrifices. That's why I took care of my brothers and sisters, because Aunt Ann-Dee taught me that's what family does—or should do."

John put down his bread. He looked Ann-Dee in the eye and cleared his throat. "According to my research, Ann-Dee Phillips was born in Florida thirty-four years ago. That's too old to be you; plus, it's not where you say you grew up. And, while it's not impossible, that's kind of young to be your aunt."

Don't waste the barbecue, John.

"I don't know who that woman could be you're talking about," said Ann-Dee. "My aunt, rest her soul, would be in her fifties if she were still alive, so . . . you're talking about another Ann-Dee altogether." She paused to pout. "I don't like the idea of someone else having my name. It should be special to me—and my aunt."

"This is the Ann-Dee Phillips whose Social Security number is on file with the FallsFest financial department."

"I can't answer for that," said Ann-Dee. "That was all Archie's job. Now let's go sit in your car until this rain stops. Maybe we can open that second bottle of champagne."

⸺⸺⸺

Gordon tapped a rapid random tune on Ruby's desk with a pen. He kept his eye trained out the trailer window. He was watching the detectives and two officers in the distance by the meet and greet ropes. Thurgood leaned back in Nancy's chair.

"You sure those are the detectives?" asked Gordon. "They look more casual than on TV."

"Same men who interviewed Mr. Sinclair," replied Thurgood. He toyed with his ponytail, unbinding it, smoothing it, rebinding it.

"How long have you had that thing?" asked Gordon.

"What? The ponytail?" said Thurgood. "Since my warrior-poet phase."

"Phase?"

"You know me, daddy-o. Make love not war. Yeah, it was a phase."

Gordon sat up. Ruby had now entered the window frame and was talking to the detectives. She gestured and laughed. The detectives laughed too. Ruby raised the paint can. Everyone looked at it.

Much nodding. Ruby laughed again and disappeared from the window. The door opened and in she walked. She plonked the can of paint onto Nancy's desk. She looked from Thurgood to Gordon.

"What's up with you two?"

"Brad radioed me," said Gordon. "A body was found in the lake next to the War Zone. The detectives checked it out and the golf cart that was abandoned there. Now they're at the meet and greet for some reason."

"That stupid War Zone!" spat Ruby. Her brows lowered. "And you couldn't tell me? We have walkie-talkies. We have phones. I just did a tight five with the po-po out there. They must think I'm a psychopath."

"Brad overheard them say the body had keys to the golf cart in one of their pockets," said Gordon. He took a deep breath and exhaled. "They were on a FallsFest keyring. They worked with the cart."

Ruby sat down on the nearest vacant chair.

"They think he had traces of blue paint on his boots. The shirt he was wearing had blue paint stains too." Gordon was running on autopilot now. "I've been going door to door with the artists, giving them a heads-up." He wanted to go home to bed. "I'm shutting the festival down."

Ruby looked at Thurgood.

"Are we insured for this?" she asked.

"Yes," replied Thurgood.

"We never got to give the guitar away," said Ruby.

"Hicks and Hampton said they'd still like to present it to the winner," said Gordon.

"Not Hicks and Hampton!" said Ruby. "Not now. Not during a murder investigation. They're nuts."

"Well, the nuts aren't backing out. They've chartered a hot air balloon and are already in the sky. Their management is hanging around to make sure they get here safely. No matter who stays or who leaves, the nuts will be here to give the guitar away."

"I wonder what their insurance is like," said Ruby.

"We'll keep it low key," said Gordon. "We're sending word around the campgrounds and hotels that the concerts are all canceled but the drawing will still take place at six o'clock."

"We need a backup plan," said Ruby.

"It might be better," said Thurgood, "to simply call the winner and award them the guitar in private."

"Can't," said Gordon. He rubbed his brow and right temple. "Some people bought tickets at the gate, with cash. The contest rules state that the winner will be selected on the last day of the festival by one of the artists drawing a three-day ticket receipt from a barrel. The ticket holder has to be present to win. I wanted the guitar to be presented onstage, in front of lots of cameras."

"I think there will be lots of cameras, Gordy, whether we like it or not," said Ruby.

⟫⟫⟫ ⟫⟫⟫ ⟫⟫⟫

Lew looked out the Schroeder kitchen window. A patrol car pulled up outside. A very young officer got out and walked toward the kitchen door.

"Mercy," said Lew. "Now what?"

There was a knock at the door.

Lew opened it to the officer. Bea popped her head up from behind Lew's shoulder.

"Gerald, how's my Gary?"

"I don't know," said the youthful Gerald. "I've been in my squad all day."

"Don't invite him in," said Nancy. "If he wants to search the house he should get a warrant."

"Nancy," said Bea, "we've nothing to find. This is Gerald. I've known him since he was a baby. How's your mother, Gerald?"

"Fine thanks, ma'am," said Officer Gerald. "I'm coming around to all the resorts to tell folks to stay off the lake. Some campers found a body."

"Oh dear, no," said Mrs. Schroeder. "Is it someone local?"

"No one I recognized," he replied. "We're guessing it's someone who was camping at the War Zone. Looks like he drank too much or took some drugs or something and went for a swim. He had meth mouth, so it's probably drug related."

"Oh, that's tragic. Poor thing," said Bea. "What's meth mouth?"

"People who use meth, their teeth get rotten. Say, Nancy?" said Gerald.

"Yes?"

"Is that your golf cart out there?" he asked.

"It's FallsFest's," replied Nancy. "But I'm using it."

"How do you like it?" asked Gerald. "My folks are thinking of getting one."

"It's fun," said Nancy. "Handy too."

"Think it's safe for a fifty-year-old to drive?"

"They're the vehicle of choice in retirement villages," said Nancy. "I'm sure your parents would be fine."

"Thanks," said Gerald.

"Don't coddle your parents just yet, Gerald," said Lew. "Fifty's the prime of life." Looking past Officer Gerald, Lew spied Chuck Nelson trotting up the hill from a nearby cabin toward the Schroeders' door.

"Officer?" said Chuck from behind Gerald.

"Yes?" Gerald turned to face Chuck.

"A colleague of mine left me a note saying he'd like to meet me at two o'clock. It's two thirty now. His note says he was meeting with Ann-Dee Phillips at a picnic area in Big Pearly Falls State Park. It all feels kind of odd."

"Detectives have been looking for that woman," said Gerald. "Been wanting to question her but can't find her."

Lew remembered Ann-Dee and the picnic items at the supermarket. He couldn't bring himself to mention it. It couldn't be true. He unconsciously began drumming his fingers on his thigh.

"Well, she might be at this park," said Chuck.

Officer Gerald excused himself and went to his vehicle to relay the new information.

"Oh, and she might be in disguise," called Chuck to Officer Gerald's back. "An auburn wig and tortoiseshell glasses."

Slim's phone rang.

"Yes?" said Slim. He listened, his face solemn. "I see. Slim Pontchartrain. I'm here for the festival." He listened some more, then nodded. "I'll be there directly. I'm about ten minutes away. Where should I . . .? Thank you." He put away his phone. Lew cocked his head. "The police would like me to identify a body. Seems the drowned man had my telephone number in his boot."

<hr />

Ann-Dee and Dale capered down the street on their way to the bodega. She was happy and full of life. Dale's hand repeatedly sought hers, but she successfully avoided every attempt at contact.

They were on their way to get ice-cream treats to celebrate Ann-Dee's newly completed demo. Ice cream may not be everyone's first choice for festive ingesting, but Dale was three months sober and neither of them entertained the idea of anything fermented.

Dale had on his lucky shirt. He wore it pretty much every other day. He said that shirt and Ann-Dee were the only reasons he was still sober ninety days after that momentous pot-smoking afternoon when he and Ann-Dee met.

Ann-Dee kept a wary eye on him. She hated Dale's lucky shirt.

She considered buying a fudgsicle today just so she could drop it on the offending talisman.

It wasn't just Dale's shirt that Ann-Dee found irritating. Dale himself was bumptious and cute like a very tall puppy, but ninety days of bumptious adoration had worn her nerves down. She didn't necessarily see his unpredictable nature as a negative—it often worked in her favor. She felt, however, that it was wise to keep him on a long leash. She had to admit though that of all the men she'd kept at a distance, Dale had been the easiest to deal with. She was now staying at his apartment rent free, with no strings.

This afforded her time and energy to nose around the local music scene, practice, write songs, and now record a demo. Dale also helped her record the demo because, it turned out, he was a talented bass-and-guitar-playing puppy. She walked a fine line keeping him interested while not encouraging him. She was an adept acrobat.

It had taken some additional acrobatics to get her demo dubbed to a cassette. Dale had to dig up the equipment from some old high-school buddies. It was all worth it though, because now she had the cassette in her pocket. She was bringing it to the bodega owner. His boom box played only cassettes. Now he would know she was going to be okay. She hadn't been around as much since she met Dale, and not at all for the last month. Now he would know why. She was full of joy to inform him he'd probably now have to get a lock for his dumpster. She giggled, a musical laugh. She didn't even know his name, but his kindness had sustained her in the days before Dale.

That old woman—the dreadful landlord's widow—almost soured the day as well. Popping out of her office (and they were almost out the door!) like a wizened beige jack-in-the-box cawing for the rent money. Dale always paid, maybe a little late, but always in a week or so. No reason to screech at them like they were criminals, when they were on their way to celebrate and share their happiness with the man who'd never treated her like a criminal. The man who'd basically kept her alive all those long months ago when she was first figuring the world out. They turned the corner to the bodega's street, each with a spring in their step. Then she saw the flashing lights. The ambulance. The police and the yellow tape. The stretcher with the bodega owner on it. Oh, the dreadful wind and rain.

—◆◆◆◆◆◆—

"You want my real story?" said Ann-Dee. "The whole truth and nothing but the truth?" She strummed her guitar as she watched John Turnbell take notes. She stopped and picked up her go-cup from the dashboard.

"I think that would be more interesting than what you've been telling me," said John. "Now, your story was interesting, don't get me wrong. It was interesting when I saw it on the Shania Twain episode of *Behind the Music* too. But I'd like to hear *your* story. I'm sure it's every bit as fascinating."

"Well . . ." She strummed the guitar some more. "Make yourself comfortable John Turnbell. It's not a long tale, but it's dense."

John topped up his glass and clicked his pen.

"My parents were survivalists—except they weren't all that good at surviving. We lived pretty deep in the woods. I didn't see another person besides them until my fourteenth birthday. My mom had books and a couple of old *Country Music* magazines though, so I had some idea that there was an outside world." Ann-Dee shook her head. "I read those magazines cover to cover at least a dozen times. I knew there was a place to find my way to after the landslide."

Ann-Dee began to pick out an old folk tune on the guitar.

"My dad used to beat my mom. You saw that coming, right? So. She went crazy. Eventually. Feral, I'd call it. One day, after Dad slugged her a good one . . ." Ann-Dee studied her fingering. "Well . . . Dad had an accident." John put his pen down. "It was bound to happen. There was just too much dynamite lying around that old homestead, plain and simple." Ann-Dee looked up at John and smiled. "Life was okay after that. For a while anyway, until we ran out of food. Dad had taught me to hunt, so I went out to try to scare something up. By the time I got back though, Mom was gone. I waited and waited. I literally searched hill and dale for her." She picked out some simple but sharp notes. "Used every bit of knowhow that dumbass old man taught me. But I never found her, and she never came back." Ann-Dee lowered the guitar to her lap. "And no one ever came looking for her either—or Dad. That's when I learned that it's possible for people to just . . . disappear."

⋘⋙ ⋘⋙ ⋘⋙

With all the dying and arresting going on, Lew wanted to know where the last of his chicks was. When Officer Gerald went to his squad car to report the Ann-Dee park intel, Lew asked Chuck if Mitch was nearby. The palms of Lew's hands were hot, but his fingers were cold.

He sure could use Mitch playing the pipes to calm him down. With this in mind, he followed Chuck back to his cabin, where Mitch welcomed him with open arms.

"Aw Lew, I'm that glad to see you," said Mitch.

"Mitchell, did you bring your pipes with you by any chance?"

"I did. I brought all my kit over from the motel. Come in."

Lew entered the living area, where Magda and Charla were playing cards at a dining table. Chuck's laptop lay near their discard pile. Chuck went to it and opened it.

"All right!" he cheered. "Moira uploaded some new stuff. Lew, there's some clips from your performance."

Lew pulled up a chair and sat down at the table. Chuck pointed to a video clip on the computer screen. "Don't tell Ruby I shot this." The clip showed Lew and the Cowboys on the FallsFest stage.

"This is just before you played 'Ghost Riders,'" said Chuck. "That guitar solo was righteous, by the way."

"Thanks," said Lew. "It felt pretty powerful at the time."

Chuck started the clip.

"Hold on," said Lew. "Can you make it bigger?"

Chuck enlarged the clip player. Lew espied Ann-Dee and Archie upstage.

"Pause it, please." The screen froze as Ann-Dee passed a beverage to Archie. The camera had just zoomed in on the two of them. Lew remembered thinking Archie seemed kind of drunk for so early in the day. He swallowed hard and thought of the antihistamine bottle in Ann-Dee's shopping basket. He'd been trying to ignore clues that pointed to people he loved, but he wasn't entirely successful. The clues started lining up for him and waving for attention. "Now look back here," said Lew. He pointed to Archie and Ann-Dee.

"Stupid Archie," said Mitch, who'd walked up behind Lew and looked over his shoulder. "I near threw my sticks at him."

"Ann-Dee hands Archie his drink. See?"

Now Charla skooched over to see. She leaned in closer to look.

Lew continued, "Gordon and Thurgood were talking today about how the police think Archie was sedated before having his head stuck in the cement." He took a breath. "I saw Ann-Dee at the grocery store later on. She'd bought a bottle of antihistamines. I know from experience they can make you drowsy. She could have slipped him a mickey in his go-cup. Maybe one or two earlier to boot."

Lew looked at Mitch and Chuck.

"Remember after the show when you chased those two away from the Hospitality Tent?" asked Lew. Mitch and Chuck nodded. "Well, I went back there and had a look around. I found two halves of an empty capsule where they'd been sitting. Looked the same as what used to live in Ann-Dee's medicine cabinet. So that's another potential dose or two."

"If Ann-Dee killed Archie," said Mitch, "how'd she get him to the StarWalk? She's mighty, but have you ever tried to move an unconscious body?"

Everyone looked at Mitch.

"I took an acting class. It was an exercise."

Lew scratched his jaw and thought.

"Maybe she used one of those FallsFest golf carts," said Lew. "Gordon let me drive one. He said they just leave the keys in them in the backstage area where fans can't go. I left the keys in the one I drove." He swallowed. "I suppose she could have even used that one." He shook his head to clear it. "I went up to the StarWalk yesterday. Looked at the, uh, the crime scene. There were ruts in the grass about where you'd figure a golf cart's tires would line up."

"Even so," said Chuck, "moving a body from the cart to the cement wouldn't be all that easy."

"I suppose she could have pushed him out of the cart and rolled him into place," said Mitch.

"Bro," said Chuck. "Please tell me this was also in acting class." Mitch nodded.

Lew stood up. "Or someone could have helped her." He paused, brought his hand up to his mouth. He let the hand fall. More memories waved. "Slim talked with Ann-Dee's bass player last night in the Twin Cities."

"From her band when she performed here?" asked Mitch. Lew nodded. "What did he say?"

He said he loved her, thought Lew.

A few moments passed.

"Police called Slim while we were both over at the Schroeders' just now," continued Lew. "Said someone with Slim's phone number in his boot was found dead in Big Pearly Lake."

Everyone in the cabin was quiet and still.

"I wish John would call," said Chuck. "Or better yet, stop by."

"You think he helped her then, this fella who drowned?" asked Mitch. "Maybe it was an accident, like he was drunk or something."

"Slim told me the man was proud of his sobriety," said Lew. "Of course, addicts do lie, and they do slip, but Slim wasn't born yesterday. If he thinks the man was clean, I believe him."

Magda spoke. "This woman is bad."

Chuck looked at Magda. "Remember the syringe in Ann-Dee's room?"

"I remember the bat," said Magda.

Lew looked at Magda, at Chuck. *What on earth?*

"While Charla and Mitch were at the vet's . . ." said Chuck.

"Charla's wee poodle had been poisoned, remember?" said Mitch.

Lew now did. He nodded.

". . . Magda and I searched Ann-Dee's hotel room," said Chuck.

"What—" said Lew.

"My husband gave me brooch when we married," said Magda. "Very old. There are not two brooches like this. It has been missing for years. I saw it on this Ann-Dee on the big screen at concert."

"We didn't find the brooch," said Chuck. "But we found syringes. I thought maybe Ann-Dee was diabetic."

"She could have injected the bass player with something," said Lew. "Made it look like he was high and drowned."

Chuck turned to Charla. "Where's your cooler with those hot dogs?" Charla looked over to its location in the kitchenette. Chuck zipped over to it and donned a pair of rubber gloves that hung by the sink. He found the hot dogs and examined them. "Each of these has a pin prick," said Chuck.

"But why would anybody . . .?" asked Charla. "Why Strudel? How'd she even know we were here?"

"You were taking pictures," Lew said to Charla. "I remember the flashes and the jumbotron. Do you have your camera here?"

Charla brought her great crocheted bag to the table, fished around in it, and withdrew the camera.

"Is there a cable to connect it to a computer?" asked Chuck. "I might have one if you don't."

Charla found the cord and handed it to him. Chuck plugged the camera into his laptop. A series of photos popped up on the screen. Everyone gathered around the computer.

"May I?" Lew asked Chuck. Chuck nodded. Lew flicked through Charla's pictorial of FallsFest.

"You're quite the shutterbug, Miss Charla," said Mitch.

"Well," said Charla, "sometimes I don't know if I took a picture or not so I keep snapping. I end up with a lot of pictures."

"Here's the proposal," said Chuck.

"Sorry, Lew," said Mitch.

"Not to be cavalier about it," said Lew, "but her jilting me may have been good for my health."

"Wow," said Chuck, "she sure looks upset."

"I think maybe the flash bothered her," said Charla.

Lew passed on to the next series of photos.

"Hey, there's us on the jumbotron!" Charla pointed. "Me and Magda and our new beatnik friend Maynard." She tucked a curl behind her ear. "I know I complain about you in beige, Magda, but you do stand out here, in the middle of all these bright colors."

"And here's a nice big close-up of Ann-Dee," said Lew. "And the brooch she always wears there on her scarf."

"That is my brooch," said Magda. "No doubt."

"Here's us on the screen again," said Charla.

Lew swiped back and forth between the photos.

"By the look on your face, Magda," said Lew, "I'd say you just recognized your brooch."

Magda nodded. Tears welled up in her eyes. Chuck took her hand.

"And here's Ann-Dee," Lew continued. "We're back to the stage. It looks different than the jumbotron pictures. See? They have a texture." He swiped to the patterned photo of Magda and Charla on the jumbotron, then back to the clear one of Ann-Dee. "This one doesn't." He studied the image. "The way her head is turned, the angle . . . I remember when I was up there and I'd look at the jumbotron . . ." He shifted and tried out various positions and angles. He tilted his head like Ann-Dee's was tilted. "Say I'm Ann-Dee and"—he pointed to a wall in the cabin—"and that wall is the jumbotron . . ." They all looked from Lew to the wall to the photo of Ann-Dee on the stage. "I'd say she was looking at the jumbotron. What do you think?"

"I think you're right," said Chuck.

Lew swiped back to the photo of Magda with Charla on the jumbotron. He looked at Magda.

"I think she was looking at you, Ms. Magda. I think she recognized you."

"Could be," said Magda. "She brought me rent money sometimes when she lived in my Derrik's building."

"Magda," said Lew, "I think Ann-Dee has killed twice already, and I think she might want to kill you."

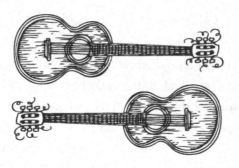

CHAPTER TWENTY

"Y ou ever watch those animal movies when you were a kid?" asked Ann-Dee. "Dale had a bunch of 'em. Bought 'em cheap out of a bin at a lumberyard or some such place. They're for kids but they're always filled with tragedy. Here, drink some more champagne, darlin'. No? How about some more of this chicken with the barbecue sauce? It's real good."

Ann-Dee picked up a smidgen of chicken without sauce and popped it into her mouth.

"These animal movies," she continued, "there's always, like, three animals: an adult and two young ones. The young ones always get inside someone's cabin and make a mess of it, tear open all the food and get it all over everything. Supposed to be funny. Let me tell you, growing up in the middle of nowhere on a mountain, where your food has to last you through a long, long stretch, maybe a hard winter, that's not funny."

Ann-Dee stirred the barbecue sauce with a spork.

"There's this one movie in particular I'm thinking about. It had a family of cougars. Well, there's always a stupid, reckless one and it's always a boy. Anyway, this stupid cougar does something careless and causes a landslide or an avalanche that kills the mother cougar. Well. That's life right there. There will always be a stupid cougar somewhere ready to mess things up. The lesson here is it's important to kill the stupid cougar before it causes the landslide. It seems cruel, but it's just survival. If I'd . . . If dad had died earlier, my mom might still be alive. You gotta take action early."

She paused and smiled at John Turnbell's empty plate.

"Do you know what it's like to have someone take care of you, help you, without wanting anything for it? When before that you've had to struggle to take care of yourself every second of your life?" She studied John Turnbell's eyes. They were a little glassy. The lids hung at half-mast. "Being with Lew was like lying down in a cool, clean bed after years of sleeping with one eye open behind a dumpster." She snickered. "That's exactly what it was like." She stirred the sauce some more.

"I thought for years that country music would make me safe. If I could just dig my way in and be successful . . . I'd be okay. I'd never sleep outside or eat someone else's garbage again. Then I met Lew. He was the sweetest backup plan I ever could have hoped for. I really felt safe with that man. He was what family was supposed to feel like. I thought I could have everything once I met him. Music, money, family, everything."

Ann-Dee studied the droop of John Turnbell's head. She listened to the rhythm of his breath.

"Stupid Archie tried to destroy what Lew and I had. But I know I could have got Lew to take me back. I'd have found a way to explain Archie to him. Some of it would be a lie, but it would work. It would be better than the truth." Ann-Dee played the guitar on her lap like a zither.

"Why'd you have to go nosing around about Social Security numbers? Who gives a damn what anyone's Social Security number is? It's ironic, because I lived so long without one."

John Turnbell slumped into the soft leather car seat behind the steering wheel.

"They wouldn't have stuck that Archie Grant murder on me," she continued. "I got it pinned on the bass player. Sure, they'd wonder eventually where that redhead with the eyeglasses who saw him at the crime scene went, but by then they'd have found Archie's stupid website. They'd have plenty of motive, and any evidence pointing toward me would be erased or laundered." She strummed her guitar. "And if that didn't work they could pin it on *my* bass player. That's why I put the keys in his pocket. I wasn't originally gonna do that, but then he stepped in that paint in the golf cart, and it just felt right. The shirt too. I had to make sure there were enough fingers pointing away from me. He had to go anyway, so, two birds as they say. Nobody was going to question an addict turning up in a lake at a music festival. He wasn't on any FallsFest payroll. It would all have eventually blown over. But you went and snooped out my Social Security number. That's not even legal, is it? You can't go around asking finance departments about Social Security numbers. I suppose it was that Nancy. I don't think she ever liked me much. Her or that Ruby." Ann-Dee scowled at the guitar strings.

"Three deaths in one place. I might get away with it. People OD and get into accidents around festivals all the time. But I better make myself scarce just in case." She peered at John Turnbell through her long false lashes. She watched his face grow slacker. "I hope I don't have to start all over—give up my music career." She brought the neck of the guitar to her temple and rest her head gently against it. "I was good, you know. A good singer. Did you write that down in your notes? Why didn't you care about that story? Lew knew I could sing. That's why he helped me. It wasn't just because I was his girlfriend.

He's been in the business long enough. I surely wasn't the first female to ask him for help. But he did help me because I have talent and star power. Ain't anybody like me. I would have been huge."

Ann-Dee strummed her guitar. A grimace wrenched her face for just a moment. She squinched her eyes shut, then opened them and stared at John.

"Well, if that's over it's because of you. I'll have to marry some old, rich dude or something—and get a new Social Security number. Whoever's number I get? That's on you too." She looked out the window. "Maybe I'll go to Boston. I met some people from there. Helpful people. Resourceful."

Ann-Dee put the guitar down. John Turnbell moved his head slowly, from facing the steering wheel to looking at Ann-Dee. His eyes followed on a five-second delay.

"Yeah, I killed Archie Grant. Stupid little creep was trying to blackmail me. Wanted me to marry him. Wanted to be my agent forever and ever, amen. You see, the night before we drove up to Falls-Fest, when I knew my performance was locked into their schedule, I told Archie I didn't need him to help me anymore. He went nuts. Going on and on about hair implants and Botox. That's when he tells me he saw me leave my landlord's office back in Memphis, after I killed the old guy. Archie said he went in after seeing me leave. Saw the body. He actually caught up with me, followed me. Saw me put the bat in the dumpster. He pulled that bat out! He's had it all this time. Saved it in case he needed it." Ann-Dee chuckled grimly. "I didn't know he could be so organized." She placed her hands on the flat face of the guitar. "So Archie informed me that he was my eternal manager and I had to break up with Lew. End of discussion. The bat has spoken. I kind of figured where he was going with that, but I thought I'd have more time to figure something out. And then he goes and proposes to me on stage, like I couldn't say no in front of the whole festival. So I 'fainted.'"

She put the lid back on the sauce, wrapped a napkin around it and put it and the empty champagne bottle into her bag.

"But when I came to, he was still around. Dogged me all the way to the hospitality tent. Reminded me about the landlord and the bat." She pinched the strings on the guitar. They made an awful sound. She put the guitar by her feet. "How do you like that? Murder was not a disqualifying factor for Archie Grant's dating profile." She took a deep breath and exhaled. "At least I got the bat back. You can bet I cleaned that baby up fast. Wiped it clean. I'm kind of glad to have it—if I can't get the brooch back. Might come in handy someday. I thought about hitting Archie with it. Would have been kind of poetic, don't you think? But he would have screamed or something. Drugs and cement are a lot quieter."

Ann-Dee pulled a sobriety medallion out of her breast pocket.

"Too bad about Dale though," she said. She examined the medallion between her fingertips. She turned it over and over. "Not a mean bone in that boy's body. I needed help moving Archie to the handprint place. He was rolled up in a sheet; but, even then, you can pretty much tell a body when you're trying to lug one around, y'know? He didn't even ask me any questions. Just hauled the damn thing to the golf cart when I asked him to." She looked out the window into the distance. "He was such a blabbermouth though. Couldn't lie or keep a secret. Silly old thing." She turned the medallion with her fingers. "I shouldn't have taken this. I took his heart. That should have been enough. He was so proud of it. But it wouldn't have looked so much like a junkie's death if he'd had it on him." She rubbed the medallion on her sleeve, gave it a kiss and dropped it in a pocket.

"Poor Dale. Another stupid cougar. Not stupid like Archie, but the poor dear just always found a way to get in trouble. So sweet but so dumb." She leaned back against the headrest, pondered the dome light. "Lew wasn't dumb. He was sweet and good and smart. And he loved me." She brought her eyes down to look at John. "He was open to all kinds of good ideas, like I was talented, like maybe I wasn't a gold digger. Like maybe I really loved him too. You and Archie Grant messed that up. You're all stupid, stupid cougars! Landslide's gonna come down on *you* this time."

Ann-Dee slipped the pen and notebook from John Turnbell's hands and put them in her pocket.

"So Chuck and the Memphis ladies are staying at the Schroeder place, huh? His cabin next to yours?"

John's eyes closed.

She found his wallet and pulled out a keycard.

"No worries. This'll help me find it."

She looked through the windshield. It was quite a view. They were at the highest point in Big Pearly Falls State Park. She could see all the way across the valley, including the ranger station and gift shop. There was a police car at the park entrance. She gathered up her bag and guitar and the picnic trash. Then she shifted the car into neutral and released the parking brake. She slipped out of the car and made her way into the woods. She didn't look back.

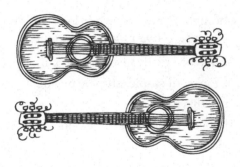

CHAPTER TWENTY-ONE

"I'll take the photos and video to the police," said Lew.

Chuck plugged a thumb drive into the laptop. He copied the photos to it.

Lew's cell phone rang. He answered it and put it on speakerphone.

"Hello, Ms. Flynn. This is Lew Sinclair."

"Lewie, I hate to ask you this, but could you help us out today? We have to select the winner of the Martin guitar and present it to them while ticket holders are still around. We've got it set up for six o'clock. Hicks and Hampton were going to do it, but—something to do with wind currents. They were going to arrive by balloon and now we're not sure what time they'll get here. I know you've been through a lot, but you know, we're show people. And we legally have to give the guitar to someone."

Lew checked the time. "I'd dearly like to, Ms. Flynn, but I've got some urgent business to take care of." Truth be told, Lew thought it would be inappropriate for him to do so after his manager's death. He told Ruby he couldn't oblige and hung up.

There was a knock at the door. Mitch opened it. He turned to Lew.

"It's a policeman," said Mitch.

"Officer Gerald!" said Chuck.

"There's the guy," said Officer Gerald to Chuck. "Are you sure about that Ann-Dee Phillips meeting with your friend? Officers went to the park. They found him in his car at the base of Big Pearly Hill. But no trace of her."

"Is he all right?" cried Chuck. He sprang up and over to Officer Gerald.

"They didn't say. They're taking him to the hospital is all I know." He winced. "It's a pretty steep hill."

"Can I go see him?"

"I guess so," said Officer Gerald. "I can take you there myself if you want. Hospital's right next to the police station. I'm on my way there now."

Chuck turned to Lew. "I can take the photos to the police station if you want to help Ruby out."

Lew considered it. He still thought him being at the raffle was in bad taste, doubly so now that John Turnbell was in the hospital—no telling what state he was in—and the bass player most likely drowned. But Ann-Dee was on the loose. She needed to be stopped. She'd always respected his opinion. Maybe he could talk her into turning herself in—if he could find her. He began forming a plan.

"I'm going to do the raffle," said Lew.

"Oh, take me with you, Mr. Sinclair," said Charla. "I want that guitar. It's one of the reasons I came to this here festival in the first place. I feel lucky."

With all that had happened at this festival, Charla felt lucky. She was a glass-half-full kind of gal.

"You might be in danger," said Lew.

"Magda's the one in danger," said Charla.

"We don't know that you're absolutely in the clear," said Lew.

"I'm going whether you take me or not. I'll drive my RV right on up to that stage."

"Aw, take her," said Mitch. "Ask them to let her stand with the security people. No one's going to try to kill her in broad daylight surrounded by bouncers and a few thousand other people. I'll stay here with Magda, erm, Mrs. Herman." He nodded to Magda.

Magda smiled at him. She put some knitting in Charla's picnic basket and took a seat by the sliding door that led out to the deck. Mitch walked to her and closed the vertical blinds. "Sorry, Mrs. Herman. It's safer this way."

Lew called Ruby back. "I guess I can make it, Ms. Flynn," he said. "And if it's okay with you, I'd like to bring a fan with me."

"You got it, Lewie," said Ruby.

"I am a little concerned for her safety though. Could you put her with the security people or some such thing?"

"Sure can," said Ruby. "Meet me backstage in half an hour."

"Should I bring Nancy with me? I'm at the Schroeder Resort."

"Nancy's got enough on her plate," said Ruby. "Until everything's okay with Gary, she's got the day off."

"Yes ma'am." Lew pocketed his phone. He looked at Mitch who was peering like a bird dog through the vertical blinds. "Maybe you oughtta stay away from the window yourself, Mitchell."

"Here," said Chuck. He sprang to the window. "Use this." He pulled down a shade. "It's one-way. Lets the light in but people outside can't see through it. Doesn't work at night though, so take that into consideration."

"I'll tell the Schroeders to keep an eye on you," said Lew. "And for heaven's sake, promise me you'll call the police if anything seems fishy."

"I give you my solemn promise," said Mitch.

Chuck, Charla, and Lew collected their gear and evidence. They stopped in at the Schroeder office to print out a screen grab from one of the clips, then set off for the festival and police station.

⸺⠶⠶⠶⸺

Lew and Charla walked up the back steps to the stage. Ruby, Gordon, and Thurgood stood before them looking out into the crowd. Lew overheard their conversation.

"A lot of people out there," said Ruby.

Gordon nodded, his chin in his hand.

"It was right to release the acts," continued Ruby.

"I know," said Gordon, "but thanks for saying it."

"I'm still forming my opinion," said Thurgood.

Lew cleared his throat. The FallsFest trio turned around. Lew held his ranch hat in his hands in deference to Ruby and Charla.

"Brought your hat, I see," said Ruby.

"Nope," said Gordon. "That won't do." He stepped toward Lew and handed him his Stetson. "This is more like it. And keep it this time. I'll hold on to the straw one until after the raffle."

Lew took the hat, nodded his thanks. "Uh, now . . ." he said. He looked at Charla and gave her a small smile. He looked back to the others. "This here is Charla, the fan I was telling you about. Charla, this is Ruby Flynn, Gordon Morgan, and Thurgood Buchwald."

"We've got everything set up for you," said Ruby. She smiled and winked at Charla. Charla smiled and winked back.

"Thank you," said Lew. "I wonder if I might ask another favor."

"Got another crease in your coat?" asked Ruby.

Lew grinned and shook his head.

"Miss Charla here feels lucky, but I was wondering, just in case, if you might let her hold the guitar before we select the winner."

· 229 ·

"As long as her hands are clean," said Thurgood.

Charla showed off the fronts and backs of her hands. Gordon picked up the guitar and offered it to her. She cradled it like a baby at first, then turned it around and began strumming "I'll Fly Away." After a few bars, she began to sing. Her voice was well suited to the song.

Even Thurgood nodded his head to the music.

"If you win, Charla," said Gordon, "we're going to ask you to sing that onstage."

"You can count on me to be a big old ham bone anytime you want, sir." She chuckled, blushed, and handed the guitar back to Gordon.

Lew made a mental note that Charla was indeed a ham bone, but was capable of blushing.

⋙∘≫ ⋘∘≫ ⋘∘≫

"I wonder if Charla has won yet," said Magda. She stood behind Mitch, who was keeping ardent watch out the sliding door.

"I imagine the shindig's just starting," said Mitch. He stretched. "I wonder what the police are making of Charles's slide show." He stood, excused himself, and headed toward the bathroom.

"I will lie down now," said Magda. "In bedroom."

"All right," said Mitch. "I'll latch the chain on the door just in case." He did so and called over his shoulder. "I'll wake you when they come back."

"Yes. Very good," said Magda. After Mitch left the room, Magda heard a noise at the front door. She saw the doorknob turn, but the lock kept it shut. Magda picked up the picnic basket, unlocked the sliding door, and slipped outside.

"There you are," said Ann-Dee. "Good things come to she who waits."

Lew looked out from the stage at the remains of the festival. The crowd wasn't exactly merry, but they weren't disgruntled either. From a music point of view, it had been a good festival despite the loss of concerts on Sunday. Lew caught snippets of conversation. Some attendees were talking about the murder. A local news crew was interviewing a few talkative fans just off the side of the stage.

Lew looked out to the festival grounds beyond the amphitheater. Many of the vendors had closed up. Some of the more mobile ones had already moved out. The beer tent was unoccupied. The saloon was dark. Most everyone respected the "no glass on festival grounds" rule; but many had brought along cans of their favorite libations. Well, thought Lew, it wasn't like they were at an actual funeral. It was a raffle at the end of a festival and the prize was a gorgeous guitar.

Lew looked for signs of security. In addition to FallsFest staff in their identifiable T-shirts, there were police on horseback, on foot, and in cars. The FallsFest cameras and jumbotron were up and running. Lew wondered if that was more for safety reasons than for entertainment purposes. Now he saw a few more TV reporters present. Their remote units were parked along the periphery of the crowd.

It was now time to make lemonade. Lew stepped aside as Ruby and Gordon rolled the ticket barrel out onto the apron of the stage. Lew followed. Gordon said a few words expressing sympathy for the families of the deceased.

Lew heard a steady *tap, tap, tap*. He looked around, then down, then up. It was Ruby's foot tapping the stage as her eyes scanned the crowd.

Gordon introduced Lew. People who had seen the Cowboys' performance clapped respectfully. Lew turned the crank on the barrel. The paper slips tumbled over and over. Lew closed his eyes and dug his hand into the middle of the barrel.

He pulled out a receipt. He paused a few moments. Ruby's foot tapped faster.

"The winner of the guitar is . . ." Lew crumpled up the receipt and put it in his pocket. "Ann-Dee Phillips!"

Ruby's foot stopped dead still. She and Gordon stepped closer to Lew. Murmurs spread throughout the crowd as people stuffed their losing ticket stubs into their pockets.

"Ladies and gentlemen," continued Lew. "We happen to have a photo of the winner." He removed a folded piece of printer paper from his back pocket. "Can I get a camera on this?" He unfolded the paper to reveal Ann-Dee's face on the jumbotron during her performance. It now appeared again on the jumbotron twenty feet wide and fifteen feet tall. The crowd began to talk. "You might remember her from this stage the other day. From the proposal?" The crowd began talking louder and looking around for Ann-Dee. "Does anybody see her here? Help us find her so we can give this handsome guitar to her."

<hr />

"Give me the brooch!" said Ann-Dee.

Magda stared at her, silent. "*You* have brooch," she said. "You wore it when you sang."

"Stop playing around," said Ann-Dee. "Fork it over. Now."

"You have *broszka!*"

"Wrong, old woman. I haven't seen it since . . . Damn!" Ann-Dee lowered the gun an inch.

"What?"

"Ain't either of us gonna get that brooch back."

"You lie to me."

"I killed your husband and all you care about is an old pin?"

Magda's eyes turned to fire.

"You *did* kill my husband!"

Ann-Dee raised the gun again. She tightened her grip.

"Why did you kill my Derrik? Why?"

"I didn't have the rent!" screamed Ann-Dee. Magda stared at her in disbelief. "I was scrambling, always scrambling, and I was tired of it. I went to his office to see if we could make an arrangement. He was holding that brooch, saying something about cleaning it for his bride."

Magda's throat clenched. She stifled the sob that was battling to escape. Ann-Dee gazed into the scene she described like it was a beautiful dream displayed right before her.

"It was in a deep-blue velvet box filled with ivory satin. The way he looked at it. The way he placed it in the satin . . . I took that baseball bat down from the wall, the one that was signed by somebody." Magda flinched. "And I took that brooch."

"How could you do this?" cried Magda.

"I was tired!" yelled Ann-Dee. "And I was angry and no one was going to care if a big old crook like him died. And I was right."

"You were wrong."

"Come on, lady. It's over. You can't outrun me and there's no one here to help you. This ends here."

A piercing mournful racket distracted Ann-Dee. It was like a high-pitched wail and a low, pained drone at the same time. She lost her focus for just a moment. Magda plunged her hand into the picnic basket and pulled out Charla's pistol.

"Where is my brooch?" cried Magda.

"It's gone. My bass player took it. I don't know what he did with it."

Magda fired twice. The second bullet knocked Ann-Dee back and she dropped her gun. She looked in disbelief at her upper arm at the blood on her sleeve. Magda fired a third time. Ann-Dee scuttled to the golf cart parked outside the Schroeder house.

"Were those gunshots?" asked Lew. "Kinda far away, but . . ."

"I'm pretty sure they came from up past the lake," said Ruby.

"The Schroeder Resort?" said Lew.

"We can get there faster if we go up the hill," said Ruby. She dragged Lew to the golf cart parked by the stage. She depressed the brake and started it up. "Hang on to your hat!" She stepped on the gas. Lew pulled the Stetson down onto his forehead. They lurched full speed ahead toward the hill. Ruby wrestled the walkie-talkie from her belt. "Code twelve at the Schroeder Resort. I'm on my way there now."

"I think the wiser person would drive away from gunshots," said Lew. They hit a bump and were airborne for a few moments.

Another gunshot confirmed the location. Ruby swerved to avoid a garbage can. Another golf cart came over the hill and flew past them in the opposite direction. The Schroeder Resort came into view. Magda stood on the cabin deck with a gun aimed at the fleeing cart.

Mitch stood beside her with his uilleann pipes, talking with great animation into a cell phone.

"Murderer!" cried Magda. She gestured after Ann-Dee. Ruby swung the cart around and gave chase. Lew looked back to make sure Magda and Mitch were all right. He believed if the woman could fly she'd have overtaken them in their pursuit.

"She's headed for the crowd!" said Ruby. She activated the walkie-talkie. "Brad! The perp's headed for the gate, but she's too close to the fans. Way too close."

The crowd parted. "It's her!" some people cried. "You won, lady!" "It's the fainting fiancée!" Some people ran after her. Two carts with security personnel shot away from the stage. Ann-Dee changed course and aimed for the StarWalk. Sirens blared. Flashing lights appeared on the hillside entry. A mounted officer galloped from behind the Norwegian taco stand. Voices came out of the walkie-talkie.

"The balloon's here! For crying out loud, the balloon's here!"

Lew looked up at the sky. A brilliant cloud of metallic gold flecks and rainbow-hued paper scraps filled the air and lilted down on the amphitheater.

Above the cloud were Hicks and Hampton leaning out of the basket of a yellow-and-purple-striped hot-air balloon. They tossed confetti by the handful in addition to that which was cascading out of the basket onto the crowd. The antic duo gradually became aware that they were floating above a high-speed chase. They retreated to the basket and reappeared with an air cannon. They studied the scene below and fired the air cannon. Four T-shirts blew down to the ground.

One landed on the backrest of Ann-Dee's cart. Hicks and Hampton reloaded. Four more shirts flew toward Ann-Dee's cart. This time, one bounced off the floorboard of the passenger side. Its band burst as it bounced up and it tangled on the steering wheel.

"Pull up beside her!" yelled Lew to Ruby.

Ruby gave him a wide-eyed look, then gunned it and circled around until she came up next to Ann-Dee's cart.

"Keep pace!" said Lew.

Ann-Dee and Ruby eyed each other. Lew climbed around behind Ruby. Hicks and Hampton fired off another shirt bomb, distracting Ann-Dee. Lew found his balance, summoned his strength, and sprang off Ruby's cart and into Ann-Dee's. He grabbed the steering wheel, struggling with Ann-Dee to control it. He stomped on her foot.

The golf cart sped faster, then hit a bump. It careened and threatened to roll over, but Lew wrenched the steering wheel in the right direction and the cart stayed on its tires—only two for a few seconds—then fell back onto all four wheels with a very consequential thud. Ann-Dee almost fell out of the cart. Another shirt attack struck Ann-Dee's gun hand. Her weapon flew to the ground. Lew put his arm around her shoulders and a foot on the brake. Ann-Dee lost her strength. She surrendered.

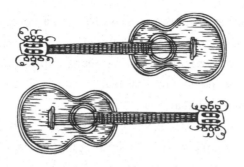

CHAPTER TWENTY-TWO

ew watched Bea Schroeder buzz around her kitchen. He breathed in the rich, round aroma of coffee simmering on the stove. He smelled bread baking in the oven and maybe, just maybe, that was the sweet, rich scent of a buttery apple pie also wafting its spell over the folks gathered in the room.

The warm glow in Lew's heart matched that of the room as he took in the special people gathered around him, sharing their time and relief and good humor. He himself was matching wits with Mr. Schroeder over a barn burner game of checkers. Mitch, Chuck, and Magda were enthralled by something on Chuck's laptop. Charla played guitar for Gordon in one corner of the room, while Ruby and Thurgood engaged in a deep discussion in the other.

A dishwasher rattled on with a rusty rasp like a trash can with a cold. Bea bent her knees slightly and gave the machine a gentle nudge with her hip. The rasp transformed into a vital purr, joining the rest of the room's hum of activity and promise.

"Now, Charles," said Bea, as she stirred a pan of thickening gravy. "How is that poor Mr. Turnbell doing?"

"They were worried about his spleen," replied Chuck. "But it looks like they won't have to remove it."

"Well, that's a relief anyway," said Bea.

"His left leg is broken in two places though," continued Chuck. "And he's pretty banged up. They're keeping an eye on him in the hospital for a few more days to make sure all his other organs work or something. He's going to be okay. That's all I care about."

Bea nodded her head while patting her chest over her heart.

"I guess what saved him were the airbags," continued Chuck. "They said his car has the best ones you can get in America. Any other car and he might not have made it. Next car I buy, I am definitely checking out the airbags."

Mr. Schroeder looked up.

"What kind of car was it, now?" he asked.

"I don't know. I didn't ask, and I didn't pay attention on the ride up," replied Chuck.

"Some journalist you are," said Mitch.

"Hey," said Chuck. "I'm a culture guy. This crime and investigative stuff's for the birds. I want no part of it. I'm sticking with food and music."

"That's what you say now," said Ruby.

"Smart man," said Lew.

"I'm serious," said Chuck. "John was lucky the police got to him when they did."

"It was exciting though," said Ruby. "Sorry, Magda. I suppose it was a little too exciting for you."

"Was worth it," replied Magda. She patted the hands of Chuck and Mitch. They beamed back at her.

"Y'all gonna come visit me and Magda down in Memphis, now, aren't you?" said Charla. "You've got a standing invitation."

"Miss Charla," said Mitch, "we've decided to drive down there with you in your RV if you'll have us."

"Yeah," said Chuck. "Moira's on her way here from Minneapolis. She wants to join us, if we're welcome. Maybe interview you for her podcast?"

"The more the merrier," said Charla. "Cheeky boys."

"I'm serious about you playing FallsFest next year, Charla," said Gordon. "You can warm up for Lew and the Cowboys. There's a guy in Memphis I want to connect you with. I think he could be your Rick Rubin."

"I told you I felt lucky, Lew," said Charla. They all laughed.

"Sometimes luck is a matter of putting yourself in its way," said Lew.

"Speaking of next year," said Ruby. "I'm thinking I'd like to scale back my workload, maybe increase Nancy's role." Mr. and Mrs. Schroeder exchanged proud winks. "This music business is getting a little too wild and wooly for me," continued Ruby. "I'm thinking of taking Thurgood up on his private-detective offer."

Everyone laughed again, but Thurgood gave Ruby a sage nod.

"Well now, Nancy might have her hands full managing the Gentlemen Cowboys," said Lew. He looked out the window over the sink. "Here she is now. And Gary!"

There were cheers all around.

Nancy and Gary entered the kitchen followed by Slim. Mr. and Mrs. Schroeder wrapped their arms around the youngsters.

"My boy is home!" cried Bea. She twirled him in a circle. Gary laughed. There was nothing stern or still about his face today. He embraced his mother.

"I still think you did it," said Lew. He laughed and clapped Gary on the shoulder, then he grabbed Gary in a heartfelt hug. He was happy to finally have all his chicks under one roof.

"I always knew he was innocent," said Mitch. "Because if Gary had killed Archie, he'd have eaten him. The Schroeders always eat what they kill."

"Now, Finbar," said Bea. "Don't be so cheeky about the dead."

Mitch winked at her and opened the oven door so she could take out the bread and pie and replace them with a casserole.

"Miss Magda," said Slim. He pulled up a chair beside her. "Mitch and Charles here told me all about your quest for your wedding brooch." He felt inside his suit jacket and found the pocket. He removed something bundled up in a pearl white satin handkerchief. He placed the bundle in Magda's palm. She opened it. Her face lit up like a child with a birthday present—or, more accurately, like a bride on her wedding day.

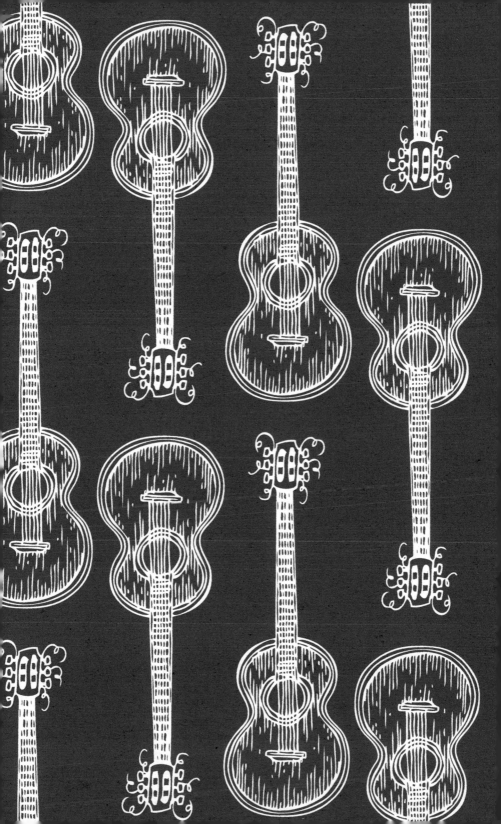

ACKNOWLEDGMENTS

And now for the Acknowledgments!

Thank you to T Bone Burnett for creating the *O Brother, Where Art Thou?* soundtrack. Its bounty of bluegrass, folk, and gospel inspired me to write a book about country music. Well, they're kissing cousins, aren't they?

Thank you to the whole team at CamCat. Special shout-out to publisher and CEO Sue Arroyo for liking my Twitter pitch and making this whole publishing adventure a reality. Thanks to art director Maryann Appel for the delightful and comic cover design. And a big thanks to my editor Elana Gibson. Her suggestions and questions made the revisions not just successful but fun to write. *Elan* is one of my favorite words and now I have one more reason why.

Thanks to Joe Demko for his insight as a performing musician. If I got something wrong about being in a band or on the road, it's because I didn't run it by him.

Thanks to Heidi Van Heel, the only other member of the bi-monthly Creative Chat Writing Group, for taking me seriously while making me laugh.

Much gratitude to Jayne Stauffer for the backstage passes.

Thank you to my early readers: Sherry Meek, Valerie Quist, Jeanne Freed, and the women of Literary Night: Janine Frank, Darla Bloch, Kathleen Plaetz, Lynn Swanson, Beth Kleven, and Annalie Plaetz. Thanks for taking the time to read my book and bravely answer my questions. Thanks also for being generous friends and introducing me to new books. And to another early reader, Molly Orth, thank you for being my liaison (and sometime spy) at book signings. We'll be sitting at Hermann's foot soon, I hope.

Special thanks to Laurie Hertzel who read a very early version that I entered in a sort of newspaper contest. My book didn't get picked, but it came close. Your kind words kept me buoyed until *Lewis* found a home at CamCat.

And love and thanks to my very own gentleman cowboy—and husband—Jeff. (He's not really a cowboy, but he is a musician and composer.) Your faith in my creativity never waivers. You have the spirit of music in you. That spirit is perhaps the most important aspect of *Lewis Sinclair and the Gentlemen Cowboys*. I hope I represented it one tiny bit as well as you do every day.

ABOUT THE AUTHOR

D. M. S. Fick's short fiction is published in the Nodin Press anthology, *Festival of Crime*. She's also an Emmy-nominated and PromaxBDA award-winning graphic designer and cartoonist.

In 2015 Ms. Fick received an Artist Initiative grant from the Minnesota State Arts Board for *The Oracle of Nuttown*, a half-hour cartoon mash-up of forest creatures, Greek mythology, and classic 1970s movies.

Ms. Fick has lived in Boston, the Twin Cities, and London. She presently resides on the Minnesota prairie with her beloved composer husband.

If you like

Lewis Sinclair and the Gentlemen Cowboys by D. M. S. Fick,

you'll also enjoy

Citizen Orlov by Jonathan Payne.

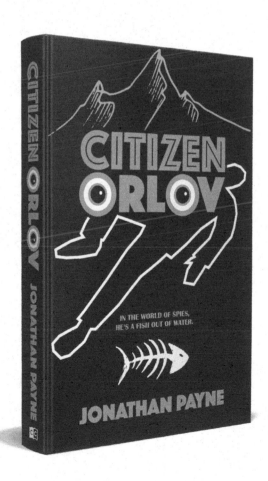

CHAPTER ONE

In which our hero meets a new and unexpected challenge

On a frigid winter's morning in a mountainous region of central Europe, Citizen Orlov, a simple fishmonger, is taking a shortcut along the dank alley behind the Ministries of Security and Intelligence when a telephone begins to ring. He thinks nothing of it and continues on his daily constitutional, his heavy boots crunching the snow between the cobbles.

The ringing continues, becoming louder with each step. A window at the back of the ministry buildings is open, just a little. The ringing telephone sits on a table next to the open window. Orlov stops, troubled by this unusual scene: there is no reason for a window to be open on such a cold day. Since this is the Ministry of either Security or Intelligence, could an open window be a security breach of some kind? Orlov is tempted to walk away. After all, this telephone call is none of his business. On the other hand, he is an upright and patriotic citizen who would not want to see national security compromised simply because no one was available to answer a telephone call. He is on the verge of stepping toward the open window when he hears footsteps ahead. A tight group of four soldiers is marching into the alley, rifles on shoulders. He freezes for a second, leans against the wall, and quickly lights a cigarette. By the time the soldiers reach him, Orlov is dragging on the cigarette and working hard to appear nonchalant. The soldiers are palace guardsmen, but the red insignia on their uniforms indicates they are part of the elite unit that protects the Crown Prince, the king's ambitious older son. Orlov nods politely, but the soldiers ignore him and march on at speed.

The telephone is still ringing. Someone very much wants an answer. Orlov stubs his cigarette on the wall and approaches the open window. The telephone is loud in his right ear. Peering through the gap, he sees a small, gloomy storeroom with neatly appointed shelves full of stationery. Finally, he can stand it no longer. He reaches through the window, picks up the receiver, and pulls it on its long and winding cable out through the window to his ear.

"Hello?" says Orlov, looking up and down the alley to check he is still alone.

"Thank God. Where have you been?" says an agitated voice, distant and crackly. Orlov is unsure what to say. The voice continues. "Kosek. Right now."

"I'm sorry?" says Orlov.

"Kosek. Agent Kosek."

Orlov peers into the storeroom again. "There's no one here," he says.

"Well, fetch him then. And hurry, for God's sake. It's important."

Orlov is sorely tempted to end the call and walk away, but the voice is so angry that he dare not.

"One minute," he says, and lays the receiver on the table. He opens the window wider and, with some considerable effort, pulls himself headfirst into the storeroom, where he tumbles onto the floor. Picking himself up, he slaps the dust from his overcoat, opens the storeroom door, and peers along the hallway; all is dark and quiet.

With some trepidation, Orlov returns to the telephone. "Hello?" he says.

"Kosek?"

"No, sorry. I'll have to take a message."

The caller is still agitated. "Well, focus on what I'm about to say. It's life and death."

Orlov's hands are shaking. "Hold on," he says, "I'll fetch some paper."

Before he can put the receiver down, the caller explodes with anger. "Are you a simpleton? Do not write this down. Remember it."

"Yes, sir. Sorry," says Orlov. "I'll remember it."

"Are you ready?"

"Yes, sir."

"Here it is. We could not—repeat not—install it in room six. Don't ask why, it's a long story."

The man is about to continue, but Orlov interrupts him. "Should I include that in the message: 'it's a long story'?"

"Mother of God," shouts the man. "Why do they always give me the village idiot? No. Forget that part. I'll start again."

"Ready," says Orlov.

This time the man speaks slower and more deliberately, as if to a child. "We could not—repeat not—install it in room six. You need to get room seven. It's hidden above the wardrobe. Push the lever up, not down. Repeat that back to me."

Orlov is now shaking all over, and he grimaces as he forces himself to focus. He repeats the message slowly but correctly.

"Whatever else you do, get that message to Kosek, in person. No one else. Lives depend on it. Understood?"

"Understood," says Orlov, and the line goes dead.

Orlov returns the receiver to the telephone and searches for something to write on. He remembers the message now, but for how long? He has no idea who Agent Kosek is, or where. Now that the caller has gone, the only sensible course of action is to make a note. He will destroy the note, once he has found Kosek. On the table he finds a pile of index cards. He writes the message verbatim on a card, folds it once, and tucks it inside his pocketbook.

Standing in the dark storeroom, Orlov wonders how to set about finding Agent Kosek. He considers climbing back into the alley, going around to the front entrance, and presenting himself as a visitor, if he could work out which ministry he is inside. But it's still early and it might take hours to be seen. Worse than that, there is a possibility he would be turned away. He imagines a surly security guard pretending to check the personnel directory, only to turn to him and say, "There's no one of that name here." Perhaps agents never use their real names. Is Kosek a real name or a pseudonym? Orlov decides the better approach is to use the one advantage currently available to him: he is inside the building.

He lowers the sash window to its original position and steps into the hallway, closing the storeroom door behind him. All remains dark and quiet. The hallway runs long and straight in both directions, punctuated only by anonymous doors. He sees nothing to suggest one direction is more promising than the other. Orlov turns right and tiptoes sheepishly along the hallway, now conscious of his boots as they squeak on the polished wooden floors. He walks on and on, eventually meeting a door that opens onto an identical dark corridor.

As he continues, Orlov becomes increasingly conscious that he is not supposed to be here. He imagines an angry bureaucrat bursting out from one of the many office doors to castigate him and march him off to be interrogated. However, he has walked the length of a train and still he has seen no one.

Finally, Orlov sees the warm glow of lamplight seeping around the edge of another dividing door up ahead. He is both relieved and apprehensive. He approaches the door cautiously and puts his ear to it. It sounds like a veritable hive of industry. He takes a deep breath and opens the door onto a scene of frenetic activity. Banks of desks are staffed by serious men, mostly young, in formal suits, both pin-stripe and plain; the few women are also young and dressed formally. Some are engaged in animated conversations; some are leaning back in chairs, smoking; others are deep into reading piles of papers. A white-haired woman is distributing china cups full of tea from a wheeled trolley. At the far end of this long room, someone is setting out chairs in front of a blackboard. Above this activity, the warm fug of cigarette smoke is illuminated by high wall lamps. Orlov hesitates, but is soon approached at high speed by a short, rotund man in a three-piece suit. He has a clipboard and a flamboyant manner.

"You're late," says the man, gesticulating. "Quickly. Overcoats over there."

"No, no. You see," Orlov says, "I'm not really here."

The man slaps him on the back, taking his coat as they walk. "You seem real to me," he laughs.

Orlov protests. "I have a message for Agent Kosek."

The man rolls his eyes. "Do not trouble yourself regarding Agent Kosek. He is late for everything. He will be here in due course."

He directs Orlov to take a seat at the back of the impromptu classroom, which is by now filling up with eager, young employees. Orlov is suddenly conscious of his age and appearance; his balding head and rough clothes stand out in this group of young, formally dressed professionals. He also feels anxious about being in this room on false pretenses. However, he need only wait until Agent Kosek appears; he will then deliver the message, make his excuses, and leave. He could still make it to the Grand Plaza in time for the market to open.

The flamboyant man, now standing in front of the blackboard, bangs his clipboard down onto a desk to bring the room to order. "Citizens," he says, "I would appreciate your attention." The room falls silent, and he continues. "I am Citizen Molnar, and I will be your instructor today."

Orlov turns to his neighbor, an earnest young man who is writing the instructor's name in a pristine leather notebook. "I'm not supposed to be here," says Orlov. The young man places a finger on his lips. Orlov smiles at him and returns his attention to Molnar, who is writing on the blackboard. Molnar proceeds to talk to the group for some time, but Orlov struggles to follow his meaning. The instructor repeatedly refers to the group as *recruits*, which adds to Orlov's sense of being in the wrong place. He becomes hot under the collar when Molnar invites every recruit to introduce themselves.

One by one the impressive young recruits stand and detail their university degrees and their training with the military or the police. When Orlov's turn comes, he stands and says, "Citizen Orlov. Fishmonger." He is surprised when a ripple of laughter runs through the group.

Orlov is about to sit down again when Molnar intervenes. "Is there anything else you'd like to tell us, citizen?"

Orlov says, "I have a message for Agent Kosek."

"Yes," says Molnar, gesturing for Orlov to sit down, "the agent will be here soon, I'm quite sure."

Orlov's hopes pick up some time later when Molnar says he wants to introduce a guest speaker. Orlov reaches inside his pocketbook to check that the message is still there. But Molnar is interrupted by a colleague whispering in his ear.

"My apologies," says Molnar. "It seems Agent Kosek has been called away on urgent business. However, I'm delighted to say that his colleague, Agent Zelle, is joining us to give you some insight into the day-to-day life of an agent. Agent Zelle."

Orlov is disappointed at the change of plan, but perhaps this colleague will be able to introduce him to Kosek. Taking her place in front of the blackboard is the most beautiful woman Orlov has ever seen. She is young and curvaceous but with a stern, serious expression. Her dark curls tumble over pearls and a flowing gown. Several of the male recruits shift uneasily in their chairs; someone coughs. Agent Zelle seems far too exotic for this stuffy, bureaucratic setting. She speaks with a soft foreign accent that Orlov does not recognize.

"Good morning, citizens," says Zelle, scanning the group slowly. "I have been asked to share with you something of what you can expect, if you are chosen to work as an agent for the ministry. I can tell you that it is a great honor, but there will also be hardship and danger."

She paces up and down in front of the blackboard, telling them stories of her life in the field. Orlov is entranced; these real-life tales sound like the adventure books he used to read as a boy. There are secret packages, safe houses, and midnight rendezvous in dangerous locations. There are car chases and shootouts, poisonings and defused bombs. It is so engrossing that, for a while, Orlov forgets that he has no business here aside from finding Kosek.

As he focuses on Zelle's lilting voice, Orlov is struck by a thought that has never before occurred to him in more than twenty years of fishmongering. Perhaps he is cut out for something more challenging, even thrilling. Perhaps, even at his age, he is capable of taking a position in a ministry such as this one where, instead of standing all day in the cold selling fish, his days would be full of adventure, danger, and even romance. Zelle's stories fill his head with possibilities. But perhaps this is foolish. After all, he and Citizen Vanev have a good business and a monopoly situation, since theirs is the only fish stall in the Grand Plaza. What's more, Vanev has always been loyal to him, and he has always tried to be loyal in return. Orlov tries to banish these silly ideas from his mind.

When Agent Zelle finishes, spontaneous applause fills the room. The agent seems surprised, almost embarrassed, and gives a slight curtsy in acknowledgement. She turns to talk to Molnar as the class breaks up and the recruits begin to mingle. Orlov sets off in the direction of Zelle, but several recruits are in his way, now forming into small groups, discussing what they have just heard. Orlov attempts to get past, saying "Excuse me. Sorry. May I. . ." but by the time he reaches the blackboard, Agent Zelle has gone.

"Is everything all right, citizen?" asks Molnar, seeing Orlov's distress.

"I really need to see Kosek," says Orlov. "It's very important. I have a message for him."

"I'm sure he'll be here, before induction is completed," says Molnar. "He always likes to meet the new recruits."

"That is what I was trying to explain," says Orlov. He gestures in the direction of the window through which he climbed. He is about to explain his entry to the building, but thinks better of it. "I'm not supposed to be here."

Molnar eyes him with a puzzled expression. "I assure you, citizen," he says, "that we rarely make mistakes." He brandishes his clipboard, showing Orlov a sheet of heavy, watermarked paper with a list of neatly typewritten names. Molnar runs his finger down the list ostentatiously, stopping in the middle of the page. "Here we are," he says. "Orlov."

CHAPTER TWO

In which our hero sets out on a journey

The next morning, Citizen Orlov forgoes his daily constitutional and sets out early for the Grand Plaza. In consideration of his new situation, he wears the dark suit he last wore at his father's funeral. It appears that the waistband has shrunk since those days, but Orlov finds that he can tuck it under his belly by wearing the trousers a little lower. This unattractive arrangement is hidden by his heavy overcoat, since it is another frigid day.

As he walks to the market, Orlov's head is full of possibilities. He understands that very few recruits are chosen to be agents. Most of the positions in the ministry are mundane and menial—clerks, copyists, mailroom operatives, and the like. And he should remember that no one has offered him anything so far. He needs to focus on delivering the telephone message. Already a day has gone by, and he has failed to find Agent Kosek. If he can find Kosek today and successfully deliver the message, perhaps that will stand him in good stead when the ministry comes to decide on the allocation of positions. Not wanting to incur the considerable wrath of his employer, Orlov determines to tell Vanev only about his short-term task, for now. He will keep the possibility of a position at the ministry to himself, until it is confirmed.

Orlov is disappointed, but not surprised, to see that Citizen Vanev has arrived at the market stall before him. Vanev—an obese, unshaven man who perpetually wears the same fish-stained overalls—is busy setting out the wooden display boxes. In a vain attempt to lessen the inevitable anger of his employer, Orlov rushes up to the stall, grabs a bag of ice, and begins to fill a display box.

"So, he's not dead after all," says Vanev.

"My apologies, citizen," says Orlov.

"What happened yesterday?" asks Vanev. "I was slaving away over cold fish all day without so much as a cigarette break."

"I have a job," says Orlov.

"Exactly," says Vanev, slamming a box full of ice into position. "And it's traditional to do your job, if you expect to get paid for it."

"No," says Orlov, "for the government."

Vanev stops in his tracks. "Doing what?"

"I'm not sure, exactly," says Orlov, "but it's very important."

"Which ministry?" asks Vanev.

Orlov hesitates. "Security. Or perhaps Intelligence."

Vanev continues. "So, you don't know what the job is or who you're working for, but you're going abandon me anyway. Sounds like an excellent plan."

"I won't be gone forever," says Orlov. "There's just one task I need to complete. It's life and death. As soon as that's done, I'll be back."

"And how long will this take?" asks Vanev.

"I just have to find someone and deliver a message. That's all."

"I need you to be here on Saturday," says Vanev, reaching over to spread a dozen haddock across the ice. "I have some political business to attend to."

"The People's Front," says Orlov.

"The People's Front," repeats Vanev. "One day, you will join us."

"I don't care for politics," says Orlov.

"I don't care for tyranny," says Vanev.

"How can you be sure a republic would be an improvement?" asks Orlov.

"How can *you* be sure you or your mother will not end up disappeared, or worse?" asks Vanev.

"Let us leave my mother out of this," says Orlov, a little more sharply than he had intended.

"I mean no offense," says Vanev. "I am merely concerned for your wellbeing, as well as my own."

"I understand," says Orlov. "But I do not share your conviction that a revolution is in the best interests of our great nation."

Vanev sighs. "It is the least terrible option available to us."

Since versions of this exchange have played out between them many times, Orlov knows it is futile. He is anxious not to be late for his appointment at the ministry.

"Do not fear, citizen," says Orlov, turning to go. "I shall return." He trudges away across the snow-covered square, pausing while a tram trundles past slowly before he continues down the hill and across the bridge into the government sector.

Orlov arrives at the foot of the stone steps that lead up to the grand front doors of the Ministries of Security, on his left, and Intelligence, on his right. He felt sure, while walking here, that he would know which door to approach, but now he is singularly lacking in enlightenment. He thinks back to the remarks made yesterday by Citizen Molnar and Agent Zelle; they had plenty to say about security, but then again, they also talked about intelligence. It could be either. He imagines being interrogated by skeptical security guards in the lobby of either or both buildings. Finding this a distinctly unattractive proposition, Orlov walks around to the back of the buildings, where the dark, narrow alley is familiar and comforting compared with the formal front entrances. He finds the rear entrance through which he and the young recruits exited the previous afternoon, but the door is closed and a surly security guard leans against it, smoking a cigarette. Orlov nods politely and keeps walking, feeling the guard's eyes following him all the way up the alley and around the corner.

Once he is out of sight, Orlov leans against the wall at the end of the Ministry of Security and enjoys a cigarette of his own. He takes a couple of peeks around the corner, but the security guard is still there. He is just about to build up the courage to try one of the front entrances when he hears voices. A gaggle of besuited men is approaching at high speed, led by Citizen Molnar. Orlov stubs his cigarette on the wall and steps forward to attract their attention. Perhaps he can follow them into the building. But Molnar speaks first.

"Ah, the very man," says Molnar, holding out a hand so that one of his aides can pass an envelope to him. He hands the envelope to Orlov. "We need you on the next train to Kufzig," he says. "Your ticket is in here. Check into Pension Residenz. Kosek will meet you there."

Orlov is stunned and for a while is unable to speak. Eventually he says, "I'm not going to be working in the mailroom?"

Molnar looks surprised, and his aides laugh. "We know talent when we see it," says Molnar. "We need you in the field."

"And Kosek will be there?" asks Orlov.

"Yes, he's expecting you," says Molnar.

"What will I be doing?" asks Orlov.

"Kosek will explain your task," says Molnar and begins to walk away.

Orlov calls after him. "How will I recognize him?"

"He will find you," Molnar replies over his shoulder.

Orlov cannot believe his good fortune. He grins involuntarily while watching Molnar and his aides disappear around the corner.

Agent Zelle's stories of espionage and danger flash through his head. He is both elated and nervous. Could he really be about to leave fish-mongering behind for the life of an agent? He opens the envelope and finds a first-class ticket to Kufzig, leaving in less than an hour. It is a small town in the mountains about two hours south of the capital. Orlov has visited it only once before, as a child. He has never before travelled in the first-class carriage of a train. He considers returning to the market to explain this change of plan to Vanev, but it is a shorter walk to the railway station. He will find Kosek, deliver the message and, all being well, return in time to cover the stall on Saturday.

ORLOV STEPS OUT onto the platform at Kufzig and pauses to admire the view while fastening his overcoat against the thin, freezing air. The picturesque little town is surrounded by rugged, snow-capped mountains. Well-dressed travelers rush past him, lifting suitcases down from the train. Others run to board before the train continues its journey south. When the train pulls away, Orlov is still in the middle of the platform, admiring the view, and finds himself engulfed by a cloud of steam.

By the time the steam has dispersed, all the other passengers have gone on their way, and Orlov is left alone on the platform with a guard, a haggard old man who limps toward his hut as though in a hurry to get out of the cold.

Orlov waves at the guard and walks toward him. "Excuse me," he says. "I'm looking for Pension Residenz."

The guard stops at the door to the hut. "Residenz, you say?"

"Yes," says Orlov. "It was recommended." He is about to say who gave the recommendation, but thinks better of it. "Is it a good place to stay? Reasonable?"

"Oh, yes," says the guard. "Quite good. And quite reasonable. Only..." He pauses.

"Only?" asks Orlov.

"Some people mistake it for Penzion Rezidence," says the guard. "It's an easy mistake to make." He heads inside the hut.

Orlov leans into the doorway. "I'm sorry," he says. "There's another pension called Rezidence? Here in Kufzig?"

"Oh yes, sir," says the guard. "It causes all sorts of confusion."

"I imagine it would," says Orlov.

"That's why I always like to check," says the guard.

"I'm quite sure it's Pension Residenz that was recommended," says Orlov, confidently.

"Straight down the hill, sir," says the guard, "a short walk along Feldgasse—that's our beautiful main street—and you can't miss it."

Orlov thanks the guard and sets out down the hill, admiring the view of the town beneath him. He was confident that Molnar had said *Residenz*, but the farther he walks, the more he wonders if he had misheard *Rezidence*. He would like to call Molnar on the telephone to confirm this but, even if he could find a telephone, he has no idea how to reach the ministry. Only now he realizes that he missed an opportunity this morning to ask Molnar which ministry he works for. Perhaps it would have been embarrassing to admit that he didn't know, but the embarrassment would have been over in a second, and then he would have been quite sure. As it stands, he will have to live with the uncertainty a little longer. He determines to ask Agent Kosek this evening, as soon as they meet. He hopes Kosek is a kind person, the sort of person who will not be cruel about this simple misunderstanding.

In any case, Orlov is bringing with him an important message, and he is therefore confident of striking up a good rapport with the agent. He will deliver the message, complete whatever task Kosek has in store for him, and return home without delay. Given Citizen

Vanev's mood this morning, he does not want to be away from the market any longer than absolutely necessary.

At the foot of the hill, Orlov sees the sign for Feldgasse and follows it into the heart of the town. The scene in front of him stirs memories of his childhood visit to Kufzig: a quaint main street with a steepled church at one end and, at the other, a square with an ornate fountain. Between these two landmarks, the busy thoroughfare is full of restaurants, bakeries, and street cafés. Half way along Feldgasse, equidistant between the church and the square, sits Pension Residenz. Like many of the pensions in this part of the world, it is a tall, elegant townhouse that was once the home of a wealthy family but has long since been converted into a boarding house, with guest rooms spanning four floors. A faded picture of Beethoven at his piano decorates the sign that hangs above the door.

Now that he has seen the sign clearly showing Pension Residenz, Orlov is feeling more confident that this is the right place. He steps into the cramped reception area and, since no one is at the desk, he rings the bell, which elicits no immediate response. While waiting, Orlov peruses the newspaper rack and sees an interesting headline: "Kufzig Prepares for Royal Visit." He considers removing the newspaper from the rack in order to read the article but, before he does so, a curious little woman in thick spectacles appears from the back office and stares at him sideways, as though her peripheral vision is better than her ability to see straight ahead.

"How may I help you?" she says.

"I'd like a room, please," says Orlov.

"You know the king is visiting?" says the woman.

"I just saw it in the newspaper," says Orlov.

"Full up," she says. "Quite full. A lot of people want to see His Majesty. Those people booked in advance. On account of our excellent views along Feldgasse. Those with a balcony can see all the way down to the fountain."

Orlov is nonplussed. "I was supposed to stay here. I have to meet someone." She shrugs and Orlov continues. "Could you tell me if," he is about to say *agent* but corrects himself just in time, "Citizen Kosek checked in yet?"

"Can't say," she says. "Against the rules."

"But he is booked to stay here?"

"Against the rules."

"May I leave a message?"

She shakes her head. Then, to Orlov's surprise, she says, "Go to the Bierkeller later." She points along the road in the direction of the square. "Every man in town will be there tonight."

"Why?" asks Orlov.

"Trust me," she says.

"Is there anywhere else to stay nearby?" says Orlov.

The woman looks at him and for a while seems to be weighing something up. "She might have a room. Across the street." She pulls a face, as though making this recommendation is distasteful. "She's always slow to fill up. On account of the inferior views."

Orlov turns to look out through the front door and across the street. "There's another boarding house opposite?"

"Directly across the street," says the woman.

"That wouldn't be Penzion Rezidence, would it?" asks Orlov.

The woman raises her eyebrows, as though he has used inappropriate language at the dinner table. "If you say so," she says and disappears into the back office.

Orlov heads outside and crosses the street, where he finds an almost identical townhouse. Hanging above the door, under the words Penzion Rezidence, is a sign with a faded picture of Gustav Mahler waving his conductor's baton. Orlov steps inside to a similar reception area. This time, he does not need to ring the bell because someone is at the desk. She looks much like the proprietor opposite, except that her spectacles are not so thick.

"Good day, sir. May I help you?" she says.

Orlov sounds a little more desperate than intended. "Do you have a room?"

The woman looks down at the ledger on the desk. "How many nights?"

"Just tonight, please," says Orlov. "I'm meeting a colleague this evening. Returning home tomorrow, I hope."

"You're not planning to stay for the royal visit, sir?" she asks.

"No, this is strictly business," says Orlov, and he enjoys how that sounds—much more impressive than fishmongering.

"Room three is the only one available," says the woman. "It doesn't have much of a view, but if you're not staying for the king, I dare say you won't mind that."

She fetches the key while Orlov signs the ledger. Room three is a drab affair on the second floor with a restricted view of the street and a shared bathroom in the hall. Since Orlov has no luggage to unpack, he decides to go out again. He takes a stroll around the town, but it is too cold for a prolonged walk. He eats an early dinner of sausages and cabbage at the least expensive restaurant on Feldgasse and then makes his way to the Bierkeller. It is mostly empty when he arrives, and he drinks two beers alone at the bar before the place begins to fill up. It is a literal cellar and a typical pub in most respects, with the addition of a small stage, complete with lights and curtains.

Orlov watches all the newcomers closely, wondering which one is Kosek. By the time he is on to his third beer, Orlov is becoming agitated that Kosek has not made himself known. He does not like the sense of being powerless.

He wants to take control of the situation.

At the other end of the bar, a serious, middle-aged man has been drinking alone for some time. He is well dressed and appears to be surveying the busy cellar with eagle eyes. Orlov might be just a simple fishmonger, but he has good intuition. He picks up his beer, walks slowly toward the man, and leans against the bar next to him. He takes a sip of beer and smiles at the man, to ensure he has been noticed. The man looks uneasy; he half-smiles back.

"Good evening," says Orlov.

"Evening," says the man.

"Are you, by any chance, Citizen Kosek?"

"Leave me alone," says the man. "I'm just here for the show." He nods toward the stage, where the lights are going up and a weaselly little man with a shaggy moustache calls the room to order.

"Ladies and gentlemen, your attention please," he says in the shrill tones of a carnival barker as oriental music begins to emanate from a tinny loudspeaker. "We are very proud to announce, by popular demand, for one night only, the return of the one, the only, Mata Hari."

To Orlov's surprise, the whole cellar erupts in applause. Some men bang their beer glasses on the tables as others stamp their feet. The cacophony dies down as the music swells. From behind the curtain emerges an exotic, barefoot dancer, dressed in nothing aside from carefully placed jewels and flowing veils. She gyrates into the center of the stage to begin her act. Only when she arrives in the full glow of the spotlights does Orlov sense that this dancer is familiar. In fact, he saw her only yesterday. It is Agent Zelle.

CamCat
Books

VISIT US ONLINE FOR MORE BOOKS TO LIVE IN:
CAMCATBOOKS.COM

SIGN UP FOR CAMCAT'S FICTION NEWSLETTER FOR
COVER REVEALS, EBOOK DEALS, AND MORE EXCLUSIVE CONTENT.

CamCatBooks   @CamCatBooks   @CamCat_Books   @CamCatBooks